# A HARD CALL

## STONEWALL INVESTIGATIONS - BOOK I

MAX WALKER

Edited By: ONE LOVE EDITING

Proofread By: Tanja Ongkiehong & Donna F.

Copyright © 2023 by Max Walker

All rights reserved.

No part of this book may be reproduced in any form or by any electronic or mechanical means, including information storage and retrieval systems, without written permission from the author, except for the use of brief quotations in a book review.

ALSO BY MAX WALKER

**The Book Club Boys**

Love and Monsters

**The Gold Brothers**

Hummingbird Heartbreak

Velvet Midnight

Heart of Summer

**The Stonewall Investigation Series**

A Hard Call

A Lethal Love

A Tangled Truth

A Lover's Game

**The Stonewall Investigation- Miami Series**

Bad Idea

Lie With Me

His First Surrender

**The Stonewall Investigation- Blue Creek Series**

Love Me Again

Ride the Wreck

Whatever It Takes

**Audiobooks:**

Find them all on Audible.

**Christmas Stories:**

Daddy Kissing Santa Claus

Daddy, It's Cold Outside

Deck the Halls

---

Receive access to a bundle of my **free stories** by signing up for my newsletter!

Tap here to sign up for my newsletter.

Be sure to connect with me on Instagram and TikTok **@maxwalkerwrites.**

Want even more Max? Then join Max After Dark for exclusive stories, audio excerpts, chat room, and more.

Max Walker

Max@MaxWalkerWrites.com

# SYNOPSIS

Zane Holden hasn't had the easiest go of things. His childhood was rough and adulthood hasn't been a walk in the park either. The only good thing in his life would be Stonewall Investigations, an investigative company he found to work primarily with the LGBTQ community. Things were ok and Zane was finally healing from a personal tragedy but the reemergence of a serial killer turns his world upside down.

Lorenzo De Luca is a cocky defense attorney dripping in Italian charm. He's well known as one of the best lawyers in New York City, a title he worked hard to achieve. When he picks up a difficult case, he finds that he needs extra help. This leads him to Stonewall, where he meets Zane for the first time and instantly feels himself falling for the mysterious and stone-cut detective.

The two men have their own hangups to work through, but both men are having a hard time denying the connection between them, even though they're trying.

When fate insists on pushing them together, Zane and Enzo give in and start exploring their feelings. They'll need to balance their budding relationship with the stress of Enzo's case, which takes them both on a twisting journey toward the truth, all while a bigger threat looms on the horizon.

# 1 ZANE

The heater in my office offered some refuge from the biting New York City winter outside, and still, my blood ran ice-cold. I pushed my chair back and stood, grabbing the photos on my desk. My eyes went over every single morbid detail as if I had to etch it all into my memory. As though I didn't have four other similar photos already burned into my brain.

"This happened yesterday?" I asked Andrew, my assistant.

"Mhmm," he said. I glanced up at him, seeing him looking as uncomfortable as I felt. His arms were crossed tight across his chest, covering the Nike logo on his black sweater, like he was creating a protective barrier around himself. He knew what this meant. He understood the nightmare that was riding into town on a skeleton horse. My eyes went back to the photo.

They were taken in the victim's bedroom. An unmade queen-sized bed sat in the center of the room, which was sparsely furnished with a few different IKEA pieces and some hand-me-down dressers. The white-and-black-striped comforter was soaked through in dark red. The man was lying face-up, wearing nothing but a pair of black briefs, his arms out and his legs together, as if someone had been above him, straddling him. His eyes were shut, his face a pale blue. From his forehead sprouted the hilt of a knife. The signature. I already knew it was an eight-inch serrated blade, sharp enough to cut through bone as if it were warm butter. The hilt was made out of ivory, white and carved with thick spirals running down the entire length.

A horn.

I dropped the photos on the table and peeled my eyes away from them. For a moment, I thought I would be sick. The waffle and coffee I had hours earlier rolled around in my stomach. I walked to the window, pulled open the latch, and lifted it up. Immediately, the sound of the New York streets erupted into the room as though an orchestra had suddenly started playing outside. Honks and shouts and laughs all blended together. Buses coming to a stop from surrounding streets, sirens fading into the distance. I looked outside, seeing people walking and going on with their lives, wearing their thick coats and heavy scarves. There was still some dirty snow piled up on a few corners, but for the most part, it had all melted away. A lady walked with her golden retriever, both wearing matching sweaters.

I took a breath. Somewhere out there, past the crazy sweater lady and the crying baby and the honking cabs, somewhere, the serial killer who had terrified the gay community years ago was coming back, out from whatever hole he had crawled into. Someone who had completely ripped my life in half and set it on fire. He was coming back out of a hole I had previously thought was his grave, but I was now realizing we had all been much too optimistic.

"Could this be a copycat?" Andrew asked. His voice was shaky.

"Maybe," I said, knowing the chances were slim. "But that crime scene is exactly like the old ones. Down to the brand of underwear he puts on the victim and the pose they're left in. The sheets look the same, too. It's all the same, and we know how obsessed this monster was—is. Shit. I can't believe he's back." Sleep tonight would be difficult to find. I wasn't normally shaken by things. It was one of the main reasons I'd gone into my line of work. I was a detective because I could look past the gruesome and see the answers when others couldn't. The figurative writing on the wall was literal for me, and the script was done in blood. It was why I opened up my own investigation agency ten years ago: Stonewall Investigations. We were an agency that worked primarily with the LGBTQ community since, statistically speaking, they were less likely to report problems to law enforcement over fear of discrimination. Of course, we took on cases from anyone who walked in through the door, but I was happy to offer a place specifically for those most scared to come and find help.

And I'd seen plenty of shit in those ten years. Most of our cases weren't as dark as murder, but some were, and those all stuck with me. But this set of murders hit much closer to home than any of the rest. My husband was taken by this monster. My Jose. He was killed in cold blood and left behind like the man in the photo. It still gnawed at my insides with a dull set of teeth, even though years separated me from the incident. Sure, time numbed some of the pain, but it never erased it fully. No, you needed more than time to erase all that. Some people turned to drugs, others alcohol, some looked to sex. I avoided all three and kept my head buried in work, distracting myself from the constant shadow left behind by the man I loved.

Except, what the fuck could I do now when work brought me right back to the same shit that had fucked me up so deeply? I felt the stress and the pain and the sorrow start to bubble up like a disgusting sewer concoction, roiling in my gut, threatening to climb up my esophagus and paint the floor. I closed my eyes and breathed, following the airflow as though it were a painting I could trace with my fingers. I stayed focused on the path of oxygen as the cold air from outside went in through my nose, falling down past my throat and filling up my heavy lungs, then followed it on the path out. I repeated this for a few more moments until the claw of anxiety eased its grip from around my heart.

"The police officer I talked to said they're working on finding any traces of DNA."

I shook my head. "They won't find anything." We all knew that. If this wasn't a copycat and was indeed the original Unicorn, then there was no way he'd left anything behind.

"I'll keep you posted on the results." Good on Andrew for batting away my negativity. He helped balance me out when things were spiraling out of control. It made him an excellent assistant and an even better friend. "The media is going to go on a feeding frenzy when the news gets out. Imagine: 'Officers buried the wrong guy; the Unicorn is back.'" Andrew shook his head, dropping it into his open hands and running his fingers up through his messy light brown head of hair.

He was right. In a few hours, news was going to break and the headlines would all be sensational. America loved a good serial killing, as terrible as that sounded. It kept people entertained while they sat safely behind screens, disconnected by distance or by knowing they weren't a target since they weren't gay. It was like watching a scary movie playing out in real time. They could send thoughts and prayers to the victims and their families and go on with their lives until the next update hit their Twitter feeds. Cable news would see their viewing numbers skyrocket and they'd start salivating, like a drug addict staring at a newfound stash of pill bottles. They'd reach with shaky hands toward a bottle, pop it open, and down it, grabbing the next one and the next one.

"Fuck," I hissed, letting it all out in one simple word.

"I've already set up a meeting between you and the police chief for three today."

"You're a rock star," I said, sitting back down at my desk. "Seriously."

"Zane." I looked up. Andrew's eyebrows were drawn up, his lips tight. "We'll get him, okay? This guy can't hide forever."

For a split second, I saw Jose standing in front of me. Not because Andrew looked anything like him, but because he would also know exactly what to say to keep me calm, to keep me focused. Growing up, I never had a grounding force. Foster families weren't always the most supportive structures in a kid's life. Some of them were; others took more of a toll on me than anything else. But then Jose came along, and I suddenly understood what it meant to have been looked out for. He would always be there at the end of the day, our naked bodies lying side by side, all our insecurities and fears laid bare, only so the other could help take them away. I always knew Jose could fight off my fears like a handsome knight taking on a fairy-tale dragon. And it wasn't like I couldn't handle myself. I had learned how from a young age. But having him around was different—he allowed me to let go of some of the burdens I was holding way too tightly. Jose was a man who had watched over me like a guardian angel.

A man who was now my guardian angel.

My attention went back down to my desk. I stuffed the photos into the black folder and closed it.

"Few more things on your agenda today, boss."

"Please tell me they're good things."

"Well, in fifteen you have naked Pilates in the park, and then in an hour you have lunch with the self-proclaimed queen of Hoboken."

I looked up and chuckled. Actually laughed. The sound came out as if I had just learned how to speak a foreign language. "Naked Pilates, huh? Are there space heaters?"

"No, it's a new thing. Tibetan, I think. Started trending after Ellen mentioned it on her show. Don't worry, your penis is *supposed* to disappear back into your body. Makes everyone feel comfortable."

"Ah, got it," I said, laughing again. "And the queen of Hoboken? What does she want?"

"Just for you to sit there and say she's pretty and that she deserves all the good things in the world while she eats a box of Jersey calzones."

"Sounds like an easy day, then."

"Nothing out of the ordinary, that's for sure." Andrew smiled. He looked at his watch. "Really, though, your twelve o'clock, Lorenzo De Luca, is downstairs." He smirked and cocked his head at me. "Sorry. That one isn't a joke."

"Thanks," I said, chuckling, knowing what Andrew meant when he apologized. My next appointment wasn't one I was very excited about, but only because I knew I wouldn't vibe well with the man. He was a popular attorney, had a ton of commercials, and would make his rounds on news networks whenever he was working on a particularly noteworthy case. He was always extremely charismatic, and the camera clearly loved him, but it was also obvious he lived a completely different life than mine. A kind of life I wouldn't enjoy. I grew up bouncing from home to home, carrying a single suitcase for the entirety of my belongings. The foster system chewed me and my siblings up and spat us out like used gum stuck to the street, ready to keep getting stepped on. I didn't have a drive for fancy suits and perfectly done hair. Colgate smiles were annoying, and unlimited black credit cards never impressed me.

I just knew I wouldn't gel with the guy, but I also knew I would try my damned hardest to solve whatever case he was bringing.

"Let's do this," I said, not knowing exactly just what I was getting into.

## 2  ENZO

*La vita è bella.* Life was beautiful. Everything couldn't have been going better for me. My Uber driver wasn't only avoiding every single red light in New York while looking damn handsome every time he glanced in the rearview mirror, but even *better* than a hot-ass driver, I was also able to convince a jury that my client was innocent of assaulting his employer. I ended up saving a man from a few years behind bars and closed another successful case. All in all, I felt pretty damn good.

"Thanks, bud," I said as the driver pulled up to my destination.

"No problem, man. Have a good one."

"You too," I said, already unlocking my phone and making sure to give him a good tip. I grabbed my briefcase and stepped out of the car and was immediately hit by the aggressively cold air. I shrugged my heavy gray peacoat on a little tighter. My breath came out in a fog as I walked toward the building. It was a beautiful brownstone with dark green ivy crawling up the facade like a well-placed mask. There was a sign above the white door that said

Stonewall Investigations, a subtle rainbow painted across the middle.

This was the place. I walked up the steps and rang the doorbell. My appointment was in ten minutes, so I wasn't in any rush. I hated getting to places late. Behind the door, I could hear the locks click. The door opened and revealed a handsome guy wearing a broad smile.

"Hi, I'm Andrew. You must be Mr. De Luca. Come in, get out of that cold."

"Thank you, thank you." I stepped inside and was immediately greeted by warmth. I looked around, feeling almost as if I were in someone's home rather than a detective agency. I liked it. It had a much different feel compared to police stations and other detective agencies I'd worked with. There was a long hallway ahead of me with a row of doors, each one with a name printed across the top on a sign that denoted which investigator was in which room. My appointment was with Zane Holden, the head honcho. I had heard only good things about him, so I was excited to get started on the case I was bringing him. It was a tough one, and I wanted to make sure I had the best of the best working on it. My law firm already had its own private investigator who was already looking into things, but I found his results were lacking in the past, so that led me to Stonewall Investigations.

"Let me go tell Zane you're here. I'll call you upstairs when he's ready." Andrew smiled as he pointed toward a comfortable-looking black bench set against the white walls, right next to the window where the bright winter sun was streaming through. There was a coat rack holding a variety of different coats with room for a couple more. I took mine off and hung it on one of the vacant copper hooks.

"Thanks, Andrew," I said, taking a seat on the bench,

the soft gray cushion proving to be comfortable and not just good for looks.

"Do you want some coffee or tea? Shouldn't be long, but we've just got a fresh brew of both going. There's also a more comfortable waiting room down the hall to the left."

"I'm okay without coffee or tea, and this bench is great. What is this? Memory foam?" I tilted up on the seat, lifting a leg and looking at the cushion. Andrew chuckled and turned toward the stairs. I noticed he was holding a thick folder in his hands, but away from his body, almost like they were tainted with something rotten inside.

"I'll be right back," Andrew assured me as he went upstairs and disappeared. The sound of knocks and then a door opening drifted down toward me. I could hear the distant murmur of conversations happening in the offices. Phones would ring every now and then, in that classic, old-timey tone, making me imagine the detectives smoking out of pipes and wearing full Sherlock Holmes regalia, feet on the table as they bantered over case details.

I entertained myself some more with my silly daydreams until Andrew reappeared. I heard his shoes hitting the steps before I heard his voice.

"Zane's ready for ya."

It felt almost like he was trying extra hard to be upbeat. Over the years of standing in a courtroom and interrogating witnesses, I'd learned how to read faces, and Andrew's face seemed a little shaken underneath that wide smile.

I got up and collected my stuff before following Andrew up the stairs. The second floor was more open than the first. It seemed like only Zane's office was up here. The landing opened into a large study-type area, with tall bookshelves full of different books and a small wooden desk placed against a bright window. Potted plants hung from the walls, their vines and leaves cascading down like hair. Zane's office was across the room, marked by a heavy dark door and a sign above it that read Zane Holden.

The door was cracked open. Andrew pushed it the rest of the way and stepped aside, allowing me in. At first, I was impressed by how nice the office was. A huge window looked out onto the street, framed by heavy red curtains held together by thick golden rope. It was a large office, furnished with pieces that would look great even in my own home, including a small side table, and a large desk facing away from the window.

But it was the man behind the desk who really blew my mind.

Never had I seen a sexier man. And never had I reacted so instantly to a man before, either. He was oozing pure sex appeal, from the way his sleeves were rolled up to show off those droolworthy forearms, to the pouty lips that were begging to be kissed, to the five-o'clock shadow that I wanted to lick. Zane was sitting behind his desk, and... holy shit. I never wanted to sit in someone's lap so damn bad before. I could see through the glass table, and his legs were spread wide, his thick thighs filling up the gray slacks he was wearing. I peeled my eyes away before I eye-fucked his crotch and ended up getting stuck in a dick trance.

Those were the worst, weren't they?

"Ciao, Mr. Holden." My hand went out in front of me before I started walking. For a hair of a second, I thought the guy wasn't going to stand up to greet me. Like it was some kind of power move. But thankfully, he stood up and reached out for my hand over his desk. He grabbed it and met my eyes. Immediately, I felt intrigued by the look behind those deep brown eyes. For some reason, I was taken back to being a kid and finding that one book out of the hundred I looked through at the library, the one with the most captivating synopsis and a head-turning cover. I was a huge reader, and those discoveries would make me one happy son of a gun.

This, somehow, was making me feel the same way.

"Lorenzo De Luca, nice to meet you."

"You can just call me Enzo," I offered, not breaking my eye contact with him even though our hands were separating.

*You can call me whatever the hell you want.*

"Okay, Enzo." He said it as though he were trying the word on. I couldn't tell if he liked it. His face was very... unreadable. I was trying. *Damn*, was I trying. But he was a solid wall of pure handsomeness and zero emotion. His squared jaw and strong brow, with eyes that glittered like precious gems, and lips that were asking me to suck on them, all of it added up to a man that made me want to drop to my knees and beg for it.

And I *never* begged.

"My assistant gave me a rundown on the case, but why don't you start from the top?"

"*Top* it is," I said, pulling the heavy black chair away from the table so I could sit down. I wondered if he noticed the slight emphasis I added to the word "top." Zane was making me want to fluff out all of my feathers and strut around him like a sex-starved peacock.

His face, still blank, gave me nothing to go off. I grabbed my briefcase and gently placed it down on the desk, opening it and pulling out two folders full of notes. I set them on the glass top and closed the briefcase, placing it back down on the floor. One of the folders, the blue one, was labeled with the name Ricardo Aventura in thick black marker. The green folder had the name Luanne Northwood.

"All right, let's get started." I pushed Ricardo's folder forward. Zane opened it and picked up the first few papers. "So, this is Ricardo," I said, knowing Zane could still listen as he read. "He's being accused of a double homicide. His neighbors were found murdered in their apartment, and Ricardo doesn't have a verifiable alibi. He swears up and down he didn't do it; the cops think otherwise and have him locked up. Considering he has a record, they didn't give him any leeway."

Zane was nodding as he put the papers down and picked up another few.

"It was a clean crime scene in terms of criminal DNA. They can't trace the gun used in the shooting either. There was no one else around during the murder, so all they really have is a videotape of a few days before the murder. In it, Ricardo is going off on Luanne and her husband. They're clearly pissed but it was someone's cell phone video so it's grainy and the audio isn't great." I took a breath, getting to the worst part. "You can hear Ricardo say something like 'you'll regret this' and then he storms back into his apartment. He insists that he said 'oh, forget this,' but it's almost impossible to be sure. They've already interviewed the person filming and came up with nothing."

He wasn't saying much, so I sat back as he went through the folders, reading the papers and asking a few questions here and there but staying silent for the most part. His lack of responses was having an odd effect on me. It was making me want to reach across the table and grab Zane's face in my hands, just to get a damn reaction from him. Obviously, I didn't want a full-blown conversation—he was looking over files—but still... I wanted something more than a nod. I wanted him to look up from the papers and at me.

"Looks like you have some things compiled already," he noted.

"My firm has a PI, too. He put a lot of it together. I can't take credit for it."

"Yeah, I saw his name on some of the papers. Any reason why you're hiring Stonewall?"

"Well, you guys have a big reputation, and I want all the help I can get. I know this guy is innocent, and I don't want to see him lose the rest of his life because of one dumb argument someone got on tape. And of course, there's also Stonewall Investigations' reputation in the gay community." I sighed, bringing up another concern I had about the case. "Ricardo is also gay. I normally wouldn't think much about his sexuality, but I'm nervous that some of the jury might be bigoted. There are a few of them who are heavy-duty Christians, and I know the prosecutor knows that, too. He'll use it to his advantage, no doubt."

That was when Zane looked up, and I was almost knocked out of the damn chair. "Plus," I said, my words forming before any coherent thoughts could back them up, "the fact that I have a hot-as-hell James Bond on the case doesn't hurt." My smiled cracked in half, my Italian accent coming in heavy toward the end.

And still, Zane didn't give me what I wanted. He gave a barely perceptible huff and a lift of his shoulders but kept that stony mask on, the one that set his lips straight and his brow pushed forward. I moved in the seat, the leather squeaking under my pants, and my hands fisted between my legs.

*What's this guy's deal?*

*And why do I want to do whatever it takes to figure it out?*

"Right," I said, brushing past my failed flirting attempt. I wasn't exactly used to failure, especially not with bedroom conquests, but I wasn't unrealistic about it, either. I hit on a good amount of men, and a few of them weren't interested for whatever reason. That was fine. I'd move on with my life and find someone else. It wasn't exactly that difficult to find guys.

Except I wanted to keep toying with Zane, if only to get some kind of reaction from him.

"Think we've got a chance of finding out who really did this?" I asked, while the gears in my brain worked overtime to think of some cutesy line that would at least get a smirk from him. Outside, the sun was beginning to reach its peak above the New York streets. It was a bright winter's day, and the sunlight felt unusually strong as it beamed through the window behind Zane, highlighting him in a way that should have only been possible in a movie.

*Or in my dreams.*

"Your PI didn't put together much."

"Yeah, we've been considering having him replaced."

Zane tilted his head, his lips pursing. "I want to be honest with you, Lorenzo."

"Enzo."

"We don't have any guarantees here, and I don't want to give you numbers since things can change on a dime. But, with that being said, I do see a few avenues I want to look deeper into. A videotape of an argument is definitely shaky, but I could see how it could be painted in court, especially coupled with the prior prostitution, which could be linked to him bringing over sketchy people and causing even more conflict with the neighbors."

He took a breath. I noticed his eyes dart to an unlabeled black folder that was set at the edge of his desk. Maybe he was being so standoffish because he had a lot on his plate?

"Well, I have faith you'll find out who really did this." I puffed my chest a bit. "I also have faith that I can create an ironclad defense out of crumbs."

"I'm sure you can," Zane said, looking back down at his folders. I couldn't tell if that was sarcasm. Was that sarcastic? I was almost going to ask but held back. Something was telling me it was my time to go and let Zane get to work. He seemed to be disengaging from me, and that was something I didn't like.

In fact, I wanted to remedy it. I wanted to see Zane again, under different circumstances, outside of talks of murder and jail time. A dinner wouldn't hurt. We'd get some good food, have some good conversation, and, hopefully, have some earth-shattering sex. All in all, it sounded like a win for everyone involved.

"Come get some food with me tonight," I said as I stood up to go. "On me."

*Cazzo. You can eat off my naked body if you want.*

Zane narrowed his eyes. I could tell he was tossing the suggestion around in his head. I smiled, hoping to sweeten the deal with a flash of my pearly whites.

"Busy tonight."

I deflated like a popped balloon. My molars ground together, my lips pursing. "Fine." I turned to leave before stopping and spinning back around. "You sure? We can do drinks instead. My buddy just opened up that bar across Central Park, near here actually. It's called Sire. I can get us a nice table."

"Sorry, Mr. De Luca." Zane didn't sound sorry in the slightest. His eyes were drawing back down to the case files

—those tantalizing eyes that I couldn't get enough of. It reminded me of visiting a museum and getting hypnotized by the collection of precious metals and gems. All kinds of rocks and crystals, glittering under precisely placed lights, made up of their own various chemical elements, each one more beautiful than the last. I felt like the longer I could stare into Zane's eyes, the more beauty I'd find.

Cazzo. I really wanted this man.

"Fine," I said again. I was having a hard time letting this one go. My rod may have been bent and broken, but I was pulling this son of a bass in, goddammit. And I knew that one important step to reeling in the catch was giving the line some slack. I wouldn't push the issue, but I'd leave it open. "I'll be there anyway in case you change your mind. You have my number. Use it."

Zane cracked a smirk. It was fleeting, but I saw it! Positive I did. That was progress. "I'll think about it."

Okay. That was as far as I was getting. I wasn't a gambling man, nor did I want to press my luck. I could tell he was interested by the glint of curiosity behind those captivating eyes of his. Of course he would show up. What did he have to lose? Free drinks and food? Hell, I'd show up to a third grader's piano recital if they were giving away free booze and pizza.

*Perfetto. I'm sure I'll see him later.*

I thought the night would end up being perfect. I never could have imagined the events that were about to come, the reason why Zane and I would be pushed together again.

## 3  ZANE

Thunder was purring up a storm as he made himself comfortable next to me on the couch. I moved one of the blue decorative pillows down to the wood floor so he could have more room. He was a fat black cat that made his heart my home, even though my nose may have despised him. Having a cat while also being allergic to said cat wasn't the ideal arrangement, but there was no letting him go the day he stumbled onto my doorstep as a kitten. That was six years ago, and a hundred nasal sprays later, I still loved him like a family member.

Besides, it helped keep me on top of cleaning my apartment. If I didn't vacuum every other day, even the Flonase would have trouble preventing the sneeze attacks.

I gave him a few head scratches and then got back to focusing on the laptop. The second my eyes turned to the screen, Thunder sensed it, got up, and stretched across the keyboard, hitting every possible key he could. I chuckled and lifted him up and set him back down to the side. It was futile. The moment my attention went back to the screen, Thunder activated his attention-grabbing systems and went into full-throttle purring, paw swiping at my fingers. I resisted for a few more minutes before he finally tired and climbed up onto the couch cushion so he could curl up behind my head. I went back to my work.

Investigations were a part of me. I loved every aspect of it. I loved turning over stones, connecting dots, and finding answers for other people's problems. Since I was a kid, I'd set out to solve problems. Especially in my teenage years, after my silence spell. Whether it was trying to figure out who was stealing my brother's lunch at school everyday, or if it was figuring out one of the neighbor's problem of someone egging their house every week. I would write out plans, set up interviews, and go on with trying to figure out the answers.

I also really enjoyed digging and looking for any unfound gems of information, which was what I was currently doing. One of the first steps to any investigation was to check social media. Many people tended to overshare through status posts and filtered pictures, but sometimes it wasn't even the oversharing that did it. I had one case a few years back where the suspected thief had posted random song lyrics but forgot he had his geotag setting on. It traced him right back to the scene of the crime, at the exact same time the robbery had occurred. Some people were simply dumb and made stupid mistakes, and social media tended to amplify the stupid by a magnitude of a thousand.

Whoever killed Luanne and Oscar wasn't stupid, though, at least not as far as I could tell. No mistakes seemed to have been made. Not yet, anyway. I needed to do serious digging. I first started by combing through Oscar's social media accounts, which took a total of three minutes. He wasn't active online, which would have thrown up a cautionary flag if he were younger, but he wasn't raised in the social media era so I didn't worry much about it.

Luanne, on the other hand, was much more active. Her profile was public, which made my job a little easier. I went through her wall posts, not noticing anything out of the ordinary—no signs of an obsessive stalker or an angry ex-husband. She would post things about her dinners and movies she'd seen. There were plenty of political posts, all with articles that looked like they were sourced out of a trash can. She had an average amount of friends and would get random comments on her wall, which was currently being flooded with "we'll miss you" posts.

Those were the ones I focused on first. It wasn't uncommon for a killer to insert themselves in some way to the deceased, whether it was a bouquet of flowers sent to the funeral or by simply writing a grieving post on social media, or in more extreme cases, showing up at the scene of the crime after it happened. Some suspected the guilty party would do it so they'd never seem suspicious, while others said the primary motive was pleasure for the murderer. They enjoyed treading knee-deep into the pile of steaming shit they left behind, leaving wrecked lives in their wake.

*I'll Always remember You, Lulu.*

That was Tonya Carpenter, an accountant based in the Bronx. Blonde, bright blue eyes, warm smile, two kids and three dogs, judging by her profile picture.

*miss you soo much, Lu*

That was Bianca Del le Rosa, who appeared to be Luanne's cousin and someone really into Harley Davidson.

*Details for the funeral have been posted. Thank you to everyone who's offered their help and hearts. Luanne will be forever missed.*

That was Susan, Luanne's sister, and someone I wrote down on the top of my list for questioning. I didn't enjoy reaching out to family members so soon after they'd lost a loved one, but I needed to make sure I caught them when their memory was the freshest. Most times a brother or a sister, a mother or father, they were the ones who knew the answer to a crime before any questions were even asked.

I kept scrolling down her wall, looking for any red flags. Once I read past the recent messages, I started seeing much less activity on her Facebook. Seemed like it took her passing to bring back old friends. The only people who wrote to her were Tonya, Susan, and Luanne's mother, Pauline. It was sporadic posting for the most part, aside from Susan, who seemed to make sure to write on her sister's wall at least three times a week from the looks of it. There were also few pictures of Luanne, and most of them were old, dating back five years or more. The more recent ones showed a smiling Luanne, skinny with big brown eyes, and her husband at Disney. There were pictures of them with Mickey, waiting in line at Thunder Mountain, standing outside of the magical castle, and looking up at the fireworks show. They seemed happy and in love, which made me wonder if there was someone else involved. That person could have easily seen these pictures and felt a spark of jealousy, strong enough to lash out at the object of their affection. But, if that were the case, which one was cheating? Was it Luanne who had another man, or was it Oscar who had a murderous side chick?

I spent the next couple of hours digging through the internet, trying to find any old blogs or secret Twitters linked to Luanne or Oscar. I did manage to find an old food blog Luanne appeared to manage for a few months and then abandoned. I checked the last post and noticed it was written a year ago, three days before Christmas. It was a recipe for "snow-covered Jell-O". She was a regular Emeril Lagasse.

I was about to click out of the page when I noticed something toward the bottom, underneath an unflattering photo of red Jell-O covered in powdered sugar. The comment read "make this for me, lu." I looked at the username: Scara-3. Clicking the username brought me to an empty profile page, with the comment history just as empty, besides the one note he left for Luanne. I noted it down, copying the username and comment.

This didn't seem like a random spam comment, whoever left it added Luanne's name to it. It also didn't feel like Oscar's account, simply because I didn't think he really knew how to use a computer, much less create an account and name himself Scara-3. From my preliminary research, Oscar was a regular guy who did well in school and had a good job with great prospects. Why would he create one anonymous page just to comment on his wife's food when he could say it to her face?

*Scara-three.... What is that supposed to mean?*

Racking my brain for the next half hour didn't do much in terms of getting an answer. If anything, I was feeling the familiar precursors of burning out. My gaze was jumping around my living room, my leg was bouncing, and my hands couldn't stay still. I had been staring at my computer for hours, and it was beginning to take its toll.

I set my laptop down on the couch and got up for a stretch. I twisted my body, holding my arm up against my chest and feeling the muscles in my shoulder flex and tug and release the tension I held inside. I switched arms and did the same. Thunder, who'd been sleeping on the top of the refrigerator, noticed I was up and leapt down onto the counter, where he could jump down onto the floor and stroll over to me, his engines purring and his tail swishing in the air. I relaxed my back and stretched my neck, reaching down to the floor as Thunder reached my ankles and rubbed himself against my legs. I gave his head a few good scratches before lifting myself back up, focusing on my breathing. It wasn't full-on meditation, but it still did the trick.

It wasn't always that way. For practically my entire life, I lived by suppressing my anxieties and fears until they just blew up and left me incapacitated. It was what happened when I lost Jose. My worst fear had become realized, and I might as well have become a paraplegic. I'd become paralyzed. Weeks passed with me lying in bed, getting up for crumbs of bread and some water. I had to give my cases to another detective at Stonewall, that was how incapacitated I felt. It wasn't until my brother had something close to an intervention and helped bring me back to myself. It was a *really* tough fucking road, but I had come a long way, and meditation had actually become a crucial tool in getting me back to working order. I made sure to set aside as much time as possible, usually half an hour as soon as I woke up and then another half before going to sleep.

I considered it now, just to hone my focus back into the investigation. I looked up at the clock on the wall, the hands pointing to ten o'clock. I'd been working since I woke up, meaning a little over thirteen hours now. Underneath the clock was a wooden bar table, painted over in a luxe navy blue, the legs solid and curved toward the bottom. It used to belong to my grandfather and was said to belong to his grandfather and so on and so on. On top, a few books were sitting with their colorful spines pointed outward, next to a white lamp, the base shaped like a deer's head, its antlers painted in solid gold.

But none of that was what caught my eye. Toward the opposite edge of the table was a framed photo. Looking back at me were two smiling men, arms wrapped around each other's sides, the thundering Niagara Falls sending up a curtain of mist behind them.

I walked to the photo, my toes feeling the hard wood beneath them, a purchase on this world, a sensation to keep me grounded as I threatened to break down some heavy-duty emotional dams. Thunder weaved through my feet and stopped when I did. He looked up and gave a chirp, as though he knew what I was doing. Was he warning me? Telling me to stop? Or was he telling me to go ahead and do it, to focus on a wound I never thought would heal completely?

He was probably just telling me he wanted food. I reached for the frame. The photo felt heavy in my hands. Like an anchor. But instead of mooring me to shore, this anchor was threatening to pull me down with it. The two faces staring back at me looked like strangers, and yet I could paint each crease, each wrinkle, each pore, all with my eyes closed from memory. Maybe not so much mine, but I knew I could damn well replicate Jose's face. I had spent hours over my years with him just looking at his face, etching his features into my mind, never knowing just how hard I'd hold on to those memories in the future. How could I have known? Never. Even with my line of work, I wouldn't have dreamed of what happened to Jose, not even in my worst nightmares.

And then, the darkest parts of my fears became real. They solidified and struck, taking away the one man I loved in this world with everything I had. He was my other half.

My entire world. He taught me what romance meant and the power that love had, and then he was taken from me. Ripped from my side, from one day to the next. He was there when I woke up and then gone before nightfall.

He was taken by the Unicorn, and now the killer was back. It made me sick thinking about it. I knew the police were hard at work trying to figure out who the killer was, but that still didn't make me feel good.

I wasn't taking the case this time, though. No. It was too personal for me. I knew I would be consumed by chasing the Unicorn if it was the only case on my desk. I decided I would put another detective on it, someone with a fresh outlook. Maybe they could see something everyone else missed. I still had to decide who that detective would be, but I already had a few ideas.

I put the photo back down. This wasn't the way Jose would have wanted me to be three years after his death. He was always such a force of energy, always wanting everyone around him to be smiling and enjoying themselves, even if it was after standing three hours in line for a new ride at Disney. He'd have everyone around us laughing and having a good time, even if they weren't part of our group. His positive energy was just that infectious. I knew he was looking down and yelling at me to go out and have some fun. And to also pick up my socks and to stop peeing on the toilet seat.

I smiled, feeling the hole that was left inside me throb with need. Thunder was looking at me from the couch, sitting next to my phone as if even he was telling me to pick it up and get out of the house.

"Fine, fine," I said to myself, walking over to the phone. What was the worst that could happen by going out?

A question I wish I had known the answer to *before* I decided to make plans.

## 4  ENZO

The night may have been young, but I wasn't getting any younger, that was for sure. I glanced at my phone for the tenth time, checking to see if I had a message before looking at the time, my patience slowly but surely getting chipped away and revealing a shiny jewel of frustration underneath. I never got stood up for a date. Granted, Zane and I never set up an official date, but *still*, you'd think he'd show up for one drink at the very least. I'd laid out the tantalizing bait: five-star grub and beer. My company would have obviously been a plus, too. Who would have turned an offer like that down?

But nope, nothing. My phone had zero alerts—oh wait! Nope, just an email from Bergdorf Goodman advertising some Prada coat (which looked really nice actually... fine, I'd buy it).

When I was done placing my order, the waitress had come around with an offer to refill my beer mug. I nodded with a smile and turned my attention back to my phone. I was sitting outside on the patio of the bar, my feet dangling from the barstool, the cold temperatures being pushed away by the huge heating lamps set throughout the outdoor area. The place was pretty packed, with couples and groups of friends claiming the nine tables outside. The din of conversation competed with the loud sounds of the surrounding city. The bar was located in Upper Manhattan, right across the street from Central Park. During the warmer months, the bar had a beautiful view of the blast of greenery that pulsed in the center of the city, but the cold had stripped away the leaves and left behind barren trees, which still had a beauty of their own, don't get me wrong.

I sighed and tried to get distracted with people-watching as they walked past holding the front of their coats tighter against their chests, talking to their friends as steam floated out from their lips. It was around eleven, so some people were just starting to go out. Others were already waiting for Ubers to get home so they could find refuge from the cold. I didn't mind being cold; I preferred it way more than being hot. I tended to get... well, let's just say the heat brought out the swamp in me. Yeah, I'd much rather be walking with a coat on than walking with a layer of sweat on. In fact, a walk home tonight sounded really nice.

*Except I don't want to do that walk alone.*

Another sigh. I had to stop that. This negative wave that was falling over me needed to get pushed back. *Shake it off.* Like my mom would say: "Chiodo scaccia chiodo," an Italian phrase for "a nail drives out another nail"—basically, one rusty nail can get pushed away by a shiny, much better nail. Or, in more blunt terms, get the fuck over it; someone else is going to come along, and chances are they're going to be better than the last.

So, I took my mother's advice and texted an old fling. Maybe he wasn't exactly a brand-new nail, but I knew I'd get a good nailing out of it, so that was worth something, right?

He lived around the block, and I knew he'd be down for some drinks and fun, so why not? Zane wasn't showing up, and that was fine. He wasn't interested, no big deal. I didn't care.

"Chiodo scaccia chiodo," I murmured to myself before taking a big swig of beer.

\*\*\*

"I seriously can't believe you said that to her." Eric was leaning over the table, his eyes locked with mine. We were already four drinks in and I was feeling it, and it looked like he was, too. His eyes looked a little cloudy.

*Nothing like Zane's...*

*Nope. No, not going there.*

Why was I so obsessed with Zane all of a sudden? I couldn't remember another man who had captured my attention so fully in the span of thirty minutes. It felt almost as if those thirty minutes had lasted the entire span of my lifetime. I felt like I knew Zane from the start. And yet, on the same token, I knew nothing about him. I had no idea what he liked to eat, or where he was from, or what he did with his free time. I didn't know what his biggest aspirations in life were or what fears he was haunted by.

I wanted to know it all. But I knew that the chances of me learning anything were slim to none. It was something I had to accept. A new, shiny nail can hammer down a rusty one.

"What else was I going to do?" I exclaimed, leaning back in the chair and looking out at the dark park across the street, pushing Zane out of my mind. "When another attorney comes at me, I'm going to fight right back. Merda," I said, throwing around one of my preferred curse words.

"I guess it's why you're one of the best lawyers in New York."

"Guess so." I took a drink of my Moscow mule. It felt weird hearing that out loud, no matter how many people reminded me about it. I grew up being far from number one, so it all still felt sort of dreamlike. Even though I was confident in myself and my abilities, I still held on to all my insecurities like a five-alarm hoarder. The kind of hoarder that keeps cat poop for years, not just old notes from high school. I had to learn how to put on a good front, strong enough to hide those insecurities.

"So, anything big you're working on now?"

I looked back from the park and my breath hitched in my chest for a split second. There was a man walking down the street wearing a heavy black coat and a navy blue beanie pulled down tight, and for a very brief moment, I thought it was Zane showing up two hours late.

*Is it... it can't be.*

But as the man drew closer, my hopes were quickly thrown into the shredder. It was just a random dude with a really hot jaw line and slightly similar build to Zane's broad-shouldered frame. I turned my attention back to Eric, who shot a glance over his shoulder.

"See someone you know?"

"No," I said, sure that he could hear the disappointment in my tone. "Thought I did."

"Oh, cuz that big guy was looking at you like he recognized you."

"Huh?" I hadn't even noticed the bigger man standing behind the Zane-wannabe. But when I looked up, the man had turned and walked away, a dark hoodie thrown over his head. I finished the last of the Moscow mule, trying to keep my mind from snapping back to picturing Zane walking down the street.

"I'm working on one big case now, yeah. But enough about work." I gave my shoulders a little shake and rolled my neck, releasing some of the tension I held in my muscles and feeling my bones pop.

"What, um, are you watching on TV nowadays?" Eric asked, tilting his head. I had to hold back a sigh. This was one of the reasons why Eric and I could never work together. He was a dud to talk to. I had more stimulating conversations with the label on a Vitamin Water bottle.

It was a common thread running through all my past relationships. No one really stimulated me, not in a way that made me want to stick around. Not after Ryan.

I thought I'd found a good one though. Oh how fucking wrong I was about that one. It took me some time to drive out that old nail. What he had done to me messed me up for a good year. But after some time, I dove back into the dating pool, only to find it was a really shallow pool. I remember being on the third date with Eric and still talking about favorite colors and TV shows. And that happened with the four guys who came before him, too. I wasn't sure if it was just my roll of the dice or if I was somehow attracting these guys. Was it my cologne? Cazzo, something was going on.

"I haven't had much time for bingeing these days, but I was watching the one with the kids and the alien thing."

"Oh yeah, that's a good one."

"Yep."

"How's your drink?"

"I finished it." I lifted the glass, giving it a twirl. "You know what, maybe we should head out."

I glanced at my watch. It was already twelve. I could

have stayed out for a few hours longer, but honestly, I just wanted to get back inside and have my fun with Eric and then get to sleep. I didn't want to keep seeing familiar faces in passing strangers. I didn't realize just how disappointed that mix-up made me until I suggest heading home. It felt as if, by going home, I was officially admitting defeat, and I just wanted to get it over with. If Zane didn't show up tonight, he wasn't interested. Simple as that. And that was fine—we'd keep a professional relationship and prove that Ricardo was innocent. Then I'd go on with my life, and Zane would go on with his.

It was the truth, and the only way this situation would play out.

*So why does that make me feel so shitty?*

We closed out and paid the check. I grabbed my coat from the back of my chair and put it on, buttoning the front to shield my chest from the cold. I buried my hands in the deep pockets and followed Eric through the gate that led out onto the street, leaving the warm refuge provided by the huge heating lamps. He looked cute in a bright blue puffy coat, his cheeks flushing pink from the chill.

My house was only five streets away, so we decided to walk it, both of us enjoying the cold after enduring a particularly hot summer. I managed to avoid some of it by taking a trip to Italy with my mother so we could visit family. Over there, the temperatures were much more tolerable and didn't have me feeling like a sweaty mess in a suit, which was exactly what I looked like every time I stepped outside the courthouse. Seriously, it was like a conditioned reaction. My body would instantly open the floodgates as soon as the stifling heat touched me. Sometimes even looking at the weather report would give me the precursors of swamp ass, and that, as *everyone* knows, is the worst kind of ass around.

"Did you see the news?" Eric asked, lifting his head, the tip of his nose turning a light pink. "About the Unicorn?"

I nodded. A chill crawled down my spine, and it wasn't from the cold. Everyone knew about the Unicorn, especially those in the gay community. He terrorized us for years, making every single gay person I knew look over their shoulders twice and triple-guess every Grindr hookup they had. We had thought it was all over when someone was found dead and the police said they'd found matching DNA, but it looked like everyone had been wrong. The Unicorn was still out there, and he wasn't done.

"I did see it," I said as we turned into a quieter street bordered by tall brownstones on either side of the street with barren trees lining the sidewalks. "Merda's fucked-up. Just have to keep your eyes open and hope the sick bastard gets caught."

"For real," Eric said. Our breaths were coming out in puffs of steam, drifting up toward the starless winter sky. "What if someone like that asks you to defend them?"

I opened my mouth but found it shutting without an answer. As a lawyer, I wasn't constitutionally bound to take on any client. It wasn't like I was a doctor; I didn't *have* to save a killer's life. But then my job wasn't to render judgment, either. I was trained to be objective and see an entire picture as opposed to just one fragment of it.

"Well," I started, thinking out my answer. "Defense attorneys never know for sure whether their client did it or not, even if they say they did it. It's impossible to *truly* know. So, if someone were to come to my firm and say they're being accused of being the Unicorn, but they know they aren't, then yeah, I'll take the case. It's my job to defend. I put together the best facts for a defense and then let the jury do the rest."

"I guess that's a good way of thinking about it," Eric said.

"It's really the only way of thinking about it," I said with a chuckle. We were almost to the intersection when I felt someone behind us. And not "down the street" behind us. I felt like someone was right on our backs. Way too close to be comfortable or normal. I steeled myself and glanced over my shoulder.

No one. I was losing it.

"You okay?"

"Yeah, thought I heard something."

"Does someone get scared of ghost stories?"

"The Unicorn isn't exactly a ghost story," I pointed out.

"Fair enough," Eric said. He was a good guy, albeit a little boring. He was going to find an equally good guy to settle down with, I didn't doubt that. Started making me wonder if *I* would ever find someone to settle down with.

We made it to the intersection. My penthouse wasn't far now. It was a beautiful, massive space that looked out onto the city from the top of a historic building. Buying the place was one of the first things I did when I started making the big bucks (after I bought mamma a new car). It was close enough to the firm that I could walk on the days when I wasn't inviting swamp ass or icicle nuts. It was also blocks away from Central Park, which was one of my favorite hangout spots. I liked getting lost on the trails, watching the squirrels battle it out for nuts and the rats for pizza slices.

The light turned red, but no one in New York waited for the crosswalk sign to click on. If there were no cars coming, New Yorkers marched right across the road, regardless of the light. We didn't have time to wait; we were always on the move, always running to catch one subway train or another.

We stepped onto the street when I noticed something from the corner of my eye. This was definitely not in my head, either. I turned to look, and that's when the fist connected with my bottom jaw. My head spun to the side, away from the assailant's fist. I fell onto Eric, who caught me and moved us backward as the man threw another fist, this one flying through the air without landing.

"What the fuck!" I spat, the iron taste of blood biting at my tongue.

"You fucking asshole." It was a man, bigger than I was, but only because he was overweight and stretching out the dark black hoodie, stained with who knew what. "You're the reason my wife's behind bars, fucking queer. I saw you at the bar, and I wanted to make you understand what you did to me. My wife. To my fucking family."

I could feel Eric next to me shrinking backward. My mind was reeling, trying to put the pieces of this sudden puzzle together. "What are you talking about?"

The man looked like he was in a rage with his bloodshot eyes reflecting the light from the streetlamp above. His pupils were blown, big black saucers staring me down. He kept reaching into the front pocket of his hoodie.

"My wife. You implicated her in the Yuma robberies. If you never brought her up, no one would have ever figured out she did it."

Merda. I knew exactly what he was talking about. I had a client wrongfully accused of robbing their employer, and that robbery happened to be a million dollars worth of precious stones. It was a case that happened to hit close to home for me, one mirroring a similar incident from my childhood. I found irrefutable evidence pointing to another woman and won the case for my client. Obviously, things didn't go well for the other lady.

"Listen," I said, putting my hands up. I wiped at my lip, my thumb coming back red with blood. "We can talk this out."

Inside, my body felt like it was boiling. I wanted to ball up a fist and send it crashing against this guy's skull. He had caught me by surprise and was continuing to piss me off. But that pocket of his—it made me nervous. I didn't want to do anything that could make this worse.

"Nah, I don't think so."

That was when my worst fear became realized. He pulled his hands out of his pocket, but this time they weren't empty. He raised a jet-black gun into the air. It was so black, it seemed as if it were sucking in all the light around it. I immediately had tunnel vision, and it centered itself straight down the barrel. Time slowed down to a crawl. My body froze, but my brain was running at a mile a second.

Things were definitely worse.

"You fucked up my life, so I think it's only fair I fucked up yours."

"No, you don't want to do that." I was surprised I still had the ability to shape words. My mouth was ash dry. I could feel my knees trembling, but I focused on steadying myself. I couldn't pass out. I couldn't show fear. I was going to get us out of this alive. It was the only option.

The man's fingers moved to hover over the trigger. I felt like I was looking at it all through a magnifying glass. I could practically see the skin cells on the tips of his fingers, the miniscule beads of sweat that formed where the pad of his pointer finger met with the cold metal of the trigger.

This was bad. Really fucking bad.

## 5  ZANE

*Pop! Pop! Pop!*
The gun sounds faded out and gave way to a fast-spitting rapper. I looked to my brother, who was eyeing the man with the loud boom box hoisted on his shoulder. He'd already asked the guy to turn down his music, but somehow the music found its way back up to full volume, battling it out with the loud sounds of the subway train speeding through the underground. Our subway car rattled as Andrei got up, using the grimy steel pole to steady himself with.

"Sir, I'm with the NYPD. Don't make me ask you to lower your music again." My brother pulled his badge out from the pocket of his jeans and showed it to the man. The guy looked from the badge to my brother, waved a hand in the air, and walked past me, leaving behind a smell reserved for sewer rats and garbage piles. He sat down on the farthest seat, giving us the stink eye for the entire rest of the ride. That was fine, though; the peace and quiet was more than worth having to deal with some attitude. The mother who had her two children with her also appreciated it, making it known when she said thank you to my brother before getting off the train.

"Thanks for coming out tonight," I said to him as we got off at our stop. My place was only four stations away from the bar we were going to, so it wasn't a long ride.

"No problem." Andrei zipped up his gray jacket and pushed his hands into the pockets of his dark jeans. The cold didn't bother me as much. I enjoyed it, much more than I liked the heat. One of my foster homes had landed me in Miami, and holy shit, did I hate it down there. The humidity stuck to you like another layer of clothing. Thankfully, that house didn't last too long. The heat wasn't the only thing I hated about that family. The next family had me reunited with Andrei again, after a four-year separation in the system. We'd stayed together ever since.

We made our way out of the subway station and up onto the busy New York City street. It was still relatively early for the city that never slept. I checked my watch. Ten thirty.

There was no damn way I was going to the same bar Enzo would be at. So, naturally, I landed at the bar that was only a street away. It wasn't my fault—it was just my brother's favorite spot and the only way to get him to come out. It was a cool bar that not only had some really great beer, but also had the best sushi I'd ever tasted. It was in the basement of a hotel, so we had to climb down a set of stairs to enter. Inside, the lights were dim and the bulbs were those old Edison types, with the spiral filaments that flickered every now and then. The walls were brick with exposed wood beams, and towering paper lamps stood next to the beams, but their light was also dim.

The place was packed, too. The loud din of conversation overtook us as we stood by the host's podium. The host was looking down at her computer, trying to find us a seat. "Are you guys okay with bar seating?"

"Sure," I said, my brother nodding in agreement. The hostess, a perky brunette with a flirty smile, led us to the two open spots at the bar. We took our seats on the stools, and she handed us the menus, her eyes lingering on my brother's. When she left, I arched a brow and spoke as I looked over the menu. "She's not your type."

"What? What do you mean she's not my type?"

"She looks like she has her shit together. You go for the messy ones."

"Not true." He wasn't even trying to put up an argument.

"Michelle?"

"Okay, fine, one."

"Andrea, Sherry, Topaz, Merlot, Sparkling Rose."

"Very funny," my brother said, laughing as he shook his head. "I have eclectic taste. Is that so bad?"

"When your eclectic taste steals everything in your fridge and then slashes your tires for no reason, then yes, yes it is bad." I was smiling, feeling good about coming out tonight. I ordered a Corona, and my brother got himself whiskey. The bartender, Shiro, was a handsome guy with short black hair and muscles that pushed against his black shirt. It was my turn to get a flirty bat of the eyelashes, and my brother didn't miss it.

"Don't even try, he's not your type."

"Oh really?"

"Yeah, he's clearly got his shit together." Andrei laughed and bumped me with his shoulder. "Seriously, though, don't try it. He's got a ring on that finger of his."

"I noticed," I replied. "I'm not one to let details slip by."

"Right, duh, Detective."

"Besides," I said as Shiro left our drinks in front of us and moved on to take care of other customers, "I'm fine without anyone. Work's got me busy, and Thunder gives me all the attention I need."

"Yeah, only when he's hungry, though."

"And how is that different than any other guy?"

Andrei lifted his glass, the light brown whiskey swirling inside. "Touché."

I drank a gulp of the cold beer. The bartender came back around and took our food orders, turning around to tap them into the computer screen. My gaze couldn't help but drift down, right toward Shiro's perky butt looking damn good in a pair of fitted black jeans. It immediately felt a few degrees hotter, and my underwear felt a size too small. I adjusted on the stool and pried my eyes away, admiring the rows of liquor bottles on the wall instead.

"But seriously, Zane, you haven't talked to anyone that's made you want to jump back into the dating pool?"

"No," I said, suddenly getting a flash of an image in my head. A face. One with big lips, a strong jawline, and a confidence in his eyes that was balanced by a deep warmth. *Lorenzo.* "No one."

"Really? Not one guy?"

"I haven't been looking."

Andrei nodded, pursing his lips. I knew what he was thinking. He wanted to tell me that I should start looking. He was always the one to push me out of my comfort zone, and it never failed to make me a better person because of it. If it weren't for him, I doubt I'd ever have gotten as far as I did. I probably would have been defeated after the second foster family. Then we were split up and I started to feel like I was collapsing back into myself, scared of testing the boundaries and pushing for the better. I stopped making friends, and I would shut down at school, to the point where some of the teachers suspected I had gone mute.

"Well," Andrei said, drinking another sip of his whiskey, "I think you should start."

I chuckled, nodding. I didn't disagree with him, but I just didn't feel an urge to go looking in the first place. It felt weird thinking about it, about having another man sleep in the same spot Jose would sleep. It didn't sit well with me. Then there was the recent news, which still had my skin crawling, so the last thing I wanted to do was date.

"We got a new case today," I said, trying to keep my anxieties at bay, even though my mind kept snapping back to the photos that were on my desk hours earlier. "The Unicorn is back."

It was as if all the air was sucked out of the bar at once. I knew it was all in my head, but I could have sworn the entire place was put on pause, the music screeching to a halt, all the attention turning to me at the mention of the killer. Then, as quick as it happened, the feeling disappeared, the bar returning back to normal, the pause button being released, and everyone getting back to whatever they were doing before I mentioned anything about the killer.

My brother's expression looked heavy, the light above us flickering for a moment. "Yeah," he said. "We've got the entire department working on it."

I took in a deep breath, filling my lungs as if I had found gold. I let it go, focusing on the sensation of the oxygen flowing through me, centering me. "I'm going to get our resources on it, too."

"You... okay with that?"

For a moment, I was going to barrel forward with a lie. But I couldn't. I shook my head, unable to hide anything from my brother. "No, no I'm not." I looked straight ahead, as if the big bottle of bourbon had suddenly become the most interesting thing in the world. "I'm going to get someone else to lead the case. Maybe Collin."

"Collin? Isn't he pretty new?"

"Yeah, only been with us for a year, but damn he's good. He sees things in goddamn dirt particles in the air. I don't know how he does it, but he knows what he's doing."

I turned away from the bourbon and looked to my brother. He was searching me, trying to make sure I was okay without asking it out loud. He'd give me this look often when we were kids, the older brother trying to assess the younger one, trying to determine whether he had to beat anyone up or not.

I managed a weak smile before finishing the rest of my beer. "I miss him."

It came out of nowhere and yet felt like it had been everything, the only thing I had been thinking about since Jose was taken from me.

My brother placed a comforting hand on my back and rubbed. "I'm sorry, Zane. I wish there was something else I could do. But I promise you—I *swear* it—we're going to find the fucker who killed Jose. Who took all those lives. This Unicorn bastard isn't going to get by us a second time."

I closed my eyes and rubbed the bridge of my nose. Another deep breath in, following it out. "I can't believe he's back."

"No one can."

"Which means Felix Ostroff was the wrong guy."

"Well, we don't know that entirely. Maybe he did do it, and this is someone picking up where he left off. Or, maybe there were two of them all along. Not like we can question him anymore, though."

I shook my head. "No, no we can't." And the reason

why we couldn't was because Felix was murdered a year ago. The prisoners were out in the yard when the leader from one of the prison gangs came up to him and shanked him with a branch they had found and whittled into a lethal stake. Felix didn't even make it to the hospital. When I got the news of his death, I remember I had felt sure that the nightmarish saga was finally behind me.

Little did I know, it may have just been beginning.

Shiro brought over the sushi we'd ordered. My brother and I went quiet as we got to work eating. My dragon roll was exactly what I needed, and the Philadelphia roll I ate afterward was exactly what I didn't even know I needed.

Basically the food was great, and it did wonders in changing the mood that had settled in the air. By the time we were done, we'd stopped talking about serial killers and had moved on to lighter topics. I asked my brother how house hunting was going, which launched us into a half-hour conversation about the pros and cons between two different houses he was considering. Finally we decided neither of them were good enough, and that it was probably time to knock out. I checked my watch and saw it was close to midnight. "All right," I said, signing the check. "Let's get out of here. I've got an early morning tomorrow."

We said our thanks to both the cute bartender and the hostess and climbed the stairs up to the street. The cold immediately hit us like a ton of bricks, forcing me to appreciate how nice being inside in the warmth was. I couldn't wait to get back home so I could blast the heater, take my clothes off, and sink into bed underneath my comforter.

That would have been the perfect end to the night.

Instead, swap perfect out for horrifying, and you've got exactly how my night *actually* ended.

## 6  ENZO

I'd never felt such a primal grip of fear close around me. Like a god-sized claw had ripped through the clouds and reached down, snapping around me and sucking the breath straight from my chest. It felt like my lungs were collapsing, as if they were made of crumpling tissue paper, while my heart was pounding to the beat of a hummingbird's racing wings. My vision tunneled in, and my feet felt as if they had been injected with pounds of cement. Fight or flight, and I was ready to do neither. I was frozen. This wasn't how I envisioned things ending.

"You gotta let us go," Eric whimpered. I could hear him shaking through his voice. This felt like it was my fault. Eric was totally innocent; he shouldn't have been here. I opened my mouth to speak but found no words. My mom would have been stunned someone found a way to keep me quiet. She always joked that I was made to be a lawyer from the second I could open my mouth and put sounds together. They weren't even words, but I was gurgling full monologues with the passion of a C-rated TV actor playing a passionate attorney.

*Mamma*, I thought, feeling as though my heart were no longer beating like a hummingbird but being torn apart by one instead. I remembered the last thing I told her, hours earlier when we had ended a call. It was a simple call, just about how the day went and what was for dinner. "Love you, Mamma," I had said, and I felt like it wasn't enough. There was so much more left to say.

The man looked at Eric. His pupils were blown. They looked like big black saucers floating in a bowl of spoiled milk. He must have been on drugs, which made this entire situation even more volatile.

"Listen to him. Let him go. You don't have an issue with him. It's with me." I found my voice. My strength. I filled my chest with as much air as I could suck in, raising myself to the man's level. "I was the one who rightfully put a criminal behind bars. Your problem is me."

I could hear Eric whisper no, but it was too late. The man retrained the barrel of the gun straight at my forehead. I felt it like it was a fire-hot brand pressed against my skin, even though he was feet away. I gulped. My hands were clammy—was that a weird thing to notice right before you died? Something else I weirdly noticed: I was about to die without having had good sex in months.

Zane should have been the one to break that dry spell. He would have kept it raining, too, I was sure of that. Maybe that's why he was so apprehensive. Because he knew, too. He felt the chemistry between us; I knew I couldn't have been the only one who felt that flame.

And, just like that, the flame was about to be extinguished before it ever even had a chance to catch. I was going to die. Time was still slowed for me. Or maybe my thoughts were coming at such a rapid pace, it felt like everything else was crawling in comparison.

I took another breath. That was when everything happened. A loud bang tore through the air. It popped my ears, taking my hearing along with my breath. My eyes slammed shut. I was shocked. The smell of gunpowder in the air followed instantly. It was acrid and stung at my nose. I expected to feel worse; getting shot wasn't something that was normally billed as painless. My eyes opened. I looked down and realized I was still standing. The man was on the floor, facedown, the gun that had been in his hand now sitting three feet away from him. People were running toward us from the other side of the street. I registered the shapes in my periphery, but I couldn't take my eyes off the man. Was he dead? Did his gun backfire?

I looked to Eric, who was as pale as loose-leaf paper. "You okay?" I asked him. I didn't realize I was shouting over the ringing in my ears.

"Mhm," he said, nodding. That was when I focused on the two shapes that were almost upon us.

Two men.

One of those men seemed like an impossibility. A glitch in the matrix. He shouldn't be here—there was no reason for it. But against all odds, there he was.

"Zane," I said, almost to myself.

"Holy shit," he said. At least, I thought that was what he said. I had to read his lips for most of it. I rubbed at my ears, trying to alleviate some of the ringing. Zane was looking me over, his big eyes scanning me from toes to scalp. They stopped on my eyes, and I immediately felt a sense of relief having Zane there. I couldn't really explain it, but it was sudden and powerful. It was a wave that flowed over and through me, easing me down from the adrenaline cliff I had climbed.

"Are you okay?"

"Yeah," I said, the ringing having subsided to a quiet whine. I wanted to say something else. Something cute. Something like "I am now that you're here," but all I could do was smile before it cracked and a few tears broke through. I rubbed at my cheeks, quickly putting myself together. I stiffened my back and strengthened that smile. Zane must have seen right through me.

*Of course he does. He's a fucking detective. Details are his forte.*

He opened his arms and wrapped them around me, and I felt safe. Safe enough to let those tears run again. I was silent, my chest pressed against Zane's. I swore I could feel his heartbeat, even through the thick bundles of clothes between us. His warmth was the antidote to everything that ailed me. He was the cure. I breathed in his scent and had to separate myself before my tears morphed into kisses.

Adrenaline did some weird shit to your body, let me tell you. One second I felt like crying, as if I were a soap opera star, and the next second I felt like fucking as if I was a porn star.

Sirens started to sound from a few streets away. Someone nearby must have heard the gunshots and called the police. I looked to Eric, who was no longer pale but instead an odd shade of green.

"Sorry, I gotta—" He almost didn't make it to the trash can but managed to impressively aim the trajectory of his vomit so that it still landed in the trash.

Moments later the police arrived, along with the EMS. Apparently, Zane's brother was also a police officer and had shot my assailant in the kneecap. The guy was going to live, and he was also going to end up behind bars. The cops took statements as the man was wheeled into an ambulance, groaning as he started to come out of shock. And just like that, everything was over.

I stood there on the now empty street with Zane and his brother, Andrei. Eric had left as soon as the police took his statement. He said he wanted to be nowhere but in his tub with the hot water running and a kiwi bath bomb thrown in. I didn't blame him, but I also didn't want to be alone. I still felt shaken, and I couldn't imagine getting any sleep.

"What... a night," I said, letting my head drop back as I ran my hands through my hair. My breath fogged in the air and rose up like a dancing cloud. "Thank you, again. Both of you. I owe you my life."

"Let's settle with just owing us a drink, eh?" Andrei was smiling. I looked between the brothers, seeing the resemblance in their strong dark brows and full pink lips, made even pinker against the cold. They had the same bright eyes, too, warm and sharp. Andrei looked like the older one, with a few more lines on his face that told me stress wasn't a stranger. Zane didn't look like he spent hours in yoga and spas, either, but he had a younger air around him.

"Fine," I said, "we'll start with drinks and work our way up."

"Sounds good," Andrei said. "All right, I'm going to follow Eric's lead and get myself home. You're okay, right?"

I nodded, feeling taken care of by the two men. Normally I was the one taking care of others. I had to defend people for a living. But now I was on the other end, with Zane and Andrei acting as my protectors. I looked to Zane, who had his eyes pinned on me. I could feel his gaze on me as if he were pressing his hands against me.

"Want to come over and have a beer? I know it's late, but maybe it'll make you fee—"

"Let's do it," I said, not even letting him finish. He had

read my mind. Going to his place and spending an hour or so with a cold beer and good conversation was exactly what I needed to bring me down to earth.

"Let's do it," Zane repeated, his lips curling into a smile.

I realized how I could never get bored of that sight. Zane wore a smile better than me wearing a custom-made Prada suit.

\*\*\*

"Thunder, huh?" I bent down to pet the big cat. His fur felt like velvet under the palm of my hand as he arched his back and rubbed his side against my leg. "That's a cool name for a cat."

"Thanks," Zane answered, looking at Thunder and cracking a genuinely warm smile. I almost thought I was hallucinating it, like a mirage in the middle of the desert. That smile was so... intoxicating. Holy shit, I didn't think Zane could get any sexier.

Well, that wasn't true. I could imagine him being a lot sexier, and that involved him wearing the smile and nothing else. He still looked as good as the last time I'd seen him, this time wearing dark jeans and a light blue shirt, his bare feet giving me a flash of the skin that I craved. But he would look way better if he just took everything off.

*I literally just saw someone get shot. Cazzo. I need to calm down.*

"So about that beer," I said as I followed Zane through his living room and into his kitchen. His apartment had a huge window that looked out on the High Line, which was a new development that brought renewed life to the Lower West Side of Manhattan. It was a pedestrian path created on the unused New York Central Railroad that wound through buildings and out toward the Hudson River. Plenty of people jogged through it daily, while tourists ambled about, admiring the different art installations and plant life along the path. It almost felt like its own little oasis that rested above the packed city streets. Currently, the path was lit up by lamps and was walked by no one. It was already, what, two in the morning? I looked to the clock on the wall, a modern piece that looked as though the big bold numbers were just floating in the air, the thick arrow pointing toward the time. Yep, two fifteen in the morning.

"Cazzo, I didn't realize how late it was."

"Cazzo?" Zane asked, handing me a cold Stella, the bottle dripping with moisture.

"Eh, literally, it translates into 'dick,' but Italians interchange it for 'fuck.'" The cap of the beer had already been popped off. I raised the bottle in the air and tilted the bottom toward Zane.

"Cheers," I said, "to my knight in North Face armor."

*There. Finally. A flirty line.*

Zane lifted his bottle and clinked it with mine, his eyes capturing my gaze like a professional hypnotist.

"Cheers," he said, "to a handsome lawyer in distress."

I narrowed my lids and drank, smiling around the bottle. Zane's eyes were glittering in the dim lighting. He brought the bottle back down to his hip. "Cazzo," he said, Italian sounding hot on him, "that's good."

"Very good," I agreed, feeling more and more at ease around Zane. This was nothing like our first meeting, where I felt like I was working on overtime just to get a smirk from the guy. It was like pushing a boulder uphill with him, and the boulder wasn't budging a damn inch. But tonight, things were completely different.

*Has to be the adrenaline. I can't get caught up in this.*

"Come on, let's hang out in the other room," he said, nodding toward an open archway that led out to his living room. I followed his steps, trying to stop my eyes from dropping down to his perky butt and completely failing. But, come on, could you blame me? His ass filled up those jeans in a way that had my mouth watering and my dick twitching. I managed to distract myself once we entered his living room, and my attention moved to his setup. It felt homey, warm. Something I wasn't really expecting from him, not that I knew why. I figured he was more the type that lived on a slightly too-old couch and preferred to eat frozen meals off a rarely cleaned wooden coffee table. Like most TV detectives I guess. But Zane, of course, was different, down to the way he decorated his space.

Everything felt new and cared for, even though there were some clearly antique pieces. Like the rustic white coffee table that was, in fact, *very* clean and displayed a potted orchid that was in full bloom, its white petals opening up around the purple pistil, creating a stunning contrast. The shiny blue pot seemed to pop right off the table. The dark blue couch looked like the most comfortable thing in the world, made for midday naps and midnight snacking. It was accented by a tall copper floor lamp, its light hanging over the couch and covering it in a soft gold.

"Wow," I said, nodding. Thunder leaped onto the couch arm with a purr and looked at me. Zane stood next to the couch, his back toward a tall bookshelf set next to a narrow window.

"Not bad, huh?"

"Not bad? I feel like I just walked into one of those magazines I only see in my dentist's office."

"I'll take that as a compliment."

"Damn right it's a compliment. My dentist has excellent taste in home magazines. You did all this yourself?"

Zane nodded, his lip quirked to the side. "I don't have a team of professionals around me at my beck and call."

I felt that jab. And guess what? I wanted to jab right back. "Hmm." I shrugged. "Too bad. I love having Chip and Joanna on speed-dial."

"*Pfft*," Zane said before taking a sip of his beer. "So what if you have the Gaineses on your phone. Not like I watch their home makeover show whenever I can or anything." He looked down at his beer, then back up at me, his gaze narrowing. "Do you really have their numbers?"

"They're right under Oprah. Wanna do a three-way call? We can put one of them on mute and have the other talk shit. Start some drama, high school style."

It took a second before Zane started cracking up. The sound of his laugh quickly had me laughing. If anyone had been looking at us through the window, as creepy a thought as that was, they wouldn't ever be able to guess the situation we had just come out of. We were both smiles and laughs as we kept talking about home makeover shows and what we loved about them. It was all easy and fun, and in that moment, I felt like I found something. A light in the middle of the darkness, something to guide me from the fear that had threatened to consume me hours earlier.

# 7  ZANE

Hours sailed by. Soon it was almost four in the morning and we were into our fourth beers, and I was pleasantly surprised at how well we were getting along. Sure, there were a few things Enzo said that reminded me about our differing personas, but for the most part, I wasn't nearly as put off as I assumed I would have been. We talked about vacation fails and embarrassing high school moments, favorite hangouts in New York (his was Central Park, while I really enjoyed the High Line) we joked about politics, and we poked fun at each other over favorite music choices. (He *actually* enjoyed Katy Perry. I almost walked out of my own apartment when I found that out.)

It didn't feel like we had just spent time giving our statements to police officers, nor did it feel like Enzo had been moments from losing his life. It was surreal thinking about it, so I didn't. Instead, I got up during a lull in the conversation and went to the kitchen for two more beers.

When I got back to the living room, Enzo seemed to have inched farther toward the center of the couch. He had been leaning on the armrest earlier. Now, he held on to a yellow pillow on his lap. I didn't mention anything, even though I definitely noticed the move.

I was almost surprised by how handsome Enzo looked. Even after the traumatic event, he still had a glow around him that lured me toward him like a moth to the full moon. His dark hair was slightly messed up, a curled strand falling down onto his forehead like a crescent-shaped shadow. His eyes were still wide and bright, even though it was likely way past both our bedtimes. He was manspreading a bit in his dark pants, which I normally would have clocked as rude, but in Enzo's case, it was actually pretty hot. It was the perfect amount of room between his legs for me to kneel down and—

"Here you go," I said, handing over the cool bottle of beer. I wasn't about to start fantasizing about Enzo, not now, not when he was sitting on the same couch that Jose and I would spend hours on, sometimes naked, sometimes not. No, this wasn't one of those nights. Besides, it wasn't like this was some random Grindr hookup. Enzo was my client, and he was someone that needed help, so I was giving it to him. If a friendship could grow from the night, then fine, I'd take it. But friendship was where it would all stop. I was sure of that.

"Thank you," Enzo said, but the way he said it made me feel like he wasn't simply talking about the beer. He looked up at me as he grabbed the bottle from my hand. Our fingertips touched for a slightest moment, and just like that, time stopped. And I'm not really one for all that fairy-tale bullshit, but I don't think it was even an exaggeration. Everything was put on pause for an indefinite amount of time. It was a connection I was being forced to recognize, even though all I wanted to do was look past it.

Then the Play button was pressed and life hit me all at

once. Thoughts of Jose came rushing at me. Of the buoyant happiness. Of the crippling loneliness. Flashes of our dates, flashes of our fights. What would he have wanted me to do?

I sat down, leaning more toward the left side of the couch. I drank, taking a big gulp. My limbs were already getting that heavy feel to them, while my fingertips seemed to lack any feeling whatsoever. I closed my eyes and let my head drop back. I rolled it around my shoulders, hearing the pops in my neck and taking some twisted satisfaction from the feeling. When I opened my eyes, I saw Enzo examining me.

He wasn't shy about it. It was that Italian bravado. He oozed confidence and didn't give a fuck what other people really thought, and so he was going to stare at your face if he damn well wanted to. I would have turned away, but I wanted to stare at him, too. I wanted to memorize the ridges of his cheekbones, the wrinkles in his forehead, the nose that'd never met a fist. His eyes scanned my face, landing on mine, holding my attention like he was a ringleader at the circus. He commanded my gaze. I swallowed, thinking it would somehow break the spell.

It didn't. I bit my lower lip lightly, a response I wasn't even fully aware I was giving. His lips quirked into a smile. When did he get so close to me? Or had I moved? I wasn't next to the armrest anymore. Enzo licked his lips—those lips that had cast a spell on me from the second he walked into my office. Tantalizing. They made me crazy for some reason. It was then I realized I had been actively avoiding looking at his lips the entire night, keeping my focus on his eyes. Now, the resistance was *definitely* futile. I was looking at those lips like I had just found the last coke in the desert.

That was when our knees touched. A touch that was swift, nothing major. And yet it had my dick waking up like an alarm had just gone off. I sat up straighter on the couch, bringing my legs closer together, moving from the electric current that ran between us. It was in that moment that, if I was letting my more primal side take over, I would have swung to the left, cupped Enzo's face in my hands, and pulled him toward me so that I could suck on his bottom lip as I ground myself down onto him.

That was my primal side. My logical side had me cemented to the couch, resisting the fire that was beginning to catch and rage inside me. It brought me back to the present, to thinking about how I was fine without needing anyone else on my couch. I didn't crave having my feet intertwined with another man's while we watched some dumb reality show, or while we lounged in bed, reading books and watching silly YouTube videos. Nope, I didn't crave that connection at all. Not anymore.

Enzo must have sensed my tensing up. He took a swig of his beer and then placed it down on the vintage *Batman* comic turned coaster. "So," Enzo said, as casually as if he were making small talk on the subway ride home from work. "Where you from?"

I couldn't help but laugh. The question was so far from left field, and Enzo's slightly awkward yet dripping-in-charm manner had me cracking up. Not to mention that smirk he had on, which quickly evolved into a full-on smile as my laughter spread to him. He sat back on the couch. He opened his legs wider, not that I was staring, but I could see from the corner of my eye.

It made me *want* to stare. I kept my eyes ahead, focusing my attention on the blank TV hanging on the wall instead.

"I'm from a lot of different places," I said. I figured the question deserved answering, even if I could have laughed it off and avoided going any deeper. Maybe it was the alcohol that had me loosening up. Yeah. It was definitely the alcohol. I took another drink. It was a smooth pale ale, exactly what I needed. "I was raised in the foster care system. I was born in Philly, but didn't stick around there for long. I'm the middle child, so it was my older brother and then my sister, who came three years after me. When I was six, both of my parents were involved in a car accident. They, uh, they both got hooked on painkillers, and they both were deemed unable to take care of us by the state."

"Damn," Enzo said in a low voice. He reached over and put a hand on my shoulder and squeezed. It was a simple yet powerful gesture.

"Both of my parents had small families with no one available to take us, and neither set of grandparents were alive, so we went into the foster system. It was okay at first, until we were moved from our first house and split up. I had a really difficult time then. My brother and I were reunited, but our sister was—"

Suddenly, the room was filled with the sound of a violent crash. It caused the both of us to jump up off the couch. I instinctively put an arm out to cover Enzo's chest, my hand landing on his beating heart.

*Thump. Thump. Thump. Thump.*

## 8  ENZO

My heart was racing. I could feel it battering my chest. I could also feel Zane's hand on me, like a warm brand against my skin, even though a shirt separated his palm from my chest. We looked around and quickly found what had caused the crashing sound.

A few feet away, the remnants of a white clay pot were lying shattered on the floor, dirt spread around like the ash left behind from a bomb. The succulents Zane had been growing were like sad little casualties of war. Then there was a dash of black as Thunder bolted from underneath a table and leaped up onto the back of the couch, where he ran right across it and jumped off to land on the nearby love seat. There, the demon cat sat on the back of the chair, his eyes dilated and staring us down.

"Um," I said, scared to move, "should we call the police? Are we being held hostage?"

"No," Zane reassured me. "Just don't look him in the eye, and don't make any sudden movements—oh, and don't feel *any* fear. He can smell fear. It drives him. Makes him hungry."

I looked to Zane, who was feigning a look of suppressed terror. I cocked my head and playfully slapped his chest. "Cazzo. I don't need another near-death experience tonight, okay?"

"Relax," Zane said, laughing. "This is Thunder's witching hour. He's never knocked anything over, but I've woken up to him body slamming the bedroom door at around this time."

"I knew there was a reason why I'm more of a dog person."

Zane chuckled at that as he walked over to Thunder, who lifted his head ever so slightly so that he could receive a few chin scratches. I turned and walked toward what I thought was the supply closet. I opened it but found Thunder's food bags instead, arranged neatly underneath a hanger of grocery bags.

*Good, so Thunder eats weight-control cat food and not firstborn children.*

"Hey, where do you keep the broom?" I asked. "Underneath your pillow so you can fight off any demon cats during the night?"

Zane laughed, a deep laugh that started in his chest. It was a sound that filled me with joy.

*Merda. Zane is really affecting me.*

"I got it, don't worry about it." Zane disappeared into the kitchen, leaving me behind with Thunder. I looked at him across the room. The moment was loaded with tension. The air felt thick, and the temperature was growing by the second. It was a standoff made for cinema. Thunder flexed his claws, his pupils turning to slits. I stuck my tongue out.

That was when Zane returned with a broom and dustpan in hand. Thunder leaped off the couch and stalked over to his water bowl. "You two getting along?" Zane asked. He was smiling. His strong jaw was an incredible complement for his warm smile. He had two sides to him, both sweet and wild, and that drove me fucking crazy.

"I don't know," I replied. "I think he's plotting to kill me."

"Probably," Zane said as he swept up the mess. This caused the muscles in his back to pop against the thin light blue shirt he was wearing. It made something else pop, too.

My dick. My dick popped. Like a fucking jack-in-the-box, it was ready to pop out of my damn jeans. I turned and looked for Thunder, making sure he wasn't hanging upside down from the ceiling holding a knife in his mouth.

"You were saying?" I asked, still interested in hearing about Zane's past. I found that I wanted to keep learning about what created the man who was standing in front of me. I wanted to know what made him tick, what he hated and what he loved and why. I wanted to know it all. I tried not to look back at Zane's mouthwatering and boner-inducing shoulders when I spoke. "About your sister?"

"Oh right, before Thunder turned possessed. I was saying how my sister was adopted by a really great family. Our case worker knew how difficult it would be to place three siblings in one home, and he'd seen plenty of kids like us end up aging out of the system and falling off the face of the earth. So he was able to find a place for my sister, and for her only. Then, when everyone saw how badly I took the separation between Andrei and I, they knew we'd need to be adopted together." Zane was still sweeping the floor, although I was sure there wasn't any more shards. "We were never adopted and ended up aging out of the system."

He stopped sweeping and looked up. For a moment, I

thought I saw a glint of moisture in his eyes, but he bent down to pick up the dustpan before I could be sure. My heart broke. How? How could there have been no one to take them? How could anyone look into Zane's deep amber eyes and turn him away? It must have left such an intense sense of rejection, even if he didn't admit it to himself. I shook my head. I wanted to turn back time and somehow fix it, all the way back to when his parents got into the car accident. I wish I could have caused them to turn left on that street instead of right. Anything to avoid the accident. He didn't deserve that kind of childhood.

And then the adulthood that followed was no dream, either. It was the complete opposite. I wasn't sure if Zane was aware, but I knew about him losing Jose all those years ago. I remember the short statement Zane had given to the media in the days following. It was seared into my memory. He wore impenetrable Oakley sunglasses that day, standing behind a mushroom patch of microphones and speaking about the man who he loved and who he promised was the last victim. We were all so sure that the Unicorn was caught back then.

I took a deep breath, trying to ignore the chill that crawled down to the bottom of my spine. Zane continued, dumping the dustpan into a white garbage bag. "It's okay, because it all happened exactly as it should have. Everything in my past led me to the place I'm at now, and I really fucking love my life. I created an organization dedicated to helping the helpless, and I help change lives in the process."

"You really have created something special with Stonewall Investigations."

"It was what I felt like I had to do. I had the idea in my head since I was sixteen. There were a few times when the idea was only that—an idea. And a fleeting one, too. Plenty of days, I was ready to give up. But my brother and I managed to find housing and get shitty jobs. My sister's family offered to help, and we used some of it, but for the most part, we strapped up our boots and stood up by ourselves."

"You're someone kids should be looking up to." I reached for the heavy bag, but Zane shook his head, walking back into the kitchen. He shuffled back wearing a pair of black sandals. I noticed because I'd been having a difficult time keeping my eyes off his feet.

What? They were sexy feet.

"I'm gonna walk this outside. I'll be back."

"And you even take out the trash. You're a rock star."

"Who else would take it out?" Zane paused by the door with an exaggerated "ahh." He smirked. "I forgot you had help following you twenty-four seven when you're at home. If I wear white gloves and a suit, would it make more sense?"

I crossed my arms. Two could play at that game. "Why don't we ditch the gloves, and we'll keep the suit but make it the birthday variety."

"Is that what you make all your butlers wear? A birthday suit? I've seen those ads on Craigslist." Zane smiled. "I wouldn't mind doing some naked cleaning."

"Oh please," I said, "not like you don't have enough money to have naked butlers running around here, too."

Zane just laughed and went out the door, the heavy wood slamming shut behind him. I was left with a smile on my face and my briefs feeling a size too small. I readjusted myself so I wasn't clearly bulging by the time Zane got back up. I looked to the clock on the wall.

Five forty-seven. Jesus. Almost instinctively, my jaws practically unhinged in a loud yawn. I covered most of it with my hand and managed to cover the entirety of the next one.

The door opened behind me, a garbageless Zane standing in the doorway. He was rubbing his biceps, the tip of his nose slightly pink. "Wow, it's cold out there."

*Come over here so I can warm you up.*

My thoughts were getting too carried away. All I wanted to do was stride over to where he stood and crush my lips against his. But I couldn't fool myself. This was all just one night, and as close as I felt like we were getting, I knew that there was still a barrier in place. Or maybe a few barriers. And although they didn't feel as unscalable as before, I could see that they still reached up into the clouds.

And so... why were we moving closer and closer to each other? Why were his hands suddenly on mine? Why did I feel the heat of his body wrap around me like a blanket? Our bodies pressed together, my crotch on his, my chest on his, my lips finding his. I could feel a gasp—was it mine or was it his? I swallowed it. I searched for his tongue and found it, and his tongue began to dance with mine. I could taste all the beer, the excitement. I could taste perfection. We fit together like a jigsaw piece, the last one that clicks in so that the entire stunning landscape is revealed in its entirety.

We stumbled backward. I reached for the couch, which I knew was closer. My fingers closed around the soft fabric. I pulled us toward it, walking around it so that I could push Zane down onto the cushions. He dropped, looking up at me with a fire in those golden amber eyes. Embers caught in my own chest, lighting me up from the inside. I leaned down, almost growling as I claimed Zane's lips once again. My hand cupped his face, my thumbs grazing the soft scruff of his five-o'clock shadow. His cock was already hard and throbbing up against my own. I ground my hips down, making sure he knew how badly I wanted him.

For a moment, I wondered if this was wrong. If I should have stopped us. Zane had seemed to make it clear he didn't want me when we initially met, and I found that those initial impressions were usually the lasting ones. Maybe I was ruining a good working relationship by reaching down and unzipping Zane's pants. Maybe I was making a mistake by pulling his pants and briefs down, and gawking at the size of the dick that sprung free. Maybe it was all a mistake... but cazzo, I didn't give a fuck. All I wanted was to try and fit that thing in my mouth.

I went down on the floor, licking my lips, making them nice and wet for Zane. I looked up and met his fiery gaze with my own. I was throbbing in my own pants, but I didn't care much about that right now. All I wanted to focus on was pleasing Zane. He was the epitome of man, sitting there with his thick thighs spread open and his heavy balls hanging. His cock was aimed up in the air, a crown of soft hair making a perfect target for my lips. I kissed him, starting at the base and working my way up, savoring the soft skin, the scent of man, the taste of him on my lips.

When I reached the head, it was already dripping wet. I sucked him into my mouth, instantly tasting his salty precome. I wanted more. I started to suck while my tongue swirled. His head dropped back onto the cushion, a moan ripping from his throat.

He was warm in my mouth, and big. It was hard trying to take it all, but damn it, I was trying. When I came up for a breath, I made sure to go down so I could suck a ball into my mouth, moving it around and looking up at Zane, who was pressing his thighs against the sides of my head. This was exactly the view I'd been fantasizing about since the second I walked into his office and saw the size of his legs through that glass table of his.

And let me tell you, reality didn't disappoint this time. The actual thing was way better than any daydream could have ever felt.

I unzipped my own pants and pulled my cock out. I used the hand that had been stroking Zane, already wet with my saliva. I spread it up and down my shaft while I went back to sucking on Zane.

"That's it, Enzo. God, that's good." His voice sounded like he was being put under a spell. I sucked him off harder, bobbing up and down. My fist tightened around my cock. He continued to encourage me, talking dirty and igniting my body on fire. When he started pulling on my hair, I almost lost it. I fucking loved it when my hair was played with, and having Zane grab a handful and using it to steer me, well, fuck, that almost made me come right then and there.

I held on, though, determined not to blow until Zane unloaded down my throat.

"Yeah, Enzo, you like that? Sucking on that big dick?"

I came up for a breath, a rope of saliva trailing behind and snapping as I spoke. "Lo adoro, Zane. I fucking love it." I went back in, licking and slurping. Zane was loving it, too, it seemed. His grip on my head got tighter, and the fire in my gut grew hotter. I wasn't going to last much longer, but judging by the incomprehensible sounds Zane was now making, he wasn't going to, either.

"Give it to me, Zane. Come for me." I jerked us both off,

licking the crown of his cock while he twitched and squeezed his thighs. He was so close.

"Do it, Zane. Come for me. I want to swallow it all." I was almost begging for it. I took him back in my mouth, and that seemed to be all he needed. He warned me with a grunt, and I made sure to keep my lips wrapped tight around him.

I felt him throb and explode in my mouth, shooting it so far down my throat I barely tasted anything before swallowing it all. The moment was enough to rocket me over the edge, my own cock spewing onto the floor as I tugged on my balls, all while Zane's twitching cock was still in my mouth.

I pulled off Zane's cock, taking a deep breath before licking my lips, tracing the smile. Zane was looking at me with dreamy eyes that had been clouded over with ecstasy. He was smiling, too. I got up and leaned in, kissing him, letting him taste himself on my tongue. He seemed to like it from the way his hands came up to hold my head, keeping me on his lips, his moan almost making me automatically sit on his lap. I held back, though.

"Looks like I've got another mess to clean up now," Zane said once our kiss broke, looking down at the puddle I'd created.

"I've got this one," I said, chuckling as I walked over to the kitchen to grab some paper towels. Zane was standing when I got back. He looked so damn good, half-naked, his cock practically glowing from how wet it still was. I had to look away before I got hard again.

"I can't believe the sun's coming up," Zane said, walking over to the window. Sure enough, there was a dark purple hue to everything outside, a sign that the sun was right around the corner.

"Merda," I said, getting up from the floor, a ball of paper

towel in my hand. "I've probably overstayed my welcome, eh?"

"Absolutely not," Zane answered quickly. He was no longer looking out the window, but instead at me. Something came over his expression then, but I couldn't read it before he looked away again.

"I'll get the guest room set up. Grab some sleep."

"Oh, no, no, don't worry about it." I waved a hand in the air. "I'll head home."

"You're not heading anywhere. Just crash here for a few hours. It's fine, trust me."

I cocked my head. Trust. If only he knew how much that word meant to me. How much I had craved to trust someone again. Zane was a man who could quickly earn my trust. Hell, I could still taste him in my mouth—he definitely had some of my trust.

"Fine," I said, "but tell me."

"What?"

"Are your pillows a hundred percent goose down, and will the blankets and bedsheets be made from a thousand-thread-count Egyptian cotton?"

Zane laughed at that as he walked away, his perky ass begging me to take a bite out of it. "The pillow's Tempur-Pedic—that's as fancy as it'll get here," he called as he disappeared into the guest room.

I smiled, trying not to let myself feel anything major. This was a fluke. The night had been a random sequence of events, some terrifying, that led to this moment. I couldn't over think anything. I had to remember that no matter how good Zane's dick tasted, it wasn't mine. We weren't meant to be a thing, and that was fine. I'd go to sleep and wake up and expect to continue on with my life.

In fact, I was positive that I wouldn't even text him after

all this. It was going to be a purely business-focused relationship between us.

Yep. No texts whatsoever. Zero communication unless it was about Ricardo's case.

*Tutto bene.* All was good.

All was good.

## 9 ZANE
### ONE WEEK LATER

I woke up to about five text messages, all from Enzo. I'd learned that he woke up about an hour and a half earlier than the time I was normally up, and by then, he would have seen a handful of funny viral videos that he thought would be hilarious to send my way. The first two times he did that, I was a little taken aback. I kept thinking there was an emergency I had slept through or something. But on the fourth time, I had almost busted a rib laughing at them, and I realized it was actually a great way to wake up.

We didn't spend the rest of the day constantly texting, but we'd send random messages whenever something came up. It was fun, and honestly, also a little weird. It made me think "hm" on a few different occasions. What exactly did this mean? Enzo was a great guy, and he was seemingly turning into a great friend, but why couldn't I shake the feeling of something more looming over every text message I sent? I was even deleting and rewriting a few so that I could get it exactly right. I never second-guessed my text messages with anyone else. And yet with Enzo, I needed a folder to hold all the drafted and trashed text messages.

I rolled out of bed and got through my morning routine, getting a few laughs from this morning's batch of texts. One of the videos was a compilation of people sliding on ice, which had me cracking up since I've been one of those people who flail around helplessly while the ice sweeps you away. Another video was of a flight attendant giving the safety presentation while impersonating at least fifteen celebrities, and doing a great job at it, too. I texted back a trio of smiley faces and pointed out that the ice one was my favorite.

*I never text smileys. What the hell is wrong with me?*

I tossed the phone onto my bed, deciding I wasn't about to become a slave to it. My closet doors were already open, so I reached in and grabbed my outfit for today. A long-sleeved button-up shirt with a plaid pattern, pink and white. My tailored navy blue pants and a light brown belt would put it all together. I wanted to look good today. A little better than I felt I normally did. I always wanted to step things up on the days I had interviews.

Well, depending on who the interview was with. If I had to be talking to a drug dealer so I could get information, I'd probably dress down a bit. Maybe throw on sneakers instead of wingtips. But today I was visiting with Susan, the deceased woman's sister, and so I wanted to look professional as well as approachable. I knew she would still be hurting from her loss, so I didn't want to come across as intimidating, either. These were all things I had to think about. Things other detectives tended to overlook led to mistakes. A lot of people don't realize that the investigation starts before you step foot out of your own door. Everything needed to be in place so I could extract the most valuable information for the case, and that meant thinking hard about everything from how I was going to dress to how I was going to introduce myself.

"Hello, Ms. Rowland. I'm Detective Holden, here about your sister, Luanne."

I was standing outside of Susan's apartment, inside of a dingy hallway. She lived over in Brooklyn, in a small efficiency that was near the iconic bridge and also right across the street from a police station. There were currently three people yelling about being handcuffed as they were getting dragged into the station, the sounds of their drunk protest coming in through an open window at the end of the hall. A police car turned down the street with its siren blaring, causing Susan to wince.

"Come inside, come," she said, stepping aside. I walked in, immediately hit with the smell of greasy cooking. The smell was almost overpowering. Maybe because it was such a small space, or maybe because the place didn't feel too clean to begin with. It was stuffy. The blinds were drawn even though it was the middle of the day, and the tan carpet appeared to have never met a vacuum. There was a space heater that was doing what it could, but the cold still nipped at me as I took my coat off.

I wondered if she had lived like this since before her sister passed, or if it was only brought on because of her death.

"Do you want water or anything?" Susan offered. She was a frail woman, despite being the younger of the two, but she carried herself with age. Rather, it looked like she carried too much of it. Her shoulders were slumped as though she'd live through decades worth of stress, and the bags under her eyes did nothing to help rejuvenate her.

"I'm okay, thank you," I said, glancing around the small room. There was an old couch pushed up against the wall which looked like it converted into a bed, although judging by the imprint of Susan's body on the cushions, she never pulled the bed out, choosing to sleep curled up on the couch instead. It told me she lived alone. She never needed the extra room to share with someone.

The kitchen, which was hard to call a kitchen since it was basically just a wall with a cheap oven and a tiny refrigerator, was kept clean from what I could see. The one block of counter held a stack of clean paper plates. The small refrigerator hummed next to it, as if it were begging for someone to put it out of its misery.

"So, you're here investigating my sister's death?"

I looked to her. She had her hands bundled together against her chest. She was wearing a thick white sweater that gave her the illusion of having some kind of bulk, but her jeans cut off near the ankles, and those were stick thin.

"I am. There was something that happened that night, and the police aren't sure they have all the details right."

"You're not police?"

"No, I'm a private detective." I avoided saying anything about Ricardo. I didn't want to taint the information Susan had, because if she also agreed that Ricardo did it, then she would immediately shut down if I said I were representing him. Instead, I stuck with the truth, that I was here to figure out what happened to Luanne.

For a second, I thought Susan was going to dig further, but she moved to the couch and sat down at the edge, her hands between her knees, her face looking up at me. She knew I was here to help, and I was determined to do exactly that.

"I just can't believe she's gone," she started, a cry getting stuck in her throat. I moved to sit next to her. I kept her personal space intact. She didn't seem like the type to gain much comfort from a stranger's touch. Instead, I decided my presence would be enough to calm her.

"She was so young, you know? I mean, I'm the young one. I'm the little sister, but she was only thirty-five. She had so much left."

"And we're going to make whoever did this pay, Susan."

"Don't they know who did it, though? That Ricardo guy? The weirdo neighbor?"

I kept my poker face solid. "He's a suspect, yes, but there's been questions brought up. I want to make sure we put the right guy behind bars."

"Well, he got in a fight with my sister and Oscar. Someone caught it on camera. That's kind of a big deal, isn't it?"

"It is." I was losing her. She was becoming defensive. The second she shut down, I knew I'd lose whatever bits of information she could have given me. "But, Susan, do you know if your sister or her husband ever made anyone else angry? For any reason? Maybe it was a car accident that wasn't even her fault, or maybe Oscar argued with someone at work?"

Susan opened her mouth to speak but closed it before saying anything. I gave her the time to search her memory. I knew that her mind must have seemed like a postapocalyptic landscape. Thoughts would be hard to string together, entire memories even harder.

"Luanne was involved with someone else."

*Bingo.*

"She was always very secretive," Susan continued, sadness coloring her features while frustration painted her voice. Her shoulders slumped farther as she spoke, her hands held loosely in her lap. "I wish she opened up to me more. Maybe I would have known more. Who she was with. But she never told me."

"That's okay, it's a start. This is a huge help."

"It is?"

"Definitely."

She took a breath, rallying herself. "Do you think maybe Oscar found out?"

I cocked my head. I didn't like speculating with people so closely connected to the deceased. But I wanted to give her some sort of peace of mind. "I don't have enough to think anything concrete yet, but I do know that I'm going to try my hardest to figure it all out."

"It's just so sad. Oscar had just gotten his promotion. Everything was set. Things could have been so great. He had just left on his first big work trip, too, a week before it all happened. He got flown out to California for a conference."

"Do you know why your sister was cheating on Oscar, then? Were there any signs of trouble in their marriage, even though the future seemed bright for them?"

Susan took another deep breath. "They never fought. Not in front of me, at least. I mean, I didn't see them that often, especially not in the last few months. They've been really busy with married life and work. They knew each other since we were all little kids. Oscar was our neighbor. He moved out of our small town and turned into a college graduate and brought Luanne along with him for the ride. She was looking into going back to school for nursing. They only just got married, a few months ago."

*So then maybe the man Luanne was seeing got jealous. Couldn't take it anymore.*

"Did she ever mention anything about this other man? Even just hair color or accent?"

Susan raked a hand through her thin brown hair. "No, I'm sorry. I wish I was more help."

"Like I said, this is a huge help."

*Not the biggest help, but it's a start.*

"Okay, good." She seemed content with that answer. I noticed her glance at the dirty clock on the wall. I could tell she was getting antsy by the way she sat on the edge of the couch cushion. This was a taxing thing, reliving your deceased sister's memory for a detective. I didn't want to add to her distress, but I did have a few more questions.

"How was the relationship between you two?" I already had a general idea through my social media research, but people always had a knack for showing their best sides on their Facebooks and Instagrams. No one saw pictures of the tears or the fears, only of the filtered vacations and carefully placed food.

"It was fine," she said. Her eyes searched mine, as if it were her turn to find the answers. "She was my big sister. I loved her. She taught me everything; she was the person I wanted to become. She had everything. A nice place, the perfect man, a great group of friends. Ever since we were little, everyone could always tell she was my guiding light. Like I said, we hadn't gotten the chance to spend much time together lately. If only I had known..." A cry got lodged in her throat. She coughed and sobbed at the same time. There was a near-empty box of tissue papers on the dirty side table. I reached for a tissue, almost knocking over a half-full glass of orange juice. I handed her the tissue, and she grabbed it with a soft thank-you and dabbed at her face.

"Okay," I said, feeling like today was a wrap with Susan. I had her number, so I'd be able to reach her when more questions arose, and hopefully she'd be in a better mental state when those questions came around. I already felt like

I'd earned her trust, and we all wanted the same thing: we wanted to find and punish the monster who did this. It paid for me to leave before she really broke down, potentially shutting me out for a while. "That's going to be it for today."

I squeezed my thighs and got up from the couch. I didn't bring a notebook this time since I wanted to make Susan feel as comfortable as possible, so I'd get into the car and dictate what I'd learned for my records.

"Please, Detective, please, figure out who did this." She got up from the couch, covering her mouth with her hand before another rogue sob escaped. "I thought it was all over when they said it was the neighbor. I just wish it was all over."

She fell into me. I opened my arms and held her, letting her cry into my chest. I guess I was wrong about her aversion to physical contact.

All I could do was hold her while she let it all out. When she pulled back, her eyes were red and puffy, but the tears had stopped flowing. She managed a trembling smile and said goodbye as she walked me out.

I zipped up my coat outside of her place. The commotion at the police station had died down. I walked down the steps toward my car. When I got inside, I put my voice memos on hold and opened up my address book instead. There was one more person I wanted to meet with before today was over.

## 10  ENZO

I hated interrogation rooms. They felt exactly how they looked like on those A&E reality TV shows. They were mostly small rooms with no windows and zero decor. Just four blank walls, a flimsy table, and a few extremely uncomfortable chairs. I had requested to get one of the larger rooms with the double-sided mirrors, but those were all "taken". I had a feeling the police chief just liked seeing me slum it, but I was fine with it.

Mainly because I was guaranteed to see Zane today, and that made any windowless room seem much brighter to me. He had called to set up a meeting with Ricardo, and he apparently had some good news to share as well. I could tell Ricardo was getting his hopes up. He was sitting next to me, and he was chatting nonstop. About what I thought Zane found, and how soon he could get back home, how he had shows to watch, and how excited he was to just do groceries.

My heart was heavy for the guy. I didn't like making any judgments on my clients, but I was almost a hundred percent certain Ricardo was innocent, and he was having to sleep on a back-breaking cot next to other men who were likely not as innocent as he was. I didn't want to feed into the growing hope, though. Not until we found out exactly what Zane knew, so I let Ricardo talk himself out. By the time Zane showed up, we were already two Styrofoam cups of coffee in.

"Oh," Zane said as he entered the room after knocking. His eyes landed on mine, and the already small room seemed to have gotten smaller. We'd been texting pretty frequently, but texts didn't have near as big an effect on me as being in the same room as Zane did. Maybe it was because the last time I'd actually seen him, he was saving my life from a crazy gunman.

"Enzo," he said. "Nice to see you again."

*Damn right it's nice to see me.*

"Very nice to see you," I said, keeping my tone as professional as I could. I smiled and reached for his hand, closing it and shaking. His big hand felt good being held in mine. Made me wonder how it would feel if I could knot our fingers together.

"Hello, Mr. Aventura," Zane said, turning to Ricardo. He smiled and looked like a fawn imprinting on its maternal figure. I cocked my head, realizing Ricardo was probably thinking exactly what I was thinking.

*Except I already know how Zane's dick tastes.*

I sat back down, just in time to prevent an obvious bulge from giving away my fiery thoughts. I normally wasn't the jealous type, but I did find myself turning a slight shade of green in the tiny room. Which was ridiculous seeing as how Zane and I weren't even anything official, so what was there to even be jealous of?

*Cazzo. Why am I acting like this?*

"So?" Ricardo started, his tone upbeat as he pulled the

chair in toward the table. "Am I free? Do we have who did it?"

Immediately, I could see the answer in Zane's eyes. "No," he said, confirming my observation. "But we are closer. I met with Susan, and she told me that Luanne had been seeing someone else."

Ricardo perked up in his seat. I watched Zane from across the table. His focus was on Ricardo, so I allowed myself extra time to stare at the smaller features on Zane's face. The prominent cupid's bow on his upper lip. The three—four—six—eight, the eight beauty marks that dotted his face, like a mystical constellation that created the symbol for some ancient deity. The long eyelashes that would be the envy of any Maybelline model.

*Annnd merda, I'm not paying any attention to what he's saying.*

I honed back in and focused on what Zane was saying. "...She wasn't able to give me any details of who this person is. She said Luanne was secretive in that way. I'm thinking that Luanne got involved with someone shady, and maybe promised that person a deadline on when she'd leave Oscar. With their recent marriage, I could see how this would infuriate the wrong person, to the point where they'd sneak in during the middle of the night and shoot both Luanne and Oscar pointblank."

*Damn. He's good.*

I realized that this was the first time I was really seeing Zane do his job. And wow... was he really fucking hot. He looked like a pit bull, hot on the bleeding trail of his prey. He was sitting strong in the chair, his chest held high and his shoulders back, like he had all the confidence in the world, even if the case was only moving inches at a time. Just looking at him made me feel like we had it in the bag.

Like I could call each of the jury members right then and there and tell them not to even worry about it. His confidence was contagious. And served as a *powerful* aphrodisiac.

Seriously, I was rock hard under that table. If I hadn't been wearing briefs, I was sure my slacks would bust in half.

"Do you know who could have potentially been the second apple of her eye?"

I looked to Ricardo, hoping that it would ease the throbbing between my thighs. "I mean, if her sister didn't know, I'm definitely not going to know."

It didn't work. My cock was aching. I fisted my hands and dropped them on my lap. Bad move. The pressure was making it worse. Or better, depending on how I was looking at it.

*Cazzo. Relax.*

Zane was making me lose control without barely having even looked at me.

"Do you remember hearing anything?" I asked, forcing my thoughts away from between my legs. "Maybe a random name? The walls at your place aren't exactly soundproof, right?"

"Right. That's what my argument with them had been about. They kept waking me up at all hours of the night with their constant fucking. And especially over the last week or so before they were killed, that's when it had gotten really bad. It was extremely loud sex. Gross sex." Ricardo shook his head and rolled his eyes.

"Straight sex?" I quipped.

"Exactly," Ricardo said, chuckling. "But seriously, it was upsetting. So I confronted them. Nicely at first. Told them to please be considerate, that we share a bedroom wall and that I'm a light sleeper. Luanne, to her credit, apologized and looked embarrassed. I felt like she wanted to run back into the apartment and forget all about it. Oscar flipped. Said that I was making shit up, and that I was just a pathetic gay prostitute, probably trying to cover for my own weird sex. That clearly got me pissed, and shit just got out of hand."

"Wait a second." Zane leaned in. "You said it had gotten worse the week before her death?"

"Yeah, it was really bad. Lots of spanking and gagging and—"

"Oscar was on a work trip that week."

Ricardo's eyebrows shot up, along with mine. Blood redirected from my dick to my brain. "So then that must have been the other guy," Ricardo said. He dropped his head in his hands, as though he'd find some answer in them. "Ugh." He exhaled loudly. "I'm trying to remember if she ever said a name. But no, no I don't think so. I would have realized then that it wasn't Oscar. Maybe the cameras caught who the guy was?"

"I called management about checking the security camera in the hallway, but they don't keep tapes longer than a couple of days unless there'd been an incident reported," Zane pointed out. "So no way of going back and checking. And whoever killed them broke in through the back, where there weren't any cameras."

"Well, it explains why Oscar reacted the way he did when you confronted him," I noted. "He must have realized Luanne was cheating on him. He was taking it all out on you."

"But then they must have made up, because I didn't hear any loud fights or anything."

"Speaking of hearing things, you're sure you didn't hear anything the night of the murder?" Zane was looking down at his notepad, but I knew his attention was a thousand percent tuned into Ricardo's answer.

"Nothing. I was in the living room, and I was... well, I was watching porn, but I like doing it with my headphones in. I didn't hear a thing."

"Right," Zane said. He glanced up from the notepad and must have seen the nerves on Ricardo's face, because he said, "I believe you."

I studied Zane's expression, wondering for a moment if he really did believe Ricardo. This investigation could easily lead back around to Ricardo, and then there'd be an entirely different situation to deal with. But Zane didn't reveal any doubt behind that confident expression.

"Wait, wait," Ricardo said. Both our heads snapped to the man. "I remember something. A guy. Yeah, it has to be him! I was closing my blinds when I saw him leaving their apartment. I thought it was one of their mutual friends or something."

"Good, good, what did you see?"

"He was a bigger guy. Long hair, down to about his shoulders. A greasy brown. He was wearing a leather jacket and looked well-put together. *Uhm.*" Ricardo was reaching the end of his memory. I could almost see the neurons in his brain firing, trying to signal for something more vivid. "A tattoo! I saw a tattoo—it was on his neck. Looked like a tilted peace sign. The bottom of it was covered by his jacket. But it was uhm, red and blue. And it had legs."

"A tilted peace sign with legs?" I shook my head. "Drugs are bad, kids."

Zane looked lost in thought. He drew something out on his notepad. Scratched it off and then sketched something else. He spun the pad around and showed it to us. On the center of the page was the peace sign, but it wasn't what I had envisioned. It looked like a scarab, with its six legs coming out the sides.

"Yeah, that's it!" Ricardo said.

*Damn. Zane really is one of the best.*

Annnd, I was hard again.

*Merda.*

## 11  ZANE

*Good.* I felt like we were getting somewhere, and that made me feel really good.

Another thing that made me feel good? Seeing Enzo again. It almost took me by surprise. I didn't realize the effect having him in the same room would have on me. We'd only really hung out that one night, and that was after a near-death experience. And although it was definitely an unforgettable night for a multitude of reasons, I wasn't sure if things would transfer over onto other meetings.

But, sure enough, I felt the spark the second I laid eyes on him. It didn't hurt that the last time we'd been together, Enzo had been on his knees and between my thighs, his tongue working circles around my dick. I was glad to find my seat as quick as I could because I knew it would be *real* damn hard trying to hide how excited I got over seeing Enzo again.

The interview itself was enough to keep my head focused and my cock quiet. I felt like we were finally getting answers, and I could feel the answer to this all at the very edge of my fingertips. The tattoo was a huge clue and something that helped narrow down the list of suspects.

"That's the symbol for the Blood Scarabs, a gang that just recently started moving in and claiming territory around New York."

"A gang?" Enzo said. He looked so cute in his stupid designer shirt and slacks. I didn't care much for brand names or famous designers, but I did have to admit, he looked good in them. Although I suspected Enzo could wear a trash bag and still make it seem like it belonged on the cover of a magazine. "Merda."

I wanted to echo Enzo's statement, but I didn't want to scare Ricardo. Because, although we were getting closer, things also just got exponentially harder. Gangs were insulated environments, hard to crack and even harder to pin down in a crime. If Luanne was actually involved with a gang member, then we were looking at an entirely different beast. A much bigger, much more lethal beast.

"Great," Ricardo said, sinking back into his chair. He must have realized the difficulty spike as well. "How in the world are we going to get a gang member to crack?"

"It's not impossible," I said, coming in to do damage control. "We have a web of contacts at Stonewall that reach out far and wide. We'll find someone who can talk. It'll take some time, but I feel confident about where this is heading." And I did. That was the truth. It was going to be harder than I initially thought, but I was always up for a challenge. It would keep me busy, keep me from obsessing about other things.

About Jose. About the Unicorn.

About Enzo.

"So the gang guy must have done it, then, right?"

"We're going to follow all of the leads and see where it

gets us." I looked to Ricardo, whose fear was apparent in his big brown eyes. He was a good-looking guy, older, with crow's feet aplenty. A warm, albeit very crooked, smile. "Please, find the person who did this. I don't want to spend the rest of my life in jail."

I saw the turmoil in his eyes. His fate was a terrifying one. I imagined that serving time for a crime you knew you didn't commit must have felt close to being buried alive. A certain desperation would claw at your throat, before it slowly gave up and gave room to numbness. Close to the emotions I'd felt when I lost Jose. A sense of losing yourself, like you've stepped to the very edge of the brink, and the pit below was endless.

"We'll get you out," Enzo reassured Ricardo. There was a sincere warmth in his tone and in the way he reached over and rubbed a hand on Ricardo's back, keeping those soft amber eyes on Rick. His eyes were like no one else's. A liquid gold, a breathtaking yellow. My favorite color, my favorite precious stone, all of it encapsulated in Enzo's gaze. And it always changed in the light, glittering like a strip of metallic gold one second and the next appearing like a deep pool of amber. I watched him, seeing such a kind soul underneath that sharp, professionally groomed face.

I turned my eyes back to Ricardo. Something had stirred a feeling in my chest. It was a familiar sensation, but one I hadn't felt in a long time. A very long time. And for once I was scared. I didn't want to feel it. Nothing—I didn't want to feel anything. I didn't have to get involved with someone, not when this case was heating up. Too much work. There wouldn't even be time to consider opening myself up to another man.

Two hard knocks sounded on the door, and an officer

came in and pointed at her watch. "He's done. Back to the cell."

She grabbed Ricardo by the shoulder and pulled him up. I was about to get up when Enzo snapped. "Hey, treat him like a person, not a dog, okay?"

"You think this is how I treat a dog?" She was already turning her back to leave. "I actually like dogs."

Enzo was about to say something else, but the cop was gone with Ricardo. I'd dealt with law enforcement my entire life, so I was a little more used to some of the shit that went down. I didn't like it, but there wasn't a ton of reform I could have done in that moment. Besides, I knew she had her fair share of shit thrown her way working in those halls, so that tough exterior was most likely a well-tuned survival mechanism. I had to focus all my energy on figuring out what happened to Luanne and Oscar, and hopefully that would put an end to Ricardo's fucked-up situation. I grabbed my notepad and tugged on my coat.

"Thank you for helping set up this meeting," I said, already half out the door. I held a hand out, which Enzo took in his. We shook but didn't let go for a few moments even though we were as still as statues.

"Zane," he started. I took my hand back, stuffing them both in the pockets of my coat. "Let's, uhm, do something tonight."

I couldn't stop myself from arching a brow. The king of smooth was a little lacking in his game. "I'm going to get working on the case."

"Okay, fine," Enzo said. I thought the conversation was done there.

"How about after?" he asked, pleasantly surprising me. "It's still early. You can work until, let's say, eight thirty."

"And then?"

"And then we'll do something."

He was recovering nicely, but I still felt like it would be smarter for me to politely decline. It wasn't the right time. I knew what Enzo was after, and I wasn't sure I could really give it to him. And he was a good man—he didn't need to be wasting time.

"Sorry, Enzo. Not tonight." I looked to his eyes, finding that beautiful golden hue that captivated me from the start. It was hard to say no to that face. Really fucking hard. But I felt like it would be the best thing for me at that point. I'd get home, jerk it off, and then focus on work. Simple as that. There were lives at stake; no need to complicate my own.

"See you, then," Enzo said. It was my sign to turn and leave. I walked out of the station, tuning out the drunken yelling and the aggressive cursing. My car was parked outside in the lot. I noticed there was a small dusting of snow on the ground, leaving behind the footprints of everyone who had just walked in and out. I looked up, seeing the heavy gray clouds starting to disperse and make room for the sunshine.

The doors to the station opened up behind me. When they shut, they silenced the chaos that was inside. "Give me one dinner," Enzo said, coming up next to me. "That's it. Come on, I owe you. You saved my life."

He was persistent, that was for sure. And that smile... goddamn that smile. No wonder he got all his clients off the hook. He just needed to flash that grin and the jury would be eating right out of his hand.

"Here, come to this address." Enzo grabbed my hand before I could protest. He was a bold one, the cocky little asshole. I was starting to really like it. He pulled a pen from his coat and bit off the top, holding it between his teeth while he spoke and scrawled on my hand. "It's an exclusive place, somewhere I doubt you've ever eaten at."

"Why? Because I'm too poor?" I cocked my head and arched a brow.

He looked up at me as he let go of my hand. "What? No, I wasn't even making a joke. Only a handful of people have eaten there, that's why. It's very limited seating. Extremely limited. Waitlist is at least four years." Enzo scoffed. "Besides, I doubt the owner of Stonewall Investigations is scavenging for pennies under the cushions."

I was intrigued. But also, I was getting slightly annoyed. Enzo had that ability—he knew how he could get under my skin so that he could light me on fire. "How do we have such priority seating, then?"

"I know the owner." Enzo grinned.

"Fine." I felt myself being reeled in by that smile of his. "I'll see you tonight."

"Perfect. See you tonight."

He was practically glowing. This was a side of him that never really showed in his various TV appearances. He was always charismatic, but there was a bravado that seemed to separate him from the viewer. It was one of the reasons why I thought I'd initially dislike him. An overconfidence that felt way too cocky for my tastes. But these moments, where he looked like a kid waking up to the best Christmas ever, felt very refreshing. Almost vulnerable. The moment had me smiling in return, big and wide and unrestrained.

Enzo left with a hug. I got in my car and started it, the engine purring to life. I sat there, letting the heater blast on and warm up the air around me. I looked at the palm of my hand.

*Bastard even has perfect handwriting.*

## 12  ENZO

I was nervous as all hell. My stomach felt like it was on its fourth skydiving trip. It was exactly the feeling I had when I'd done it years ago. Stepping up to the edge of the plane was probably the scariest part, and then willing your body to jump was another experience entirely. But I remember that fear, the kind that made your stomach twirl and your body suddenly feel light as a feather. An anxiety that came from fear of the unknown. I had no idea how my skydiving experience was going to turn out, although of course I had clear hope that everything would work out okay and I'd still be able to move all four of my limbs.

As for tonight, I had zero idea of how the date was going to go. I could only hope that things would go well and that the night would reveal something between the both of us.

That's what my romantic side was aching for me to believe. My other side—the more analytical side—pushed me toward the realization that I was looking at all this through rose-colored glasses. Sure we had a good connection, and our bodies clearly reacted for the other, but Zane was still holding up walls and I had no idea if I was the one meant to bring them down. He'd lost the man he loved in a way that still haunted him to this day. That was a hard cross to bear, and although I was more than willing to take on some of the weight, I knew it would all depend on if Zane was ready to share it.

My Alexa started ringing. The timer I'd set must have run out.

"Alexa, sto—" Shit, she didn't hear her name. "Alexa, Alexa." I moved closer to the flashing cylinder. "Ale—Oh my god. Alexa! Stop!" The damned thing stopped ringing. I rolled my eyes and walked into my kitchen. The smell of parmesan, ricotta, mozzarella cheese, and basil drifted out of the oven and filled the room, adding to the already delicious scent in the air.

I had been working in the kitchen for a couple of hours now, and I loved every second of it. I was running around, kneading dough on one flour-covered counter while hurrying over to another counter so I could prepare and cut vegetables. Another counter was dedicated to the meat. I used the sink in the island to wash things, while the space next to the sink was dedicated to the lasagna noodles. There were a couple of other stations for the salad and breads, which made me grateful for the fact that I had a kitchen big enough to accommodate it all. I remember being little and watching my grandma at work, utilizing every inch of space in her tiny kitchen, eventually having to use the tables in the shared yard to hold some of the bowls. I was always fascinated whenever she was in the kitchen. It was like watching a magic show every single time. Spices would fly like fairy dust in the air, while the old oven would shoot up a jet of flame every time it turned on, adding a little pyrotechnics to the show. I think that's where I got my love of cooking because although my mamma enjoys it, she also wasn't against ordering takeout more often than not. Which I didn't mind growing up, because it meant I got to spend extra time in the kitchen when I convinced her I could whip up a better meal than Rachel's Mediterranean Chicken next door.

Also, spoiler alert: Rachel wasn't even Mediterranean. Shocker, I know.

I checked my watch. Zane was due any minute now. I opened the oven and checked my work.

"Perfetto," I said to myself. The colors were all exactly how I wanted them, crisp and gold, meaning it was cooked to perfection. The oozing cheese and sizzling beef verified my suspicions. I slid on the blue silicone oven mitts and pulled the baking dish out, setting it on top of the oven so that it could cool. I admired my work for a moment. Lasagna was all about layers, and it looked like I nailed them. There were also some colorful sweet peppers thrown in for a crunch.

Two white plates sat on the counter next to the oven. I grabbed some marinara sauce and added a dab and a stroke on each corner of the plate, almost making it look like it was done with a paintbrush. I grabbed some parsley and set it on the top of the plate. I'd watched enough cooking shows to know that plating mattered almost as much as the actual food. I wanted to present something nice for Zane, something he was going to remember, aside from how great it tasted (because, let's be real, we all know my lasagna tastes incredible).

"Alexa, what time is it?" I asked, wiping my forehead with a paper towel.

"I'm sorry. I'm not equipped to answer that question."

"Jesus." She must have not heard me right. "Alexa, what *time* is it?"

"It is currently 8:30 p.m.," she said in her pleasant yet slightly unsettling voice.

And as if we'd rehearsed his cue, the doorbell rang throughout the house. I looked around the kitchen, happy that I was able to contain most of the mess, and then looked down at myself. *Merde.* I wasn't exactly looking sharp. I had flour marks on the sides of my shirt and a dollop of marinara sauce right on my thigh.

"Great," I said, hurrying to the sink. "He's going to think I'm on my period."

The doorbell rang once more, and the marinara stain was only getting worse. I thought of the second-best option: pulling my pants off and folding them up to throw into the laundry closet on my way to the front door. I considered opening the door in just my black Calvins, but I decided it may have been too much for a first date (even though all I wanted to do was hang out with Zane in our underwear... or out of them). So I grabbed a pair of gray running shorts from the closet and tugged them on, almost tripping down the hall.

"Zane!" I said, opening the door and opening my arms. Zane was standing there, looking dapper as hell in a casual navy sports jacket and a nice shirt tucked into a pair of dark skinny jeans that drew my eyes straight to the bulge in his crotch. "Sorry about my last-minute wardrobe malfunction," I said as we hugged.

"That's okay," Zane said, stepping into my home. "I thought it was just a look you were going for." He looked me up and down, a smirk breaking on those big lips of his. "The 'sexy alcoholic just waking up from a bender and still looking hot' kind of look."

I threw darts at him through my eyes.

He chuckled and looked around. "Wow, your place is incredible."

"Thank you," I said, offering to take his jacket. He took it off and handed it over with a smile. I had a coat rack by the door, one that was gifted to me by one of my clients. It was definitely a conversation piece. It was made up of shed deer antlers, which was something I didn't even know was a thing. But apparently deer shed their antlers like my mamma sheds her hair in my shower every time she comes to visit.

It helped that my interior-design style was already a little eclectic, kind of like Zane's. He was now admiring a tall white marble bookshelf that held books and trinkets from all of my different travels. I walked over to stand next to him. Instantly, I was put into a trance from his scent alone. It was a cologne I didn't recognize. A little sweet, but a lot of man. Spices and oak and sea salt.

"Where's this from?" Zane was pointing at a small elephant carved out of brilliant jade, its bright and vibrant greens immediately drawing the eye.

"I went on a volunteer trip to Thailand a few years ago. Spent the summer helping a village with building projects, and I also held classes at night. Simple stuff at first, but some of them learned really fast. I was teaching some basic law concepts by the end of it."

I was smiling, remembering my time in the village. It was difficult at first, adjusting to having almost zero electricity and having to shower outdoors, but it was an experience I'd never regret.

"They had two elephants in the village: Delilah and Erica. I grew close with Erica's caretaker. He found this jade rock years ago, and he ended up carving Erica out of it and giving it to me as a gift on the day I left. He said it was a thank-you from the entire village."

Zane looked from the elephant to me, his eyebrows drawn up. "That's an incredible gift. I didn't think—"

"I'd ever work for free? See, I'm full of surprises."

"That's not what I was going to say." Zane quirked his lips. "But since you said it." He smiled and nudged his shoulder into me. It was a small gesture, but it might as well have knocked the earth off its axis. At least that's how I felt. There was something so playful and at ease in the way things felt. There was absolutely zero tension or awkwardness in the air. It was almost like I was standing next to an old friend, reviving memories from years ago.

"What I *was* going to say is, I didn't think you knew how to complete any manual labor."

"Ha. Ha. Ha," I deadpanned before breaking into a smile. It felt like a moment that would have been perfectly punctuated by a kiss. If it were any other guy, I would have gone for it. But with Zane, things were different. It felt like I was coaxing one of the rarest, flightiest birds in all the world. And the last thing I wanted was to spook him or scare him off. Nope. I wanted to grab this rare Amazonian Tweety Bird and never let go.

So, instead of the kiss, I turned and walked away. "Let me give you the grand tour," I said, motioning toward the hallway that wound through the rest of the penthouse. "Or do you want to start upstairs?" I pointed toward the spiral staircase that led to the second floor.

"Let's go with dealer's choice."

"All right, all right," I said, nodding. "Follow me, we'll do the first floor. I'll keep the upstairs for the big climax."

"Of the tour?"

"Right, yeah."

"Gotcha," Zane said, chuckling behind me as I led him through the foyer.

The nerves I'd been feeling earlier were dispersed the second I opened my door and laid eyes on Zane. A sense of ease had come over me. It was similar to coming home after a long day at school and getting a whiff of the addictive pastries your mom was making in the kitchen. It was a sense of comfort that told me it was all going to be all right. Tonight was going to go off without a hitch, even if everything had somehow managed to go wrong. Because it didn't matter if the entire world was crashing down around us; I was pretty sure Zane and I would find a way to make a good time out of it.

## 13  ZANE

I'd be lying if I said I wasn't nervous. This entire situation revved up my adrenaline like a NASCAR driver was behind the wheel of my nervous system. A date. I hadn't done one of those in, fuck, who knows how long. I didn't even want to put a number to the time—it would've only served to freak me out even more.

I tried to tell myself that it wasn't a big deal. We'd already spent time together, and it went perfectly fine. Hell, it went better than fine. So there was no reason this time would be any different.

*Which could be exactly why I'm so scared...*

Was that the reason? Was I nervous because there was now something that could be messed up? But that would have meant admitting I felt something for Enzo, and I wasn't sure if I was at that conclusion yet. There were still questions that needed answering. Questions I had to ask myself.

"It smells great in here," I said, following my nose as we walked through Enzo's home. His place was insane. It was obvious he had money in almost every aspect of his home, down to the perfectly maintained blue-and-gold Persian rug underneath the white leather couch that, I could safely say, was definitely more expensive than most of my own furniture put together. And yet, with all of that being said, I didn't *feel* like I was with someone who had a bottomless bank account. That was refreshing. I had been around people with a quarter of Enzo's wealth, and they always made it something to be known, something to hold over others because in their twisted heads it meant they were better than them.

Enzo was nothing like that, which was exactly why I could joke around with him about it. I could poke fun at his affinity for bellhops and caviar, and he'd laugh and find something to poke me back with. He didn't take himself too seriously. He was down-to-earth and funny and had a good heart and, holy shit, I was starting to feel something for him.

"Right," Enzo said, clapping his hands, "so the exclusive dinner I promised you is actually *here*. Welcome to Casa di De Luca. We're not meeting at my place for just predrinks like I had said."

I smiled, already figuring out the surprise the second Enzo opened the door, looking like he had just been running around trying to make everything perfect. He looked like a man who had zero plans of leaving the house anytime soon. Plus, the mouthwatering scent that filled the space made me think his kitchen was being put to use. I let him think he got this one over me, though. It was kind of cute.

"Ah, so you do actually know the owner."

"Very intimately, yes." Enzo crossed his arms. "Did you not believe me?"

"I'm learning to believe everything you say..."

"Good."

"Is a big ol' steaming pile of dogshit," I added in a stage whisper.

Enzo's jaw dropped and he chortled out a laugh. It was infectious. I really liked the sound of his laughs. They were a little obnoxious, but that's what I liked about them. Something about him not really caring how he sounded, just that he was expressing his joy. I laughed along with him.

"You're going to eat those words when I get you a dinner with the Gaineses."

"And Oprah?"

"Okay, maybe that one was a little bit of an exaggeration."

"Mhmm," I said. His eyes were glowing under the bright overhead lighting. We were standing in the dining room, which was painted a light gray. A tall chrome vase held a beautiful sunflower arrangement in the corner of the room, bringing a pop of stunning yellow. A wide archway led into the kitchen, where the delicious scent was originating.

"Need any help?" I asked, nodding toward the kitchen.

"Nope, you sit down, I'm going to get everything ready. Let me change first."

"Don't," I said quickly.

"I look ridiculous."

"It's cute. And besides, you look really comfortable. Why squeeze into skinny jeans when you can hang out in gym shorts?"

Enzo considered me for a moment. He chewed on the inside of his lip before smiling and shrugging. "If you insist, *signore*."

*Damn.*

I couldn't help thinking it.

*The smallest word he says in Italian gets me hard.*

"I do," I said, pulling a chair out from the table and ignoring the pulse in my briefs. He really did look comfortable in the shorts, and, on the more selfish side of my request, he also looked *sexy. as. fuck.* They were the short running kind of shorts, made of a thin material that ended inches above his knees and showed off his muscular thighs and biteable calves. That mixed with his button-up dress shirt, and he was a hot, sexy mess I could stare at all damn night.

Enzo came back into the dining room, walking past a large white sliding barn door. His dining room was just as perfectly decorated as the rest of his home. There was the regal-looking wooden table that held a centerpiece of five orchids, all in bloom, in shades of whites and pinks that balanced with the white shadow boxes on the wall holding a variety of succulents in different pots. Each shadow box had a window looking out from behind the plant, giving a peek of the New York skyline below. There was a copper statue of a jaguar wearing a studded leather collar, sitting like a king looking down on his city. It was set against the opposite corner as the sunflowers, its eyes looking at the dinner table as though it were expecting its next meal at any moment.

"That's one of my favorite pieces," Enzo said, setting a glass of red wine in front of me.

"Thank you." I grabbed the glass by the stem. "Cheers." I looked up at Enzo, and he smiled down on me as our glasses clinked.

"Cheers," he said, lifting the glass to his lips. I looked away, drinking the merlot.

"So how did the investigating go this afternoon? Find anything else out?" Enzo pulled out the chair next to me and sat down. There was a big white marble bowl of chips with a row of dips set in front of it. He reached for a chip and dunked it in the dark green sauce.

"Nothing useful," I said, shaking my head. "I reached out to a contact who might be able to get me in touch with the Blood Scarabs, but it's still shaky. They aren't exactly open to speaking to strangers."

"How would that even work?" Enzo asked. He looked concerned, the way his wrinkles popped up between his brows. "Would you meet them somewhere public? Like a Starbucks? You'd have backup, right?"

"Yes. I'd first order us all a round of Venti caramel and white chocolate Frappuccinos, then we'd get down to business."

"I pegged you as more of a latte guy."

I chuckled at that. "You're right, actually. I do prefer lattes. But no, we wouldn't be meeting anywhere public, and there wouldn't be any backup. I'm not part of the police force, I can't just call for a gang of guys with guns. No, this one is just me. I'd be going in undercover. I'd be posing as a hopeful initiate."

"Seriously? Undercover? But you aren't exactly an unknown figure. People know you head Stonewall Investigations, right?"

"Right, which is why we've got an excellent makeup artist working with us. She can transform anyone. It's incredible what some prosthetics and a little contouring can do to change someone's face. Throw on a wig and a hat and no one would recognize me."

"I can point you out of a crowd in seconds, guaranteed." Enzo's eyes were back to scanning my face again. "You sure you're safe?"

"I'm never sure," I said, being honest. "But that isn't going to stop me from doing my job."

"And you think he'll talk? To an initiate?"

"I can be pretty good at getting the truth out." I drank more of the merlot, savoring the bitter smoothness.

"Have you had to do it before? Go undercover?"

"Plenty of times. Not all as dangerous as getting involved with a gang, but some were. It comes with the territory. I can't throw handcuffs on someone and drag them to the station for questioning. My answers have to come through other means. I've had to pose as a drug dealer, a bank robber, an arsonist. And then there are other jobs where the cover isn't as intense. Like this one job I had." I sat back in the chair, still tasting the merlot on my tongue. "A young man came to us about being fired for being gay. He wanted us to find some kind of proof. The man who fired him was very wealthy and powerful and was also huge in the evangelical community. He had a lot of influence, but he also had a few weaknesses. I discovered a couple after weeks of research. One of those weaknesses was hiring a gay masseur company known for specializing in happy endings."

"Woh," Enzo said, swirling his glass and raising it to his lips.

"Right. And another thing? He enjoyed filming his encounters. So, instead of going undercover as a gang initiate, I went into this man's life as a masseur."

"Merda... did you have to give him a happy ending?"

"No spoilers," I said, smirking. "But no, I didn't. What happened was, I 'coincidentally' bumped into him at his neighborhood grocery store. I apologized and grabbed his wrist for a second. Enough to trap him. I pretended I had no idea who he was and told him he seemed like someone who was holding their shoulders a little tense. I offered him my company card: Hill's Massages, guaranteed to leave you happy."

Enzo almost did a spit take with his wine. "Seriously? You made cards saying that?"

"Mhmm," I said, smiling. "And he took the bait. He made an appointment with me that same night. I show up at his place, looking like a masseur ready to do business. I was wearing all white and acting real serene. He wanted me to set up the table outside in his backyard, which opened out to a massive lake. I set up and call him over. That's when he breaks the news: he wants to record the session. Perfect. I nodded and let him set up the camera. He's lying down, and before I start, I begin with asking him some questions. I feign recognition suddenly, realizing that him and I go to the same church. He almost rolled off the table in surprise. He sits up and looks me up and down. I can tell he's attracted and wants to keep going, but he's also rattled. Those are the best moments to draw out confessions."

"You're good," Enzo said, smiling around the lip of his wine glass.

"I asked him, point-blank, about firing Paul for being gay. Told him Paul was a good friend of mine. He was astonished and denied it. He told me to get out of his house. I walked backward, toward the house. His face was beet red. I asked him again and again, and he denied it. One last time, told him God was watching. He cracked. Said, 'Fine, yes, I fired him because he's a practicing homosexual' as if being gay was something like a religion or a medical profession. As if it could be turned on and off. That was probably how he was able to go to sleep at night, justifying his own behaviors by thinking he was turning it off."

"What a coglione."

"Coglio-what?"

"Coglione," Enzo repeated, emphasizing his Italian accent. "It means testicle."

It was my turn to almost do a spit take of wine. I swallowed it down before I laughed. "I've never called someone a testicle before, but I feel like it fits."

"Oh, definitely. Italians have a thing with balls. We have like five different ways of saying testicle, and all mean slightly different things. A coglione signifies a dumbass."

"Well, I ended up maneuvering myself next to the camera, which the testicle had forgotten was set up. I reached and grabbed the entire camera off the tripod and ran." Enzo's eyebrows shot up as I told the story. "He runs after me, but he's naked and his towel drops and tangles him up, plus he's older, so he's not as quick. I'm halfway through his house when I manage to get the memory card out of the camera. I leave the camera behind and bolt with the videotaped confession. Case closed."

Enzo's eyes were glinting as he looked at me. He was beginning to remind me a little of Jose, who'd look at me just the same way.

*This wine must be real damn strong...*

## 14  ENZO

"That was damn good lasagna." Zane sat back in his chair and lifted a napkin to his lips. His plate was scraped clean, adding a testament to his words. And that was his second serving. I got up from the table and grabbed both of the plates.

"Here, let me," he said, reaching for the dirty plates. I shook my head and dodged his attempts at helping me. I couldn't stop him from following me to the kitchen, though. He tailed me with our glasses in hand. I could practically feel his shape behind me. Like I'd be able to draw him out if I closed my eyes and had some pen and paper.

The entire night, I'd been acutely aware of Zane's presence. Of his body. Of his being. I was taking it all in, and it all felt so damn right. It was almost scary how well the night had been going. There wasn't an ounce of awkwardness or a moment of wishing things would end. It was the total opposite—I was hoping things never ended. Our conversations were so animated and both of us were so involved, it was stimulating every damn part of me.

Seriously. Every single part.

I placed the dishes in the dishwasher and grabbed the glasses from Zane. "We done with these?" I looked at the clock that was above the sink. It was only eleven.

"Oh, I wasn't bringing them to clean them. I was looking for refills."

"Smart." I smiled as I set them down on the counter and walked over to my wine fridge. It was opposite my actual fridge and had a glass door allowing anyone to look in at the rows of white wines. There was a section that wasn't chilled for the reds. "Another red, or do you want some white?"

"Let's go with a pinot grigio."

"White it is," I said, noting his choice of wine. Pinot grigio happened to be my favorite, and it was also a wine native to Italy. Coincidence? I think not. There was one bottle of pinot with a deep gold wax covering that called my name. I grabbed it and pulled it out. "This is a 2002 Elena Walch from Italy."

"Sounds great," Zane said in a tone that told me he didn't care much about the origin. He looked from the bottle in my hands to my eyes. We held that eye contact for a loaded moment. I wasn't breaking. I wasn't going to look away. Zane should have learned that about me. I was the type to go for the full eye contact. Eye fucking was a real thing, and I felt like I was *real* fucking good at it. Zane, on the other hand, would normally look away. I had noticed he didn't hold my gaze for as long as I would have liked. That was changing, though. He was standing his ground more and holding eye contact. Even over the course of the dinner, I could tell he was meeting my eyes and keeping them for longer and longer. It meant something to me. Not only was it a sign of progress, but it was also eye contact filled with a tension that was only getting harder and harder to ignore.

I walked to the counter and set the wine down.

"So, what part of Italy are you from?" Zane asked.

"Both my parents were born in Palermo. It's a small city in Southern Italy. It's the warmest city in all of Europe, they say. We go back a couple of times every few years.

There was a warmth that was spreading out from my core, and it had nothing to do with the warm weather in my parents' hometown. The heat was tightening my balls, making my heart beat quicker, making my lips tingle. I turned, ignoring the wine bottle and refocusing on Zane, who was leaning back against the counter with his arms across his chest, making the slits on his shirt pop open and giving me a peek at the furry, muscular chest beneath. I wanted to run my fingers through the dark hair. My tongue.

My dick.

It throbbed in my briefs. Soon, there'd be no hiding the bulge. Zane was looking at me, truly looking at me. His beautiful deep brown eyes were captivating. Words were said without either of our lips moving.

In seconds flat, I crossed the distance that separated us. My hands went up to his face as his fingers dug into my hips. He pulled me onto him as my mouth found his. A moan escaped us both. His lips were soft, his stubble rough. The taste of wine was still on both our tongues as we probed the other's mouth. My fingers went up to get lost in Zane's head of hair. He had a short cut, though long enough for me to mess up on the top. I bundled some in a fist and tugged his head back, sucking on his bottom lip, feeling Zane push his body forward onto mine as a sign that he liked it.

Well, judging by how hard his dick was, he fucking loved it.

I pulled his head back a little harder, exposing his neck. We were both about the same size in height, so I craned my head to suck on his sensitive flesh. I moved on to a new spot before I felt like I was leaving a hickey. He was moaning and grinding his hard dick against mine, sending waves of ecstasy coursing through my body. I was seeing stars, and not in the way that happens when you hit your head. No, these were from being launched out of the earth's stratosphere and into space. The kind of stars you saw only through a dream (or because your buddy had a really great batch of mushrooms... it was college, could you really blame me?).

In this case, I was seeing stars because of how high I felt from Zane's kiss. From his tongue, the way it felt against mine. I was high from the feeling of his hard, muscular body pushing against mine. Of the way he smelled, a scent I wanted to bottle up and use on a daily basis.

Cazzo. Zane was unwinding me. I let go of his hair and dropped my hands down to his hips. My hands slid between us, running over his hardness, feeling the thickness of it through his pants. I could feel it throbbing when I squeezed. It drove me crazy.

"I want you, Zane." My words fell out in a growl. Zane's gaze was filled with fire. Our eyes locked. There was something in Zane I hadn't seen before. Maybe glimpses of, but never the full thing. Lust. Hunger. Zane was looking at me like a lion would stare down a plate of thick, raw, bleeding meat.

And I wanted to feed him. My fingers found the zipper to Zane's pants. I pulled it down, the zip sounding in the room like a chorus of angels. With his pants open, I buried my hand between his thighs, feeling the warmth, holding his balls in my hand, the soft material of his blue briefs creating a barrier I needed to rip off. I could feel the heat of him against my palm, and it was mesmerizing. It spread through me as our lips met again, and this time our kiss was even hotter.

My hand moved up from his balls to the band of his briefs. I tugged them down, feeling his soft fur brush against the back of my fingers. I moaned into Zane's mouth as I slipped my hand into his briefs, immediately feeling my hand get slick with his precome. I grabbed his velvety soft length and almost came right then and there. Just holding his rock-hard cock in my hand was enough to unwind me and send me rocketing to another level.

I gave him two good strokes before I couldn't take it anymore. His cock needed to be between my lips. His taste was all I wanted on my tongue. I broke from the kiss and smiled as I slipped my hand out of his briefs and grabbed on to the waistband. With one tug, they fell down to Zane's ankles, his cock springing forward. My smile grew wider.

"Wow, that's a *cazzo*," I said, my jaw practically on the floor. Which was a good thing because anyone would need an unhingeable jaw to fit that entire thing in their mouth.

Zane put a hand around himself, his thumb on the base, as though I needed it there for scale. "From what I can see, you have a big cazzo yourself." His eyes were turned down to the huge bulge in my shorts. I could have provided shelter for a family of four with how big the tent was.

"Your Italian makes me even bigger," I said, rubbing myself over my shorts with one hand and stroking his bare cock off with another.

"It's impressive, right?" Zane said, smirking. "*Grazie.*"

I cocked my head, smiling. "I could see a few spots for improvement," I teased, "but that's nothing a great tutor can't help you with."

"And where would I find this great Italian tutor? Do you have any suggestions? Not sure I can think of anyone."

"Oh really? You can't think of one person you'd want to tutor you in the beautiful and romantic lingua Italiana?"

Zane licked his lower lip, a move that drove me wild. He was grabbing his balls while I stroked him off. All the while our eyes remained locked together, fire spreading through both of our bodies. I could feel it, the heat rising inside of him. He was warm in my hand, throbbing with a need to come. "Nope, no one's coming to mind."

"Bene," I said, shrugging. "I'm sure someone will pop up."

"Hopefully," Zane said, slowly moving his hips so his cock was sliding across my palm. I used his precome as lube, slicking up his shaft with his own juices. "Oh wait," he said, "I almost forgot."

My eyebrows arched up excitedly. I was having fun playing with Zane while also *playing* with him.

"One of our detectives. She's Italian. She can teach me."

My eyebrows drew together, and my mouth twisted into a sarcastic grin, all while my grip was still closed around Zane's pulsing shaft.

"Well, good luck with that." I dropped my shorts and briefs to the floor. We were both naked from the waist down. "I doubt her extracurricular activities would have been as fun as mine, though."

"Oh, really?" Zane asked, but he wasn't looking into my eyes anymore. He was staring down at my dick, hard and pink in the air, the tip wet with my own precome. "What would you have me do—" Zane looked up, back into my eyes, his own filled with even more hunger. "—*Professor?*"

I moved forward, grabbing his hips and pushing our cocks together, feeling the heat from his roll off and spread through mine. It was such an intense sensation. I loved it.

Knowing how hard I made him and feeling it against my body, it was exactly what I wanted.

"Well, for one," I said, kissing him between words, "I'll teach you the 'off-book' words."

"What are a few?"

"How about a phrase to start with?"

"Sure, teach me."

"Okay, how about 'succhiami il cazzo.'"

Zane's head tilted. He was smiling as he tried the words out under his breath before committing. "Say it one more time," he said, his hand sliding down my side to reach for our cocks. He grabbed both of us in his hand and started to rub. I could feel the soft skin of his cock against mine while his fingers worked the other side. It was magical.

"Succhiami il cazzo," I repeated, trying to enunciate some more but finding that the pleasure shooting through my balls was too much for me to focus on much else.

"Schucchu-mama al cazzo," Zane tried, butchering the first part but sounding so damn adorable doing it. I don't know how he did it, but he managed to be both smoldering hot and cheek-pinching cute at the same damn time.

"It means 'suck my cock,'" I said, grinning, "and since you asked so nicely."

I dropped to my knees, licking my lips as I went in for tonight's main course.

## 15   ZANE

Enzo's mouth felt like heaven. Seriously, like cloud fucking nine. He was a magician with his tongue. It swirled and whirled and got my toes curled. I was rocketing past the moon when he swallowed my cock down to the halfway point. He moaned around my dick, using his free hand to stroke the rest of my shaft before grabbing and massaging my balls. I groaned, a deep sound that originated in my chest. Who knew learning a new language could be so fun?

A piece of me, the one that realized 'holy shit, this is happening again,' kind of froze up. But that side of me wasn't as loud as the primal side. The one that felt the intense connection between Enzo and I and was ready to watch it explode (preferably all over my chest).

"*Fuccck*, Enzo, that feels so good."

Enzo stopped for a breath. We both took off our shirts. "It tastes so good, too." He was smirking at me, his lips shiny and plump as they went back to work. He took more of me down his throat this time. I started thrusting my hips forward, slowly at first. His hands came up from grabbing his own cock to dig into my thighs. I loved it. I started pumping faster, fucking his mouth harder. He looked up at me, almost begging for more. I was balls-deep now. Thrusting. He was taking it, swallowing it all. My hands gripped on to his hair like I was holding on to reins.

"Fuck, fuck, *fuck*." My balls were seconds from emptying. My teeth ground together. "I'm going to come," I warned, feeling the crest of the impending tsunami.

Enzo didn't miss a beat. He continued to bob up and down, slurping on my cock, squeezing my ass and pushing me deeper down his throat. I couldn't hold back anymore. My hands squeezed on to Enzo's head as my cock erupted, blowing load after load down Enzo's throat. My entire body spasmed, my thighs twitching, my toes pushing down into the floor.

Enzo swallowed every last bit of what I had to give him. He squeezed my ass one last time for good measure before kissing his way up my body, sucking on my nipples and sending pure lightning straight through me. He reached my lips. I could smell my sex on him. I could taste myself on his lips, on his tongue. I loved it. The salty sweetness mixed with Enzo's own taste created an intoxicating mixture that was already making me hard again.

But it was my turn to have some fun with Enzo. "I think it's time for the tour of the bedroom."

"I think so, too," Enzo responded, kissing me before turning around and leading the way. We left our clothes discarded in a pile, which allowed me to stare at Enzo's ass the entire way up to his room. It was fucking perfect. I'd never seen a nicer ass. I had to give it a good slap as we climbed the stairs. The crack sounded through the apartment.

"Ow," Enzo said. "Do it again." He stopped abruptly

and bent over a bit. I smiled, but instead of slapping his ass, I leaned in and bit it, sucking in the sensitive flesh, leaving a mark on his left butt cheek. I had to make it even. I did the same on the other side while reaching between his legs and grabbing his balls in my hand to give them a tug.

"Oh fuck," Enzo purred. My other hand went up to his lower back and pushed him farther down, exposing more of his ass in the air. I started to lick from the top to the bottom, and Enzo was turning into Jell-O because of it. "Oh, oh, gah, cazzo, right there, baby, fuck." Enzo was just stringing random words together as my tongue licked around his hole. He moved forward from the sudden sensation, but I pushed him back, spreading his cheeks so that I had better access. I went in like Enzo had just served me cake.

And I fucking *loved* cake.

My tongue danced around Enzo's sensitive flesh, marking him as mine. I kissed and sucked and probed, and Enzo was shaking like a fawn just finding its legs. He was moaning and pushing his ass back onto me, giving me more of him. I loved it. I reached between his legs again and grabbed his cock, feeling it rock hard and throbbing in my hand as I ate him out. I ran my palm over his tip, feeling it come back slick with precome. I used it to lube up as I jerked him off, moaning into his ass, feeling him getting tenser and tenser. He was getting close.

"Oh cazzo, proprio lì," Enzo said, slipping into full Italian mode. It had me leaking again, my cock spilling some leftover come onto the white marble stone steps.

"Fuck, Zane, you're going to make me blow."

I continued lapping at his crack and tugging on his cock. His entire body quivered underneath me for a moment before I felt his cock spasm and his hips jerk forward. His body convulsed as he shot his come onto the stone steps. I watched him, feeling intensely satisfied by it all. When Enzo regained control of his muscles again, he stood up and turned. I climbed a couple of steps until we were even, our eyes locked in, our faces wearing drunken smiles.

"Wow," Enzo said, leaning in to kiss me. "I thought I was going to pass out there for a second. Cazzo, Zane. We didn't even make it to the climax—"

"Actu—"

"Of the tour," Enzo said, finishing his thought by reaching down and grabbing my semihard dick, as if it were a punctuation mark.

"Well, let's go. I'm still down for a tour."

\*\*\*

The climax of the tour rerouted from the bedroom to the shower. My body felt like I'd spent a day at the spa. Fuck that, it was like I'd lived at a spa my entire life. Every single muscle was relaxed. My dick hung heavy and limp as I got into the shower, noticing Enzo's dick was still hard.

*An Italian stallion, that's for sure.*

I almost fucking purred when I grabbed his hips and pulled him close. The water fell straight down from the dual showerheads that simulated rainfall. His shower was huge, more than big enough for two sweaty men coming down from some incredible sex to soap up in.

I kept kissing him, my hand sliding up to grab his still-tight balls. I squeezed them, pushing my body against him, feeling his hard shaft against my stomach. The water fell down in warm droplets, truly making it feel like we were standing outside in the rain. I closed my eyes and let myself feel every single thing coming over me. Not only just the water, but also the emotions. I was feeling things I hadn't felt in years. This kind of warmth and comfort was alien to me. Having someone so close to me, having their naked body on mine. The concept of intimacy felt like a dust-covered fossil, something that died long ago for me. I'd buried it with my husband's coffin.

Something caught in my throat. It wasn't a moan. I pulled back, our bodies still touching, our eyes locked on each other, but our lips no longer pressed together. The water fell down Enzo's face in heavy drops. The white marble that surrounded us was reflected back to me through the droplets, almost making it seem like he was glittering.

"This is..."

"Perfetto," Enzo said, smiling.

I paused, feeling his word land in my chest. Not to mention, whenever he said the tiniest thing in Italian, I immediately perked up. "It is," I said, leaning forward for another kiss. This one was short, though. I drew back and looked into Enzo's eyes. They were so warm, so kind, something I was ashamed to say I hadn't noticed when we'd first met. Maybe I was just tainted by the character he portrayed on his televised interviews. This cocky, always-on defense attorney who won case after case was actually a much more multifaceted man than he let on. It was intriguing and made me want to learn even more about him. I hadn't felt that way about someone else in a long time.

Enzo quirked his lips. "Zane," he said, my name sounding like the beginning to my favorite song. "What are you thinking? I see something behind those eyes. Something bothering you?"

I felt myself crumbling. All the carefully constructed walls I had spent years fortifying were now falling in a cascade of bricks. I was naked, both physically and emotionally. Unbidden tears started to fall down my cheeks, mixing with the water from the shower. I didn't know that a simple question could unwind me in such a powerful fashion. Or maybe it wasn't the question, but who was asking it that had me so raw. It was getting more difficult by the day trying to keep certain parts of myself separate from Enzo, the parts I hadn't shared with anyone since Jose.

"I miss him," I said, being a hundred percent honest with Enzo. "Jose. We were married, and everything was good, great, and then it happened—"

"I know," Enzo said, sparing me from having to say it out loud. Having to relive envisioning the photos of his body, of the horn rising from his forehead. "I was waiting for the right time to bring it up, or until you felt comfortable enough to talk about it. Zane. I'm so profoundly sorry for what happened. My heart breaks knowing that you'll always have a piece of yours missing."

"Thank you," I said, finding a powerful sense of comfort inside Enzo's warm eyes, which were also moistened, and not from the shower. "I don't know what the hell's coming over me. This probably isn't the best time to talk about my dead husband."

The words fell into the shower like nuclear warheads. "There's never a 'right' time," Enzo quickly replied, not letting it shake him. Good. I needed that. Normally I was the solid support, but right now, I was wavering. I was letting it all out. I was naked and bare and allowing Enzo to see a part of myself I kept locked in. "I'm just happy that you can talk about it with me, at any time. Because I want to hear it. I want to hear about what pains you, and I want to hear about what makes you laugh. I want to hear about it all. Jose was such a huge part of your life, the last thing I want is for you to think you can never talk about him again. His spirit will always be inside your heart, shining through.

You carry his memory, and in that way, you keep him alive."

He was right, but the sadness was still heavy on my chest. "It's scary." My gaze dropped to our feet, puddles forming around them as water collected before it disappeared down the drain. "Everything felt so damn right. I was the happiest I'd ever been with him. And then, from one day to the next, he was taken and my entire life got flipped around. I still have whiplash." I took a breath. The warm water was relaxing my muscles, making me feel even more relaxed, more vulnerable. "And I'm scared I'm allowing it to happen again."

"How so?"

"By falling for you, Enzo." There it was. An admission of something both of us knew was true from the beginning. I had been falling for the cocky defense attorney from the second he walked into my office, and I had a feeling he could say the same about me. "The happiness I felt back then, I can feel it happening with you. It's fucking scary. I don't know what to do."

*Not to mention the Unicorn is back. He's fucking back.*

I didn't even want to say it out loud, not now. As if those words were somehow poison designed to boil away my insides.

Enzo's hands rose up to cup my head. He was looking into my eyes, anchoring me. "I feel happiest when I'm with you, too, Zane. I can find that I trust you, so much more than I've trusted anyone in recent years. And I think that means something. It's scary. I'll be a hundred percent honest with you, Zane. I'm scared, too. I can't say I'll ever completely understand your pain, but I do feel echoes of it in my own past. I was betrayed by someone, and a relationship I thought was golden turned out to actually be a pile of shit prettied up with gold wrapping paper." Enzo shook his head, letting go of me. "To be honest, I should have smelled it a mile away."

We both smiled. I could sense Enzo was peeling back a layer, showing me something underneath that not many other people got to see.

"But I didn't understand that," Enzo continued. "I thought it was perfect, and I lost it and a sense of myself, too. It took me a few years, but I've come to realize that I can't live my life bound to that really shitty circumstance. Sure, it can shape me, but it certainly won't define me. It was a little bit of a life-changing realization."

He was completely right. I was allowing my one traumatic experience to reverberate and affect my life in ways I didn't even grasp.

"That's a good way to think about it," I said.

"Damn right it is." Enzo turned then and raised his head toward the water. He turned back to face me, his cheeks puffed out. Before I could realize, he spit a stream of water onto my chest and smiled. "You'll get hit with a dolphin jet every time you say something obvious," Enzo said.

"That's not fair."

Enzo raised his face and lower it, a stream of water shooting out of his mouth. "That's obvious."

We both started cracking up. When we were finally catching our breaths, I opened my arms and took him in. I had to hold him. Had to make sure he was real. This was all too good to be real, but somehow it was. I never thought I'd be feeling this way after Jose again, and a part of me thought I'd feel guilty if I ever did. But talking about him with Enzo had a therapeutic effect, like a cool aloe balm spread over a sore burn.

We stayed in that shower a while longer, our conversation turning lighter, our laughs coming more freely. We landed in Enzo's bed, rolling around in a tangle of naked, damp limbs.

Although I was tired the next day from barely getting any sleep, I knew that I was forever changed after that night at Enzo's.

## 16  ENZO
### A WEEK LATER

"You're fucking *smitten*," Candice said, her rivers of auburn brown hair shining in the afternoon sunlight that fell in through her office window in rays of gold, appearing like some kind of drapery over the arm of the couch she was resting on. Our firm was located on the topmost floor of a building that looked down on the always chaotic Times Square. I loved it. I loved being able to look outside and see crowds of people at all hours of the day. The energy drove me, and today was no different. I was looking outside, down at a large crowd of tourists gathered around a sword-swallowing street performer as I talked to Candice about Zane. She was my partner in the firm and also one of my closest friends. We'd met in law school and had become inseparable since, both of us knowing we were bound to have our own firm one day. Fast-forward a few years, and we were sitting at the top of Times Square in an office that had *De Luca, Lively & Associates* written behind a lit-up waterfall as you walked in.

"I'm not smitten, Candice." I watched as the sword swallower started juggling what appeared to be eggs. Some of his audience members seemed like they were getting too cold, standing outside while waiting for the big sword-swallowing finale. "I'm fucking sprung."

Candice laughed at that. She was sitting on the red couch against the far wall. She'd kicked off her red bottoms and posted her feet up on the armrest, her hands behind her head. It was like a reverse therapy session, where the therapist lies down and the patient stands up. "What are you going to do about it?"

"Watch it all disintegrate in front of me, most likely. It's what always happens."

"Oh shut up, Enzo. You haven't even given yourself opportunities to watch your chances wither up."

*Merda.* She was right.

"When was the last time you dated someone seriously? Not since that Ryan guy, right?"

"You're right, it's been a while."

*Not since Ryan.*

But Candice didn't know the entire story about Ryan. He'd only lasted three months, but those three months were some of the worst months of my entire life, not to mention the following ones as well. I didn't know why I still hadn't talked about the extent of what Ryan did to me, not even with Candice, but I just couldn't bring it up. When that man left my life, I wanted all signs of him gone, too, and that meant not even bringing his name up in conversation.

But that was almost three years ago. I had moved on from what he did to me. Especially over the past year, I really found myself accepting what had happened and allowing myself to trust other men again. I started sleeping around and having fun, something that had been absent since Ryan entered my life. But I still never fully felt myself open up around anyone. Not until Zane.

I felt like I made peace with what Ryan did to me, and that may have been one of the reasons why Zane was even coming into my life at that point. I was making room in my life for someone who actually mattered. Someone who deserved my attention.

*Of course, he could always turn out to be a major coglione, too, but I highly doubt that.*

No, Zane wasn't like Ryan. There had been red flags from the start with that guy, which I ignored because he was a hot Instagram model and I thought that was all I needed.

Oh, how much I'd learned.

"You act so different with men compared to your cases. Thank God, because if you treated our cases like you treated guys you cared about, I don't think we'd ever get anything done. You diddly-daddle too much."

"I do not *diddly-daddle*," I said, "unless we're on the second date."

We both laughed. The sword swallower down below moved on to his final act, pulling out a (surely fake) sword from out of a long black box. I wondered how his fingers weren't freezing off in the cold. He wasn't even wearing a coat, sticking to a look that reminded me of someone who'd travel the country chasing behind a punk rock band.

"Seriously, though, I'm nervous to make the wrong move. That's never happened to me before. I can pick up and keep men entertained like it was my second profession. But with Zane, the table's been flipped. Nothing feels the same. I'm constantly on my toes, making sure I don't scare him off somehow."

"Have you guys had sex yet?"

"No," I replied, watching as the man below raised the sword up high into the air.

"Wow," she replied, whistling. "It is serious, then."

"We've hooked up, and that's been explosive enough, I don't think my body can handle full-on sex with him."

"Well, if I see you walking into the office like a penguin, I'll make sure to cover and tell the associates you had a really rough spin class."

I snorted at that. "Thank you. I knew I could always count on you."

"Obviously," Candice said. The sword went down the man's throat. Well, at least that's what everyone around him thought. From my angle, I could clearly see the sword retract back into the hilt, his throat a black hole holding nothing but his tonsils.

*All smoke and mirrors.*

"How do you know I wouldn't be the one topping?"

"Babe... come on," she said as she sat up on the couch. She laughed as her hazel eyes dropped below my waist. "With an ass like that, it would be criminal if you weren't a bottom. You'd seriously need to go to gay jail."

"Is that the one where everyone drops the soap on purpose?"

"Exactly," she said, laughing.

"Doesn't sound too bad." I moved away from the window, laughing along with Candice. These moments were very much needed, especially with the stress of Ricardo's case hovering over me. Sleep had been hard to come by the past few days. With the court date approaching like a shadowy monster with its fangs bared, my gears were working on full throttle. I had another interview with him the other day and walked away feeling positive that he couldn't have done it. I was working on overtime putting together a good defense in case Zane's investigation didn't pan out. It seemed like he was onto something, but that meant he had to talk to a gang member in order to figure it out, and that part scared me. If anything happened to Zane, I knew I would feel like I was the one responsible. I'd been the man who hired him and sent him off onto danger's path. Of course, that was in his job description, but still, it made me nervous.

"Okay, fine. Say you do end up surviving a sexual encounter with Zane, all limbs and holes intact, what would you see happening from there?"

Damn it. Candice was good. Explicit, but also good. That's why I loved her. Her sharpness was also invaluable in the courtroom, where she could shred apart a counterargument like it was a block of parmesan going through a grater.

"I see us… I don't know. Being happy. Life feels good when I'm around him. Truly beautiful. Trust me, I like my life from before I met him, but when I'm with Zane, everything is different. La vita è più dolce con lui." I sat down in her big leather chair. "Life is sweeter with him in it."

"Okay, so maybe you should go into this thinking positive thoughts, not that you're going to see anything disintegrate. It sounds like things are off to a great start, and nothing you do is going to ruin that, so just let things ride out the way they should. I've got a feeling you found a good match."

"We'll see," I said, feeling hopeful and confident inside but knowing there were still some hurdles to jump.

That was when the buzzer on Candice's intercom blurted through the room. "Hi, Ms. Lively, is Enzo meeting with you?"

I immediately recognized my assistant's voice. I reached across the desk and pressed the button. "Hey, Liz. Yeah, I'm here. What do you need?"

"I've got a call for you."

"Tell them I'll call back in ten."

"Sounds urgent. He told me to tell you it was Zane about Ricardo's case. Told me you wouldn't want to miss him."

Candice gave a suspicious cough, one that sounded more like a laugh. "I'll buzz you when I'm in my office so you can give me the call," I said, hopping up from the chair.

"Be sure not to miss him," Candice said as she took her place behind her desk, watching me with a smile as I closed the door, flashing a certain finger behind my back on the way out.

## 17  ZANE

I didn't have to wait long for Enzo to pick up the phone, which was good because I could hear the welcome party getting started downstairs. We were celebrating (albeit, a little late) our two newest detectives becoming part of the team. I'd need to join them soon.

"Ciao, Zane, how are you?" Enzo's Italian accent was already getting my thoughts revved up and headed in a direction they shouldn't.

"I'm doing well, you?"

"Better now that I can hear your voice." The flirty line drew a warmth to my cheeks that felt foreign to me. "You have news about Ricardo?"

"Yes, yes," I said, looking at my computer screen and trying to hone back in on the task at hand. "I dug around and reached out to a few contacts. Two of them led me to a man named Herberto Torres, a defect of the Blood Scarabs. They have the idea that he might talk and go against the leader, who we're suspecting is the man Luanne was having an affair with. If I can get Herberto to testify or put in a statement, preferably not anonymously, then you can build an even stronger case for Ricardo's innocence."

"That's incredible!" Enzo exclaimed. I liked hearing him sound this happy. He was normally an upbeat guy, but I could hear the excitement in his voice. "You're a magician, Zane. A fucking magician. So when are you going to talk to this Herberto guy?"

"I've got a meeting set up with him in three weeks. He's out of the country right now but should be back for a short window of time."

"Are you sure you aren't being set up?"

I shrugged and looked out the window. It was the afternoon, so the sun hung high in the air, beating down on the concrete jungle as if it were trying desperately to get us warm again. This most recent cold front was already wearing out its welcome.

"My contacts are trustworthy, so I'm placing my trust with them. They can't control what Herberto does, but I'm sure that he's a defect."

"Isn't it impossible to leave a gang? Don't they hunt you down and sell your parts on eBay or something?"

"Yes, there's actually a website specifically for gangsters. It's called gBay."

"Sounds like their G-spot."

"Basically," I said, chuckling while Enzo laughed. I couldn't ever get tired of hearing Enzo laugh. "You're right, though. Most gangs do have 'lifetime memberships' so to speak. Although, I have a feeling it's harder to cancel a gym membership than it is getting out of the Bloods or the Crypts."

"They make those things impossible to get out of! The last gym membership I had to cancel, they had me send a postcard by raven while I tap-danced dressed up in a bear costume. And it could only happen during a full-blood blue moon."

"Well... that just sounds like a Friday night to me."

Enzo found that hilarious. "Why aren't I ever invited to your Friday-night bear parties?"

"No, no. The *bear* parties are on Saturdays. Fridays we just tap-dance."

"Got it. So Saturdays are when everyone gets down and dirty with big hairy guys?"

"Correct."

"I'll be there."

"Good," I said.

"Bene," Enzo said. "Have you been practicing your Italian?"

"My tutor's been too busy for any lessons." I glanced at the door, making sure it was closed all the way. The last thing I wanted was for someone to be standing outside a cracked door and hearing me flirting.

"So you haven't done any self-study, eh?" Enzo's tone was shifting. I could hear it in the way his accent became more pronounced. I noticed it was a tell of his. Happened whenever he was horny.

"I'm waiting for the professional to come around," I said, shifting in my chair. I shook a leg under the table, attempting to redirect blood flow away from my crotch.

"This weekend, then. I think you're due for a lesson."

"I agree." I squeezed my thighs together, my dick already at half-mast. "Seriously, though, you've had a busy week. Have things calmed down?" I was trying to stop myself from popping a full-on erection, so I had to steer the conversation back on track.

"Work's been crazy. Ricardo's case is my priority, but there are so many other fires to put out. All hands are on deck right now. I think I've slept a total of seven hours over the past four days."

"Shit, sorry," I said, finding that my dick wasn't responding to any distractions. I dropped a hand on my lap and squeezed. "You deserve some relaxation time. Maybe a good full-body massage."

*Fuck. Now I'm the one throwing around innuendos.*

"Well, maybe you can pay for your next Italian lesson with an oiled-up massage."

"Sounds like a fair deal." My hand started rubbing over my slacks. "Free Saturday night?"

"For you, I'll make time." I could hear the smile in Enzo's voice. "I already can't wait."

"Neither can I." I looked down at the bulge in my hands, my gray slacks looking strained.

"So," Enzo started, his tone shifting slightly. "Back to business for a second. What do you think? Think the gang leader did it?"

I shrugged, looking out the window again. "It's a hard call."

There was a moment of silence from the other line. "Hard call, huh?"

"Yeah," I said, narrowing my eyes. I wasn't sure if he could figure out the smirk in my voice or not. "Very hard."

"You know what else is hard now, right?" He asked the question knowing damn well I could guess the answer. "It's a handful of a situation."

"I think I've got an idea," I responded, my tone dropping a note. "I've actually gotten a hard situation in my hands, too."

"Really?" Enzo asked. "I think this might be a good time to FaceTime. You know. Just so I can help out with your hard call."

"And I'll help out with yours," I said, stroking myself over my slacks.

Just hearing Enzo take on that sexy, gravelly, Italian stallion–type voice made my dick rock solid. I spread my legs open underneath my desk, giving myself room to grow in my pants. My eyes shut and my breath drew in for a sharp moment.

My cell phone rang from the corner of my desk. Enzo's name was on the screen, requesting a FaceTime connection. I smiled as I realized the bastard had already hung up the phone call we were on and redialed me from his cell. I shook my head, still smiling as I answered his FaceTime. In seconds, a handsome and slightly pink Enzo was smiling back at me. He looked like he hadn't been sleeping recently, and normally that would be an insult, but Enzo somehow made extreme exhaustion and sleep deprivation look sexy. His dark hair was messed up with a lock falling down onto his forehead, and his five-o'clock shadow was more like a twelve-o'clock beard. It was really fucking hot. I could picture him kissing his way down my chest, his beard scratching my skin, his soft lips against me.

"You're looking good," Enzo said, holding the phone at a high angle so that I could see everything above his waist. One of his hands was conspicuously out of the shot.

"And you're looking *bellissimo*," I said, stumbling on my Italian, but trying.

Enzo's eyebrows shot up. "Wow, maybe someone has been practicing on their own. Maybe you're ready for a pop quiz."

"Go ahead," I said, glancing at my frame on the screen for a second. I was holding the phone straight in front of my face so Enzo couldn't see the massive erection I was sporting. I had to admit, the afternoon sunlight was working real well with my face on the screen.

"Okay," Enzo said, the arm not holding his phone moving up and down. "Let's start with some easy words."

I had a feeling I was going to ace this quiz.

## 18  ENZO

I was rock hard. I didn't even have to be on the phone with Zane for two seconds before I popped a boner. How did that happen? What kind of power did this man have over me and my dick? It was an instant reaction, as if I had trained my own dick to stand to attention at the first sign of contact with Zane, whether that be through the phone or in person. Cazzo. It was almost childish with how crazy my hormones were acting.

But I also couldn't control it. Zane just set me off in so many different ways. I couldn't help but steer the conversation toward how fucking horny I was. The moment Zane started playing along, I practically had my pants down to my ankles. I double-checked to make sure my office door was locked before unzipping and dropping them, my briefs following seconds later. I sat down in my office chair, spinning it around so that my back was to the office door and I was looking out toward Times Square. I had the corner office, which meant my window wrapped around and gave a much more impressive view compared to Candice's. But she was closer to the kitchen, so it wasn't like she lost giving up the corner office.

I palmed my balls as I pulled Zane up on FaceTime. I made sure he could only see me from my waist up. I wanted to give him a little bit of a tease before we ended up Facesexing.

"Okay, so for the quiz," I said, thinking up different naughty words I could throw his way. "You know what 'cazzo' means. How about 'pompino'?"

Zane narrowed his eyes. He looked so good, even just being on a phone screen. He was the type of man that took great photos and looked great in person, too. A double fucking whammy of hot. I tugged on my balls.

"Pompino?" Zane repeated. "Like a penis... pump?"

I couldn't hold back the laugh at his guess. "Close-ish." I also couldn't tell that face he was flat-out wrong. "It actually means blowjob."

"Ah, that was my next answer."

"Right, right."

"Okay, what's another critical sex term I should learn."

I arched a brow. "Do I sense sarcasm? Because I could stop these lessons and leave you with palle blu."

"Blue... blue balls."

"See, you *are* learning." I felt my own balls tighten, my cock leaking down onto the bottom of my light blue dress shirt, staining the fabric with dark spots.

"What do I get for answering right?" Zane asked. I noticed one of his arms wasn't in frame. He must have been taking some serious notes.

"Satisfaction in knowing you're bettering yourself through the beauty of language." I smiled at him while I let go of my balls and gripped my shaft in a tight fist. I ran my thumb over my leaking slit, wiping off the clear fluid and rubbing it all over the head.

"I'm definitely looking for some satisfaction," Zane said, his tone taking on a more gravelly pitch. I licked my lips and rolled my chair back. I held my phone out farther, my eyes honed in on Zane's. He was smirking.

"Okay, try this phrase on for size: 'Voglio il tuo cazzo.' You already know 'cazzo,' and the first word is similar to yearning for something."

"Okay, okay. So..." Zane took a moment, looking offscreen and thinking of what the translation could be. His jawline looked dangerously sharp in the light. My cock throbbed in my grip. "Hmm, yearning... dick... want... I want your dick?"

I nodded, clearly impressed. "Good job," I said, chuckling. "You pass with flying colors."

"All right, Professor. Let me try this out." He was grinning. I glanced at the window holding my video. Zane still couldn't see my cock, but my arm movements were definitely no secret anymore. An inch farther out and the camera would clearly catch the head of my dick leaking onto my hand as I stroked, getting off to the idea of Zane doing the exact same thing. "Vog—Voglian—Vlogging ew your cazzo."

I almost snorted. Zane's Italian still had a ways to go, but damn it, he sounded so damn cute, and his attempts were admirable for sure. Besides, I was a patient teacher, and I had a feeling I could spend hours training that tongue of his.

"Is that a request?" I asked, biting my lower lip as I dropped the camera lens a few more inches. My eyes were out of the frame, but my cock was taking up half the screen.

"Damn," Zane said, his voice sounding huskier. "I wish I could reach through the screen right now."

"So do I," I said, stroking myself for Zane. I could see him staring, his mouth slightly ajar, his arm moving faster as he played with himself offscreen. I ran my thumb over the tip again, lifting it to show off the string of clear precome that created a rope between my thumb and my cock.

"Fuck, I just want to lick that up." Zane was holding his phone out farther, showing me how badly he wanted to lick it up. He was rock hard, his pants discarded and his thick, hairy thighs opened wide. Zane was such a sexy specimen of a man. He went to the gym at least five times a week, and that clearly showed in the way he was built. I could picture him suffocating me with those muscular thighs of his, and I'd die perfectly happy. I, on the other hand, tried to make it to the gym at least twice a week. I ate really well, which helped offset my lack of exercise. I didn't have a picture-perfect six-pack, but I never felt like I needed to have a set myself. It was definitely a nice bonus that Zane had a six-pack I wanted to make my regular dinner plate, but it was certainly by no means a requirement.

"Cazzo, Zane. You're beautiful." My fist squeezed tighter. I swallowed and stretched my legs out. "Imagine me sitting on your lap, baby. Close your eyes." My tone grew deeper, matching the huskiness that had overcome Zane. I watched as he listened to me, closing his eyes and dropped his head back while one hand held the phone and the other one worked his swollen dick. "Imagine me climbing on top of you, my legs squeezing yours, my cock getting your abs wet with precome. Picture me reaching back, grabbing you in my hands. I can practically feel you, Zane. I could feel your weight, your hard, thick cock in my hand. I'd guide it to my tight hole. I'd spit in my other hand and use it to get myself slick. Ready for you."

Zane was grunting. I could tell he was keeping his volume contained because he was normally much louder. I smiled, my balls sending electric shocks of pure pleasure racing through me. Seeing him getting close was making me push toward the edge.

"Oh fuck, Enzo, you have me so hard. I'm so close."

"Yeah you are," I answered, wishing I could moan it into his ear instead of my cell phone. But honestly, I'd take whatever I could get at that point. If he wanted to write me dirty letters like we were some kind of prison pen pals, I'd totally take it. We could share the same bunk in whatever gay prison Candice was secretly creating. "And I haven't even put it in yet. Imagine how you'd feel when I push my ass back, taking the head of your cock inside me. I'd gasp, feeling my body get used to how big you are. But I wouldn't be able to hold back for very long. I know I'd slide down on you, taking the entire thing in my ass, making you see stars, our bodies becoming one being. I'd look you in the eyes and smash our lips together while you start to fuck me. Faster and harder. Oh, Zane, ti voglio dentro di me."

"Oh fuck, *fuck*, Enzo. You're going to make me—"

Suddenly, a couple of knocks stopped us both in our horny tracks. I wasn't sure if it had come from my office or Zane's for a second, but judging by how wide Zane's eyes were, it seemed like he was sure the knocks were on his door.

"Fuck," Zane said into the camera. His cheeks were flushed pink, his cock still in his hand, hard and ready to blow.

## 19  ZANE

*Are you fucking kidding me?*

"One second," I called to whoever was waiting outside my locked door. I set my phone down and propped it up on the base of a lamp. Enzo could still see my face; meanwhile, I had a full view of him still jerking himself off. I reached down and grabbed my pants, pulling them up as I stood.

"Nice view," Enzo said from my phone.

"Just wanted to let you know the party's started downstairs." It was Andrew.

"Got it. Be there after this call."

"Perfect," Andrew said from the other side of the door. I let out a relieved exhale and sat back down in my chair, dropping the pants back to the ground.

"No, no," Enzo said. "Stand up."

I looked into the camera, chewing on my bottom lip as I stood up so that my cock was smack in the center of the shot. Enzo could see every vein, every pulse, every stroke. I'd never performed for someone like this, which may have been why I found it so fucking hot. I continued to jerk myself off, watching the screen on my propped phone so that I could watch Enzo. He still held the phone up high, and I could see his lower jaw, his lips, his hard dick. His dirty talk had really spun me up and left me on the brink.

"Oh, Zane, you're so sexy, baby. I want to be kneeling between your legs, looking up at you as I take you in my mouth. I want to taste you on my tongue. I want you to blow your salty, sweet load down my throat."

My balls were almost inside my body as I felt myself falling off the edge. "Fuck, Enzo, fuck." My body tensed as my cock erupted with come, ropes of it splattering across the floor with audible thuds as they hit the floor. I was seeing stars. My fist opened and closed on my twitching cock as my knees threatened to buckle. I shook my shoulders and opened my eyes right in time to watch Enzo blow his load onto his chest. He had lifted his shirt, but the come shot up to his chin, making him wince back, and I laughed with blissed-out glee.

Every muscle in my body felt relaxed as I sat back down in my chair, my hands limp at my sides, a wide, toothy smile on my face as Enzo came back down to earth and aimed the camera back at his face. His eyes were so damn beautiful, even through a phone screen. I wished I could kiss him. Feel those lips on mine, let our sticky bodies dry up together before we hopped in the shower to do it all again.

"Wow," Enzo said, wiping off his chin with a thumb. He put it to his lips and smiled as he sucked it. Fuck, how I wanted his thumb in my mouth. "That was a productive call."

"Definitely was," I said, giving Enzo's eyes a look that told him exactly what I still wanted to do to him.

"Hope I helped that hard situation of yours," he said, knowing damn well he gave me exactly what I needed.

"You helped." I glanced at my wristwatch, the black-and-gold face telling me that it was pushing two in the afternoon.

"All right," Enzo said. He was pulling up his underwear from the floor, lifting his ass off his seat and tugging them on. He was still bulging in those sexy red-and-white briefs. "Go to your party before they start the fun without you. Let me know if anything else comes up about Herberto." He was looking straight down the barrel. "And Zane, please, stay safe."

"Of course," I said, trying to assure him. I could tell he was serious. I smiled and gave him a wink. "I might need help with another situation tonight if you're available."

Enzo smiled back at me. "I should have a hand free."

"Perfect."

"Bene," Enzo said. We said our goodbyes again and hung up the call. I sat back in my chair for a moment, soft dick still in my hand, my breathing soft and slow. My entire world felt like there was a hazy, dreamlike quality to it. I hadn't felt this good in so long, I let it wash over me. And not only did I feel good, but I was also excited. I couldn't wait until later, when I could actually hold Enzo in my hands, touch him and kiss him and suck him. It was enough to start getting me hard again.

I shook it off and stood up, pulling up my pants and looking down at the sticky white mess on the dark hardwood. I grabbed some tissues and cleaned it up, throwing it away in the black wastebin sitting next to a tall and leafy pot of bamboo.

Typically I wasn't a huge fan of big festivities, but I was feeling like I could take on the world right then, so I wasn't bothered as I locked up my office and made my way downstairs toward the common area. Every step I took felt like a little cloud was underneath the soles of my feet, giving me a bounce that was probably obvious to anyone paying close attention.

The building was set up to have four offices on the first floor and mine on the top. We also owned the building next door, which made space for ten more detectives. Today we were celebrating two new detectives joining Stonewall Investigations. We were a close-knit bunch and often worked together on different cases, so the extra help was something we were all looking forward to. I made sure to choose the two candidates who not only were the most experienced, but also the two that I felt could gel with the rest of the team.

"There he is!" Andrew called from the far side of the room, drawing everyone's attention to me as I walked in. The common room was packed with smiling faces. There were balloons of all different colors floating throughout the room, their white strings falling down like roots, giving the impression of a perpetual rainbow hanging above. "Zane, we've been holding off on the speeches. You're up first."

*A speech? Shit, I wasn't ready for all that.*

Everyone's eyes were on me as the crowd formed a semicircle around me. That was when Andrew waved a hand in the air. "I'm just teasing, there's no speeches planned."

My eyes narrowed at him before laughing. "Hi, everyone," I said, giving a big general wave. "I won't give a speech because I know half of you would probably fall asleep standing, but I do want to welcome the two newest additions to our Stonewall family. Where's Leo and— Ah, there they are. Come up here. Everyone, give a round of applause for Leo and Wanda."

The two of them came up to shake my hand, big smiles

on both their faces. Leo was the younger of the pair, although Wanda didn't appear a day over twenty-one. They both stood with proud shoulders and strong chests, both having military experience. Leo had come from another private investigators' office, where he was the top-producing detective, but the company had gone under. Thankfully for me, because it freed up one of the best detectives in all of New York.

Wanda was just as good, but she was slightly more green. She'd worked as a police officer after coming back home from a yearlong tour in Iraq. She left the force when she realized she wanted to solve crimes before they happened instead of responding to them as they happened. She studied up mostly on her own before working for a well-known law firm. She was a "say it the way I see it" kind of woman, and I liked that about her. Both she and Leo had come dressed a little nicer than we all normally dressed for work, with Wanda wearing an expensive-looking dark blue dress cut just above her knees and Leo wearing a white button-up with khakis and a casual gray sports jacket.

"These two are sharp and determined. I've got confidence that our team just got much, much stronger." Another round of applause and a few hoots. "All right, so let's go around and say something about ourselves that makes us special. Andrew, you first."

"Me, oh, um, well, let's see."

"Kidding, kidding." The crowd laughed at that. Andrew's cheeks turned pink after he got a dose of his own medicine. I laughed along, glad that we could all get along so well. "Leo, Wanda, you guys want to say anything?"

Wanda stepped forward, her heavy black heels sounding on the floor. "Hi, everyone! I've met all of you by now, and I just want to say I'm really excited to be working with you all. Our community needs people fighting for it, and I think we're doing just that. I'm ready to help out and solve cases." She clapped along with the rest before stepping to the side so Leo could step forward.

"Hey, everyone," he said, a little more bashful than Wanda. He didn't seem as comfortable with all the attention turned to him. "I think I've met pretty much all of you already, too, and like Wanda said, I'm excited to be part of the team. I see a lot of good things happening. For all of us." He looked around, keeping his hands in his pockets as the rest of the gang clapped. He bowed his head and smiled, taking a step back and standing in line with Wanda and me.

"Perfect," I said, gaining back the attention of the room. "So we've got subs, I hear, along with a cookie platter and some beer in the fridge. Everyone, take some time to relax and recharge. We all know that rested minds solve the cases. An hour or so away from your desk won't be the end of the world."

I could already tell Ryland and Collin were itching to get back to their offices. I didn't blame them; they were working on important cases. I knew they would step out in five minutes or so, which was completely fine with me. Andrew was standing with Theresa, a hawk-eyed detective with a penchant for dating bad guys, and Alejandro, a detective who could solve a Rubik's cube while working on a sudoku puzzle all while auditioning for *American Idol*. And he'd probably win, too. Seriously, that guy had a voice in him that blew off whatever roof he was standing under, and the roofs next door to that, too.

I walked over to them, bringing Wanda with me while Leo chatted with Mark and Owen, two detectives who worked best when they were together. We were all thinking the same thing about the two of them, but neither of the men ever confirmed any suspicions. For now, they were two detectives who had an excellent working relationship between them.

"Posted up next to the cookie tray, good strategy." I put an arm around Andrew's shoulders and gave him a little hello shake. He bit into a cookie and spoke, covering his mouth with his hand.

"I've learned from the best," he said.

He was right. I would have done the exact same thing had I gotten here earlier. I reached for a white-chocolate-chip cookie and broke it in half, offering the rest to Wanda.

"Thank you, but I'm trying to watch my figure. I have a wedding coming up."

"No kidding!" Andrew managed to swallow the rest of his cookie. "When?"

"Two months from now," Wanda said, beaming from ear to ear. "We're having a small ceremony back at her parents' farm in Texas."

"How exciting," Andrew replied. He appeared to be genuinely excited, and so was I. It was hard not to be with how infectious Wanda's joy about the wedding was. "Well, we're going to have to meet the lucky lady soon. Is everything already set, or are you both still running around like chickens without their heads? Oh wait, is that insensitive? Since the wedding's at the farm?"

The group laughed along at Andrew's sudden fear of offending Wanda, a clearly badass woman who'd probably seen a headless chicken or two in her lifetime.

"Both of us have our heads attached, thankfully. We're both just excited for the big day, now. It's not traditional with an aisle or church or anything. She'll be wearing a beautiful dress, but not a wedding dress. I'll be wearing a suit. A kickass suit if I'm being honest. And we'll walk out to our close family and friends with my sister playing the piano."

"I love it," Andrew said, lifting his hands to his chest. "If you need someone to release doves or set off fireworks, let me know. I'm your guy."

"Got it," Wanda said, laughing. I laughed along, although this talk of weddings was driving my thoughts back to my own wedding, a day that was straight out of one of my wildest, happiest dreams. A dream was all it felt like, now. It didn't feel like it actually happened.

The welcome party continued on for a bit, with everyone mingling and chatting about cases, family life, or what was the newest hot-topic show on TV. At one point during the party, I looked around the room and felt really damn good about the team I had put together. And this was only at the New York office. I had many more talented detectives all around the United States, working to help the underserved when no one else would.

A chime rang through the room over the chatter. "Oh, that's the doorbell. Let me go check who's here." Andrew set his red cup down on the table and walked out of the room and into the hallway. I was left standing with Alejandro, one of the first detectives I ever hired at Stonewall. We were discussing a case he was working on involving a hit-and-run where the driver fled the scene.

"I think you're definitely on the right—" I was cut off by Andrew, who had run back into the room and straight for me.

"Zane," he said, sounding slightly out of breath. His face was ghost pale. "You have to come."

"What happened?" I asked, hurrying out of the room with Andrew leading the way down the hall. I could tell the party behind me was cut short as people followed along, no doubt picking up on the concern.

Andrew reached the open door and stepped aside. The cold New York air blew in from outside, the tree branches making a chorus of noise as they whipped together. I looked down and saw a black box, about the size of a shoebox, but it was square. The lid had already been removed, no doubt by Andrew.

Inside the box was a red velvet pillow, its luxe fabric shimmering in the sunlight. On top of the pillow, right on the center, was a black figurine. A horse... no, there was one long, menacing horn protruding from its forehead. And there was a note folded up and pierced right down the center.

"Fuck," I said, while someone behind me gasped.

## 20  ENZO
### THREE WEEKS LATER

The city was warming up. Still not shorts-wearing weather yet, but we were getting there. I no longer had to put on seven different layers just so I could keep my blood from freezing in my veins.

Okay, maybe that was a little too dramatic, but it had gotten really cold. Especially at one point last week when the temperature had dropped out of nowhere for a few days. Thankfully, I was sleeping over at Zane's and had his huge body to keep me warm under the covers at night. Seriously, he was a human space heater. The amount of heat that man generated was insane.

It wasn't the only night I had slept over, either. Come to think of it, we really only slept apart probably four nights out of the past three weeks. I don't know how it became such a regular thing, but I do know that it did, and I wasn't complaining.

It really started that night I went over to Zane's, the same night he had received that package. It had rocked me to the core, and I could tell Zane was shaken by it, too. I slept over that night, and the next, and the next. He stayed at my place some other nights, and then I went back to his. It felt good, waking up and feeling him next to me, knowing that the same thing would happen the next time I woke up.

Today, though, I was spending the night at my parents' house. It was my pa's birthday tomorrow, and I told them I'd take them on an early-morning flight to the Hamptons, one of my dad's favorite places to spend time at. They lived across the bridge in Jersey, inside of a beautiful gated community that my mamma always called "Pig Fair" even though the official name of the community was Fig Pear Lakeside. She always said that was a dumb name and thought pig fair was much funnier, saying she could imagine the Albertsons next door to her wrangling around mud-covered pigs inside of their pristinely clean mansion. My mamma always wondered how many housekeepers they had to hire because keeping things as clean as they did was a full-time job for a multitude of hands.

My parents' house was smaller than the Albertsons', but only because my mamma had insisted on picking the smallest option she could. And smaller by not that much. Instead of a seven-bedroom mansion, my parents had a five-bedroom home, with a basement that served as a fitness center and a private backyard with a massive in-ground pool. She hated the idea of taking money from me even though I wanted to buy her the biggest place on the block, so she thought a smaller option would be less of a financial ask and also less of a burden. She refused to hire any help for around the house, so she often busied herself with cleaning while listening to one of her favorite talk shows in the background.

My phone started to ring as I pulled through the big black gates that marked the entrance to the community. I reached between my legs (where I liked to keep my phone, okay?) and saw it was Zane calling.

"Hey, Zane."

"Enzo, I've got bad news."

"Not another package," I said, pulling into my parents' driveway, the cobblestone sounding beneath my tires. The last time Zane called me with bad news, it was to say a serial killer had left a surprise package on his front doorstep. That was a really dark day and one I never wanted to repeat again.

I recalled the note that had been left with the unicorn: *"Heard the queer Scooby gang was back on my trail again. Have fun. I know I will."* Thinking about it was enough to send chills crawling down my spine.

The fear of the Unicorn was enough to paralyze the entire gay community. Gay clubs were empty most nights, and the gayborhoods were all on high alert. Everyone always checked on their neighbors, and people tried to make sure no one had to be out on the streets by themselves at a late hour. The NYPD tried to assure everyone they were working hard to protect the community, but with their track record against the LGBTQ community, it was a little doubtful. And to know that the monster's eye was turned in Zane's direction filled me with a constant hum of anxiety mixed with dread.

I still had to believe that the cops would find the killer before he struck again. And if they didn't, then Stonewall Investigations would find the monster. Hell, I'd bet they would find the killer before the cops. Zane had a few detectives working on it and said that they were the best brains around. Hopefully the right person would be put behind bars and the terror would be put to rest once and for all.

"No, no," Zane answered, "thank God. No note."

I gave a sigh of relief as I put my car in park. "So what is it?"

"About Ricardo's case. I was supposed to be meeting with Herberto, the ex-gang member."

"Right. What about him?"

"He's backing out. He doesn't want to talk to me anymore. Thinks he's being tailed and doesn't want to risk getting his fingers and toes cut off if he gets caught being a rat."

"Merda. He won't talk at all?" I could feel a sense of defeat settle on me like a net meant to trap me. "The jury meets in two months to deliberate a verdict. I don't know if we have a shot if we can't get this guy to testify against the gang leader. I'm starting to think that the prosecution found something on him, too."

I had met with the prosecution a week ago because they wanted to offer a plea deal. We flat out denied it because Ricardo felt solid in his innocence and I had thought Herberto was going to bat for us. Now things had changed, and the decision couldn't be taken back. Whatever happened from here on out would fall squarely on my shoulders. I needed to pull together the defense and get Ricardo off. No leaning on witness testimonies.

"When one door closes, another one opens."

"Since when do you speak to me in riddles, eh?" I got out of my car. Mamma was already running outside, a thick coat being held shut with two hands against her chest. "What does that mean?"

"I've got someone else I want to interview."

"Son!" She was on me before I could even close my car door. "You're going to get sick! Your jacket isn't even shut. Jesus, Enzo."

"Zane," I said, focusing on the phone call while my

mother walked around the car and stopped at the trunk. "Mamma, I didn't bring any laundry."

"Enzo, are you sure? Everything's clean?"

"Yes, Mamma, I promise. Everything's minty fresh."

"Minty, huh? You like that tingle in your briefs?" Zane toyed on the phone. "Tell Mamma Sofia I say hello."

I focused back in on the call. I couldn't get distracted. Zane was being vague, and I didn't like it. There was a reason why he was holding back, I just wasn't sure what that was yet. "Wait, who are you going to go see?"

"Someone who could have answers. I'm actually parking now. I'll call you when I've got those answers."

"Zane." I was getting frustrated, but I wasn't going to push anything. Zane was a grown man, and he knew what he was doing. He'd tell me if something was wrong. Hell, maybe he was being secretive because he was planning a surprise party. Most likely that wasn't the reason, but I liked being optimistic. "Stay safe."

"I will," Zane said and hung up.

"Mamma, I *swear*, I don't have any dirty laundry for you to do." She stepped away from the trunk, her arms crossed and her head tilted. I cracked a smile and took her in my arms for a tight hug. She was a tiny Italian firecracker, with dark red hair that matched her fiery personality.

"Oh, son! Enzo, look at you, honey, you're too thin. What, being a famous lawyer isn't enough to put some good food on the table?"

I cocked my head, laughing as my mamma smiled and took me into another hug, this one tighter than the last. I was perfectly healthy and well sized (although I could stand to lose a few pounds off the middle). She just loved to feed me and get me even bigger. Aside from food, she also had a love for comedy and didn't mind throwing around some jokes, her sarcastic edge always cracking everyone up. It reminded me a little of Zane, who wasn't scared to pull the punches when it came to joking. I loved that about him, and I learned how to take it from my mother.

"Okay, come in, come in. I'm just teasing you."

"I know, Mamma."

"Who was that on the phone, eh? Business or pleasure?"

"A little bit of both, actually."

"Oi!" my pa called from his seat on the couch as I entered the foyer. He was sitting cross-legged and petting Francis, their ancient golden retriever who had more white hair than gold. She struggled up onto her feet and slowly ambled over to my side, where I gave her some really great head scratches.

"Ciao, Pa," I said, getting a couple of licks on the cheek from Franny.

"He was just talking to *the one* on the phone, Matteo!" She practically sang out "the one" as if she were in a Disney movie all of a sudden. My mother jumped twenty steps ahead whenever it came to my relationships. She had always wanted to see me with someone (although no one would probably ever be good enough by her standards) and always got incredibly excited when there was a prospect of someone serious on the horizon.

I laughed as I got up from my squat and wiped at my cheek. "Relax, there, Ma. He's a good one, but it's still early."

Pa had gotten up from his seat and came over to give me a hug, although his hugs were more like slaps on the back hard enough to dislodge a lung. Even though he was getting up there in age, he still had all the strength he had back when he worked in the fields. Thankfully, my success allowed him to basically retire from all that backbreaking work before he actually did break his back.

"Can he cook?" Pa asked, holding both my shoulders. I always felt like a kid when he did that—didn't matter if I was a thirty-two-year-old man or a fifteen-year-old kid.

"You know what... I'm actually not sure."

"Get rid of him," Mamma said as though I were canceling a cable plan.

"Mamma, meet him first. I promise you, you'll like him. I know I do. It was amore a prima vista."

"Bene." Mamma put her hands up in the air. "If you say so. I'm not the one sleeping with him."

"I certainly hope not," Pa said.

"Let's, uh, go eat and stop talking about my sex life." I disappeared into the kitchen while my parents laughed behind me. It was nice being back under their roof, with the constant love and attention. I wasn't going to lie, I loved it. Italians weren't exactly known for flying the coop very early, and when we did, it was always nice to fly back to the coop more often than not.

Especially now, after that phone call with Zane. Even with my parents' lighthearted jokes and carefree attitudes, I was still feeling a sense that everything wasn't right. There was something up, and I felt like Zane was in the center of it.

*Amore a prima vista. Love at first sight... Goddamnit, Zane. Don't do anything stupid.*

## 21 ZANE

So Herberto, the defected gang member, was a bust, but that was okay because I landed an even bigger fish. I got myself a meeting with the big bad himself, Tito Gomez. He was the one who Ricardo was saying had the affair with Luanne, and the way I was sure of that was because Tito was the only one in the gang who had the scarab tattoo on his neck.

I learned that bit of information when I had spent an afternoon drinking (mostly glasses of water) at a bar the Blood Scarabs were said to frequent. Sure enough, a few showed up and opened up to me, thinking I was someone ready and willing to join their ranks. See, members got a sort of "bonus" if they recruited new initiates that were actually worth it. They saw a gruff-looking guy trying to start trouble and thought I'd make a good addition to the gang. They weren't exactly fountains of information, but they did break down some of their hierarchy (things I already knew) as well as the information about the tattoo (something I hadn't known).

It took a week after that for me to be able to set up a

meeting with Tito himself, but I managed it. I was going in under the guise of me wanting to interview the leader of local gangs for a documentary set to air on a prestigious network. I had gotten whiffs of Tito's egotism and had a feeling he'd be the type to take the bait. I promised him anonymity on the show, but he wouldn't take it. Said he wanted everyone to know where his turf was.

I had Helen completely change my face, making sure I'd be unrecognizable if you held a picture of the real me side by side. Looking in the mirror was an odd experience, but I got used to it after a few times. The new, rougher nose and the rounder jaw threw me off, but not as much as the slight unibrow I was now sporting, along with brows that protruded way more than my normal ones. A pair of round glasses made me even more of a new person, and the bald cap Helen expertly blended into my face took the look to a whole other level.

"I'm actually parking now. I'll call you when I've got those answers," I said, as I pulled up to the designated meeting spot. It was an old apartment building used solely for filming. I told him I'd rent the entire place out for him so we could assure privacy, and I did. We'd be the only ones in the entire building.

"Stay safe," Enzo said. His voice helped calm some of the nerves that were riling up inside me, although I could tell Enzo was growing upset with my roundabout answers about my next interview. I felt bad I wasn't telling him exactly what I was up to, but I knew how he'd react. He'd worry about the meeting for the entire time I'd be in it, and it would completely take him out of the time he set aside to spend with his family. I didn't want to do that to him. There was nothing he'd be able to do if things went sour anyway. I told Andrew where I'd be, and he would call the police if I didn't contact him in a few hours. That was the most that I could do to guarantee my safety.

Well, that and the heavy black pistol sitting underneath layers of my clothes. I needed to bring some kind of insurance.

I got out of my car, noticing there was no one else parked in the empty parking lot. I wondered what poor Uber driver had to pick up Tito, who was sitting outside the studios on a bench. He looked me over, up and down, his beady eyes practically drilling holes into me as he sized me up. I gave a nod and got the camera equipment from the back of my car. With two heavy bags slung over my shoulder, I locked the car and started toward Tito, who didn't bother standing up as I drew closer.

"You the film dude?"

"Yes, I'm Thomas. We've been talking over the phone. I'm the one directing and producing this."

"Cool, cool." He got up, his heavy North Face jacket reminding me of a bulletproof vest. I wondered what insurance Tito brought with him. I couldn't let my guard down. This was a hardened criminal who could have potentially murdered two people while they slept. I'd need to be extra careful and make sure I didn't push it. If I sensed Tito getting anxious, I knew I had to cut the interview right then and there. I didn't want him feeling like a cornered dog, because those were the ones that always bit.

We entered the building through the side, where there was a padlock holding the keys to the place. I had been given the password, so I set the numbers and tugged it open, retrieving the key inside and opening the heavy red door. The building was located over in Brooklyn and had definitely been an old apartment before it was converted into a filming space, most likely by some business-savvy millennial seeing a need for studios.

The lights clicked on by themselves as we walked through the hall, past rows of closed doors marked with a number. Since we had the entire place rented, we could choose whichever room, but the coordinator had told me the upstairs room had a view that would look great on camera, and I wanted Tito to think this was a legit production. He needed to, because it would keep me safe if he thought I had an entire production company knowing my whereabouts, and it would also lower his walls enough to talk to me. I knew he wouldn't speak to me on camera about a recent murder, especially if he were involved, but I had an idea that could have him talking before he even realized we were filming.

We reached the topmost floor. I unlocked the door and walked into an airy room, empty of any furniture except for two chairs smack in the center. Big lights had already been set up around the chairs. Behind Tito's chair was the massive window that looked out to the Brooklyn Bridge, which was only about seven blocks away. It was definitely an impressive backdrop, and Tito was ogling it the entire time while I setup the camera and moved around some of the lights.

"Thanks for offering to do this," I said, sitting across from Tito once everything was set up and we were both wearing mics, ready to go. The scarab tattoo on his neck seemed to crawl with every pulse of his artery. His eyes were small, set into a face that was scarred from knife fights and broken bottles. He wore the wounds proudly, badges of honor that said he had made it out alive. He was wearing a black shirt that was baggy on his muscular frame. I could tell he lifted plenty of weights, a habit he probably picked up during his time in prison. He smelled like what I would imagine prison to smell like, too. It wasn't pleasant.

Tito responded with a nod. His hands were held in a loose fist on his lap. I had given him a once-over when he was standing by the window without his coat on, and I didn't notice any conspicuous bulges telling me he was carrying a weapon, but I assumed he was regardless. He shifted in the plastic chair, the material creaking under his weight. The camera's lens clicked and whirred as it refocused on its subject.

"We filming yet?"

"No, Tito."

We were.

"Okay, good." He sat back in the chair, unaware of the fact that I had colored over the little red light on the camera with a heavy black permanent marker. I'd been rolling since I set the camera on the tripod.

"So, before we start filming anything, I want to ask you some questions to get you comfortable. Loosen things up. I like my interviews being as natural as I can get them. Some of my past interviewees say this is the therapy part of my films, before the camera ever even comes on. I might ask some tough questions, but it's only to get you thinking—"

"Yeah, yeah, man. Whatever, just ask your fucking questions."

Perfect. The bait was set. He'd be more open to talking now.

"All right, let's get started. How long have you been the leader of the Blood Scarabs?" I held a notepad in my hand. I had written out a predetermined set of questions on there even though I didn't need to. I got through about halfway down the list by the time I felt comfortable enough to start broaching the topic of Luanne and Oscar.

"So, recently, a big news story broke about a couple murdered in their sleep." I paid close attention to every detail in his expression, but it was stone cold. He wasn't giving me shit. "There was a report that the Blood Scarabs were somehow involved. Do you think rumors like that hurt or help you?"

It was a bullshit question, with a bullshit premise. There was a total of zero reports about Tito's gang being involved in the murder, but I was betting on the fact that Tito wouldn't follow up with a request for sources. Instead, I wanted to plant the seed of thought involving him and Luanne, and I wanted that to take control, to throw him off enough that he'd crack under further questioning.

"They help," Tito said, crossing his arms, tilting his head. He was smiling. "We want stories out there, even if they aren't all true."

"Because it strengthens your street rep." I noticed his attempt at throwing in doubt on whether or not they were involved. "But if something isn't true, wouldn't it hurt if someone else finds that out?"

"Nah, that shit don't matter. Once it's out there, it's out there, man."

"So, if it is because of your gang, how do you take credit without getting locked up?"

"Word spreads, but as long as there's no evidence, what are those *pinche* cops going to do?"

I was nervous, although I was an expert at not showing it. I could feel my heartbeat pounding in my throat, but I knew Tito had no way of knowing that, so I kept my chest proud and my tone even. "If you did it, would you want to take credit for it or let your entire gang take credit?" I was trying to prod at his egotism, the same thing that got him sitting in front of a secretly recording camera.

"Yeah, but still, I won't advertise shit. If I did it, then bitches find out and get put in their place. But I don't need to be fucking shouting it from the roof."

I took a moment, as if the next question had just come to my head, even though it was the one question I'd been wanting to ask since I arrived. I allowed some of my fear to show through, to make him believe this next question was difficult for me to ask.

"Tito," I started, a small quiver in my voice, "did you do it? Did you kill them?"

"Are you fucking kidding me?" Tito scoffed, his yellow teeth looking like chipped canines. "Seriously, man? You kidding me?"

"No," I said, staring the hyena down. "Were you involved in some way with the murder of Luanne and Oscar?"

Tito shook his head. His eyes were beady, the whites of them darkened by popped blood vessels. Fistfights must have been his style. Although, judging by the way his hand hovered by his hip, concealed carry was probably the case. I was on high alert. This was the most dangerous part of my job, but it was crucial. Sometimes, catching criminals off guard was the best way to catch them red-handed. They would bluster over their answers and incriminate themselves somehow without too much intervention. That was when I'd catch them on the mike taped against my chest. New York was a one-party consent state, so secret recordings could be used in court as long as I came in to testify. All I had to do was get this asshole to break and say he did it. Then I'd get the fuck out of there and get Ricardo out of jail. First, though, I'd pull off the prosthetic nose because it was getting really uncomfortable.

Tito was different than I was expecting. He was smarter

than most. The couple of face tattoos he had would make people think otherwise, but I could sense it. He was sharp. "It wasn't me. I wouldn't kill anyone for that *puta*."

I couldn't speak Spanish fluently, but I definitely recognized the word for "bitch." My eyes narrowed. "Sounds like you two knew each other. You didn't get along?"

"Nah, we got along just fine. She loved having my dick deep in her ass, man." He shrugged. "I just don't think she's worth killing anyone for. I've got plenty other bitches I could call for a fuck. She was one of the best, but there'll be another. One that won't make me post shit on her stupid ass food blog."

I looked at him, trying to spot a chip in his armor. "And you would sleep with her where? Her own apartment?" I made sure not to let on that I knew exactly where he slept with Luanne.

"Yeah, fucking bitch, she never wanted to give me a copy of the key, so she would leave it outside." He laughed at that. It was a biting, acidic sound. "Probably what got that dumb bitch killed."

"So she'd leave a key just for you outside?"

"Yeah. She liked it when I came inside the house without telling her. She'd tell me the days her *pinche* husband would be out of the house, and I'd just show up whenever I wanted. If anything changed, the key wouldn't be inside the frog and I'd find someone else to bang. She always made sure she had the key when we were done, too —she probably thought I'd take it." He scoffed at that. "*Puta madre*, I'm in a gang; I'm not a thief. Speaking of her husband, why don't you look into him, eh? He was into some fucked-up shit."

Well... that was unexpected. My interest was immediately piqued, but I didn't want to show it. This could easily be Tito trying to throw me a bone so he could keep me off the real trail.

"What kind of shit?"

"All I know is that she mentioned something about him not being innocent. That he was worse than she was."

I was getting frustrated, and that's exactly what Tito wanted. I controlled my expressions, making sure I wasn't feeding into his pleasure. "Help me figure this out," I said, my tone making it clear I wasn't playing around, "before the cops start focusing on you."

That got his attention. The last thing a gang member wanted was for the police to start digging around. Even if he was innocent, they'd still find something worthwhile. He stared me down, expecting me to break. I held strong. This wasn't the first time I'd been intimidated, and I knew it wouldn't be the last.

He shook his head. "Fuck that, man. Why are you even bugging over this bitch? They already have the guy that did it."

"Ricardo?"

"*Si, ese.*"

I cocked my head. "So he was involved with Luanne? You're saying a gay prostitute was sexually involved with a woman and fell hard enough for her to kill two people in their sleep?"

"No, man. You fucking dense, aren't you? I think he was involved with Oscar."

"Bullshit." He was trying to throw me. Either way, my interest was piqued. "Why'd you think that?"

"Because that fucking weak-ass bitch came up to me crying for drugs the second I left Luanne's place one night. He told me that he'd do anything. Suck my dick if I wanted. Told me I could ask Luanne's husband how good he was."

I didn't say anything. All I did was read his face, studying it for any miniscule tell that would denote he was lying. A recurring twitch of the lip, a nervous tic that only grew worse, a rapid success of nervous glances down to the floor.

Nothing. The guy was giving better poker face than a Gaga song.

"Why, eh?" Tito asked, leaning in. "Why you so interested in what happened with *esa puta*?"

"It was a rumor on the street that I wanted to get clarified."

"Well, you just clarified it." He sat back in his chair, throwing a tattooed arm onto the back of it. "The only thing I'm responsible for is fucking that woman until she couldn't walk straight. I think it was that fairy they have behind bars. Has to be. He was getting some good dick from that *puta*'s husband, then he had too much coke one night and lost his goddamn mind. The night I saw her she was all fucked-up in the head. She looked crazy. Like she'd just got back from fight club or some shit. She probably went off on that Ricardo bitch, since she knew Oscar was up to shit. And it had to be something she considered worse than sucking my nuts."

It took a lot for me to restrain myself. I couldn't lose control even though I wanted to deck this guy. "What do you mean? What did she look like?"

"Her shirt was torn up and her hair was a fucking mess, like someone tried yanking it out of the dumbass ponytail she always put it in."

This was new. I had to keep digging, though. I felt like I was on the brink of something. I had to push. "Tito, be honest with me. Did you get in a fight with Luanne? Were you upset she married Oscar? Did she promise you she'd be with you?"

He sucked in his bottom lip and tilted his head back, as if he were looking down at me even though he was sitting just across from me. "I'm fucking done with this." He was cracking. I told myself I would quit while I was ahead, but I was feeling greedy. I needed to figure out everything he knew.

"Did she accidently leave the keys in the frog that night? Did you walk in on them and fly into a fit of jealousy?"

"Fuck off," Tito spat, getting up from his chair. "Interview's fucking over." He smacked the camera and sent it flying across the room. It bounced on the floor with a loud crack. I was up on my feet, sure to show that I wasn't intimidated.

"Good luck figuring out who killed her." He started walking, although I noticed him watching me through the reflection of the window in the door. "Shame. She was one of the best fucks I've had."

I let Tito leave. When he was gone, I picked up the camera, turning it on only to hear it give its last dying clicks and whirls. I looked around the big empty room. This meeting was supposed to solve it all. Tito was the missing link, the one who had a connection, a motive, and a means. But there were no answers. Instead, I was left with a broken camera and more questions than I had answers for.

*Except there's one person who has more answers than he was letting on.*

## 22　ENZO

I *really* hated interrogation rooms. This one was smaller than the last. It was as if the chief had a running joke with the rest of the department: how small of a box could they stick us in before we ran out of air? Next, I expected to be sent into an Amazon delivery box, with holes poked through the sides for ventilation. This was a huge contrast compared to the massive, open backyard I was lounging in just hours earlier before Zane called me telling me to get to the station ASAP. My parents weren't the happiest of campers, but they also understood how high the stakes were. I promised I'd fly back to them when I got the chance.

We sat at the table, Ricardo practically on top of me from how little space there was for our chair. Zane was sitting across from me. He was looking good, even under the terrible fluorescent lighting. He hadn't given me many details over the phone, only telling me that things weren't where he wanted them to be. He had more questions for Ricardo. That worried me. With Herberto falling through, the last thing I needed was the attention turning back to Ricardo, who still had zero in terms of an alibi.

"Well, what's the news?" Ricardo asked, looking between Zane and me. He looked like a scared little tropical bird in his orange jumpsuit.

"I had a meeting," Zane said. He was looking at Ricardo. I noticed he'd been mostly avoiding my gaze since he came in. "It was with Tito, the head of the Blood Scarabs."

Both Ricardo and I made some kind of sounds, akin to "wha the fuh?" between the both of us. "Wait, seriously?" Ricardo asked after the shock had washed over the both of us.

"Yes. I managed to set up an interview. He was under the impression that I was there filming a documentary. I wanted him to open up to me about Luanne before we started 'filming,' and he did. He told me that he was seeing her and that he had been over that time you saw him."

"Great! So that's it! And you got this all on camera? Jesus, you're good. Your—what? Why does your face still look like that? Why aren't you both smiling?"

I was looking at Zane, realizing what was happening. The last thing I wanted to do was smile. I clicked into defense attorney mode. "Zane, what else did you find? Nothing to incriminate Ricardo, right?"

Zane looked at me then, one of the first times since we'd started this. His eyes were pools of chaos. Something was troubling him, and that troubled me. "Ricardo, did you ask Tito for drugs? Did you offer him oral sex for them?"

My eyeballs almost dropped out of my skull. I looked to Ricardo, who I expected to spit out a flat denial, but he was turning beet red and was fumbling for his words. "I... uh, well, I..."

"Ricky," I said, shaking my head. "Cazzo."

"I'm sorry," he said, dropping his head into his hands.

"I'm sorry. I'm so sorry. I didn't want anyone finding out I was on drugs again—that's why I kept quiet about Tito."

Zane sat up in his chair. "Ricardo, I need you to be honest with us. Did you get in a fight with Luanne? On the same day you saw Tito leaving the apartment?"

"What? No! The only time I ever fought—and it wasn't even a fight, it was a heated argument—it was when it was caught on camera. I'd never fight with Luanne. Just that asshole Oscar."

"Which brings me to my next question."

Great, what the hell was next? That Ricardo was sleeping with Oscar?

"Were you sleeping with Oscar?"

"Cazzo," I said, almost to myself this time.

Ricardo was a terrible liar. He was redder than a baboon's ass, which was coincidentally how I was starting to feel. "Ricky, why weren't you honest with us from the start?"

"It sounded bad, okay? Even to me, it sounded bad. But it wasn't even a big deal! Me and Oscar were a one-night thing," Ricardo said. The hope that had been in his eyes when he'd first sat down was now replaced by a sense of defeat. "It was the same day as the fight we had." Ricardo dropped his head, his cheeks burning like they were set on fire. "I'm sorry. I don't know what happened. I saw Luanne had left the house, and I couldn't help it. I went over and knocked. I wanted Oscar to apologize to me. To personally say he was sorry for what he said to me."

"He apologized all right," Zane said, massaging the bridge of his nose. I looked to him, trying to read his expression. He was in detective mode, and that meant everything on him was a blank slate. He wasn't giving any indication as to whether or not he was believing Ricardo, and that made me nervous. I definitely believed him, but that wouldn't matter at the end of the day. If Zane couldn't find anything, then all that mattered was what the jury believed, and he had a feeling they would lean toward Zane's train of thought.

If only Tito had confessed. Then we would have had a slam dunk case...

*Tito.*

This entire whirlwind of a situation stopped me from realizing just how much danger Zane had put himself in. But that wasn't all. Zane had lied to me. He could have died, and I would have been thinking he was in his office googling shit the entire time. I would have found out from a call or a knock on my door, never guessing that Zane was even in danger in the first place. Why didn't he just tell me he was meeting with Tito? It wasn't like I'd follow him and mess shit up somehow. Cazzo, I was a grown-ass fucking man; I could handle it. I just couldn't handle lies, even if they were roundabout lies through omission. I didn't like feeling a lack of trust. It made me angry. It sparked a resentment in me that was left behind from the implosion of my last relationship.

"Well, Tito said that Luanne looked as if she'd just gotten back from fight club that night he went over. She was in an altercation with someone." Zane's gaze was pinned on Ricardo. I tamped down my growing anger and focused on the issue at hand. We'd deal with the trust thing later. "Are you sure she didn't find out about you and Oscar? She didn't maybe come over and get into a fight with you?"

"No," Ricardo said, shaking his head. He seemed confident in his answer, but now there was an unshakable fog of questions hanging over everyone's heads. Doubt. It was a cruel spectre. "I swear. I didn't do it. You guys have to believe me. Enzo, you're my lawyer—you believe me, right?"

"Ricky, I will craft the best defense for you as I can, regardless of the circumstances." I didn't want to give him an affirmation; I wanted to give him the truth.

"It's still not over," Zane said. He must have read the despair written across Ricardo's forehead. He looked like he had nothing left. "If Tito isn't lying, then maybe whoever got into a fight with Luanne could be the one responsible."

"The only people I ever see going to that house are mailmen, food delivery men, and their families. I've seen one of their parents, I think Oscar's, stay there for at least a month. Luanne's sister visits a lot, too. Her car's always parked half in my spot—it's like she does it on purpose. Those are the only connections I know they have, and I don't see any of them beating up Luanne."

I sighed. The fact that I felt like we were being held inside of a cat's litter box didn't help. This place stank and it was tiny and there were zero windows. I was feeling anxious, but I had to control it. My confidence needed to override. I was an award-winning defense attorney. I was going to get Ricardo off even before I hired Zane's help; I'd be able to make him a free man without it, too.

"All right," I said, feeling upset with Zane and worried for Ricardo. "To wrap things up: we still have no clue who did it. All we know is Ricardo had a one-night angry, self-hating gay fuck with Oscar, and Luanne was in a secret fight club. Two things the jury is going to *looove*."

Zane looked to me. This was the first time that our eyes locked for a substantial amount of time. He was piecing things together, I could tell. He was realizing where my mood was heading. "Enzo, I'm going to find out who did this. Don't worry."

I wanted to trust him, but that was hard to find at the moment. I put a reassuring hand on Ricardo's back, as he was currently slumped forward with his head inside the cave created by his arms. "You'll be okay. There's no way the prosecution can prove anything beyond reasonable doubt."

"I didn't do it," he said, the sound of his voice bouncing off the table and echoing in his cave.

## 23  ZANE

The mild chill in the air was much more preferable to the stuffy heat inside of that investigation room. Seriously, could they find anything smaller for us next time? I expected them to lead us into a goddamn broom closet. The sounds of the city were also better than the drunken howls and the angry yells inside. I much preferred listening to taxi cabs honking.

"Do you think he did it?" Enzo asked me point-blank. He had his arms crossed against his chest. He looked really good, dressed like someone who was just lounging in the Hamptons hours earlier. A pair of dark blue pants and a white shirt made him look sharp but also relaxed. The jacket he had on was clearly tailored to fit him and only him. I wanted to jump him right there and then. Tear off the designer jacket and pants, get down to his bare skin.

"I'm not sure," I said, wanting to be a hundred percent honest with Enzo. Especially since I had to skirt around the truth earlier. He didn't seem to be upset about Tito, although there was something in his posture that felt off to me. Almost as if he was guarding himself. "Now there's an even bigger motive for him to do it, besides the fight. If he had a relationship with Oscar, that kicks things up to an entirely different level. And the fact that he was asking Tito for drugs, it tells me he's the type to act on his impulses."

"Yeah, but I don't think those impulses were ever to kill anyone. Much less two people."

"You're right. I never said he did do it. I'm going to chase down the lead Tito gave me and hope it gives us something." We walked down the steps of the station, stopping in the street. Tall skyscrapers were blocking the sun from hitting us, casting heavy shadows. We stopped at the intersection and turned to face each other. I was going to catch the subway back to the office, but I was hit with an idea for something we could both do.

Before I spoke, I noticed Enzo's eyes bouncing between mine, dropping down to my lips before darting back up to my eyes. "When were you going to tell me you were going to go meet with Tito?"

*Shit.*

So Enzo *was* angry. I could sense it in the way the muscles on his jaw flexed. This was new. Something I hadn't been on the receiving end of. For a second, I was taken aback. I wasn't certain how to react, and that made me want to close up.

"You didn't need to know."

"Are you kidding?" Enzo's voice rose, and his hands danced in the air. He always spoke with his hands, but when emotions started to rise, Enzo's hands took on their own special choreography. "You go to meet with a convicted criminal and lunatic gang leader, and you don't think it's important to bring it up to me? Say hey, Enzo, listen, I really care about you and want you to know that this is where I'll be and what I'll be doing in case you never hear from me again."

Now I was getting angry. Investigating was my job; he had to stick to the courtroom and slay the monsters in there while I hunted down the ones out on the street. "It's just part of the job," I said, my tone turning defensive. "I didn't want to get you worried."

"Well, you succeeded in doing that, except now I'm going to assume you're off infiltrating *uno cazzo* terrorist organization every time you tell me you're going out to grab some coffee." Enzo threw his hands up into the air. "Cristo, Zane! *Trust*, man. That's number one for me. I want to trust you."

"It was never my intention to lie to you. If you asked, I wouldn't have lied."

"I did ask, Zane. You just didn't answer. That's lie-adjacent, and enough to make me question things."

"Question what, Enzo? What are you questioning?"

The fire between us was growing. "Don't fucking pretend like you're suddenly dumb, Zane. You're the smartest damn detective in this city—don't act like you don't have the answer already."

I did. But I wanted him to say it. I wanted to hear it coming from his lips. "Tell me, Enzo, what are you questioning?"

"Us. This. Whatever we're doing."

"Well, *stop*. Stop questioning it." I was looking him right down the eyes. There was a heat between us that singed away the cold in the air. I realized then that I was never feeling anger toward Enzo. No, I could never be angry at the man. It was passion that had been rattling against my rib cage. I just hadn't felt it in so long, I couldn't recognize it at first. "I didn't tell you about Tito because I care about you, Enzo. More than I've cared about anyone in a very long time. I want you to be there when I wake up and there when I go to sleep, every single damn day. And you're right, I should have told you. I was dumb in keeping it from you. But you can trust me, Enzo. I swear to you."

I reached and grabbed his hands in mine. The station was located on a side street that wasn't as populated. We were standing outside of a bodega, the smell of deli sandwiches wafting out from the open door. People were crossing the street, going around us, completely oblivious to the intense moment Enzo and I were having.

"Trust me," I said again, squeezing Enzo's hands. He was looking at me, but the anger in his stance seemed to dissipate like evaporating water. He relaxed, his face dropping before picking back up again with the hint of a smile playing on his lips.

"I do, Zane. It's just difficult. I haven't had the best track record with placing my trust in the right person, and I really don't want to relive that merda."

"You won't." I had no idea what Enzo was talking about, but I wanted to. I wanted to know who hurt him in the past, who made him laugh, who made him cry. I wanted to learn about all the experiences that shaped him. I brought his hands up to my lips and kissed them, looking deep into his eyes as I did. "I'll never hurt you."

Our hands came back down to our sides, but our eyes stayed locked. "Come on," I said, nodding toward the subway entrance. "I want to walk this off with you. You're not busy now, are you?" I glanced at my watch. It was five in the afternoon on a Friday, and I figured Enzo could probably spare a couple of hours. I'd probably be up all night working on Ricardo's case anyway—might as well take some time to clear my head with Enzo by my side.

"No, I'm not," he said, cocking his head. I still felt a little bit of wariness in the air, but I was determined to change that. I would prove to him that I was a man who he could trust.

"Okay, cool," I said, happy to see the flicker of his smile grow brighter. "Let's go."

"Where are we going?"

"You'll see," I said. "I promise, it's somewhere we can talk seriously and have a really deep one-on-one."

\*\*\*

The Museum of Sex was blasted in neon pink through the glass next to the ticket counter. It was a dimly lit room with smiling employees welcoming everyone to the world-famous museum. I had been wanting to come (ha. ha.) and see it for a while and thought it would be the perfect place to go and lift (ha. ha. *ha*) Enzo's mood. Seemed like I was right, because he was giggling like a little Italian schoolboy as we got our tickets and walked over to the entrance.

"There's a bar downstairs—you both are more than welcome to start there, or you can go up the stairs and start your journey through the history of sex." The woman taking tickets at the bottom of the stairs opened her hand to take ours, smiling at us both. Everyone who worked there seemed to be so happy. I didn't have to really wonder why, though.

"I can't believe I was in the Hamptons this morning and now I'm climbing the stairs into a sex museum."

"Isn't life grand?" I said over my shoulder as I led the way. The stairs opened up on a floor where another attendant was standing. It was a narrow hallway with dark walls, the light also dim except for the doorway behind the attendant. That was brightly lit and spewing its light out into the hallway.

"This is the boobie jump house. We've got a group just finishing up in there, do you guys want to bounce?" the man asked, once again smiling from ear to ear.

"Boobie... jump house." Enzo almost snorted. I had made sure to pay extra for the experience because I figured Enzo would get a huge kick out of it.

"Hell yeah we want to bounce," I replied.

"Just take your shoes off before going in."

We both slipped off our shoes ("Wouldn't wanna hurt the boobies, eh, Zane?") and opened the door into a brightly lit bounce house, except this wasn't your typical kids' birthday party bounce house. The floor was two huge boobs, inflated and ready to be bounced on. But that wasn't all. Around the bouncy boob house were other big inflated balls, all painted to look like different breasts.

"This is a gay man's worst nightmare," I said as we fell in, both of us laughing as we bounced up on the nipple.

"I might get night terrors after this, Zane." He was pushing himself up onto his feet. "Will you be there to cradle my shaking body?"

"Of course," I said, getting up onto my unsteady feet but failing to find my balance and falling back down, only to bounce up and land on my side. There was a dark areola right smack on my face. I batted it away with a hand, watching the ball hit the wall and bounce back, straight for Enzo's head.

"Ow!" he said, rubbing the spot. "You almost gave me a boob-cussion!"

It was all so silly and so fun and such a perfect way to wind down after a chaotic day. It felt good being able to play around with Enzo, even though tensions may have been higher than normal. We were two grown-ass men; we weren't going to hold on to petty arguments because in the grand scheme of things, if we were going to work, we'd need to get past way bigger obstacles.

We laughed and bounced around for our allotted time before another group was allowed to come in. We collected our shoes and bounced out of the boob house through the back door, into a pink hallway that reminded everyone to check for breast cancer. The hallway then opened up onto the first floor of the museum exhibits. This room was also dark, with windows set in the gray walls looking into different exhibits, a plaque next to each window giving some background as to what was inside. In the center of the room was a huge wooden bike with a long pole attached to the front. It took us both a second to realize there was a dildo on the pole, and it was moving whenever someone hopped on the bike and pedaled.

"How much do you think that would cost to get installed in my bedroom?" Enzo asked, leaning toward me. I could smell the faint oakiness of cologne on him mixed with the outside. "I'm looking for a good cardio machine."

"I'll ask on our way out." We laughed as we walked around the exhibit, looking into the windows at all the old-time sex objects. There were dildos made of leather with authentic raccoon tails attached, sex dolls that were from the '60s, a cock-and-ball torture thing that made my own balls suck themselves back into my body. All the while, Enzo was walking by my side, making jokey comments and laughing the entire time. There were other people in the room, but they all disappeared around us. I couldn't describe any of their faces because I was so caught up in the moment with Enzo.

It was there, surrounded by ancient sex toys in a dimly lit room, that I realized, *holy shit, I think I love this man.*

## 24  ENZO

We were sitting at the bar, holding flutes of bubbling cotton candy champagne in our hands. This little excursion had been an excellent idea. It was exactly what we needed. I was getting upset with Zane, but that all seemed like a distant memory. He had apologized and realized his mistake, and I had to believe he was telling me the truth. I could see where he had been coming from, too. He wasn't completely in the wrong. It's not like he lied to me so he could hook up with the guy. He skirted around the truth to protect me.

Cazzo. Maybe I did overreact.

Whatever. We were good now, and that's what mattered. Hell, we were better than good. If anything, that little mini-fight we had only made me more sure that this was right. That Zane *was* a good man and that what we had was real. It also revealed the passion on both of our sides, otherwise neither of us would have really cared. If he were any other detective, I wouldn't have been so upset not knowing about the meeting. Merde, I wouldn't be upset at all. But since it was Zane, my emotions were on an entirely different level.

"That was an experience," Zane said.

"Which was your favorite floor?"

"I liked the third floor."

"The one with the deer orgy replica happening in the middle of the room?"

Zane chuckled. "Yeah, that one. I liked how they showed connections with homosexuality and the animal kingdom. The dildo bike on the first floor was a highlight, too."

I nodded. The champagne fizzed its way down my throat. I could taste the subtle sweetness of the cotton candy. "The third floor was a good one. The boob jump house was fun, too."

"Couldn't have jumped on some aeriolas with a better partner," Zane said. His eyes were practically glowing as he looked at me. I couldn't be sure of it, but I felt like something had changed between us since my small outburst. Shifted. Settled into place. Like a key finally fitting into its ring. I took another swig of champagne. We kept talking about the museum for a little longer as the lounge area began filling up with more and more people.

We were on our third glasses of champagne by the time the music kicked up a notch and people started hitting the dance floor.

"So," Zane started. Our conversation had been growing deeper, so I expected an interesting question coming. "What got you into being a defense attorney?"

His eyes glittered with the neon lights that were spaced around the lounge area. It was a disco-themed bar that was getting more and more packed with people as the minutes ticked by. There were huge disco balls hanging from the ceiling, along with a sizeable dance floor and red velvet couches to lounge on against the walls. Explicit black-and-white photos taken by the famous Bill Bernstein were hung up on the walls, mostly depicting gay men in various states of undress, dancing, kissing, fucking, and blowing inside different disco clubs.

"I was really into *Law and Order* growing up."

"Seriously?"

"Dun. Dun," I said, dramatically replicating the opening of the show before laughing. "No, not really." I took a sip of the champagne, smiling around the glass, watching Zane watch me. "It's a little bit more of an involved story." I set my glass down on the bar. A disco classic was playing through the speakers, making my foot tap against the floor to the beat. I was expecting a good question, and I got one. "I was seven when both my parents had immigrated from Italy and moved to Jersey. I took it in stride, thinking it was a huge grand adventure. I was excited to be going to a new school and making new friends and eating American food. I expected the entire country to be like a huge theme park, where everyone gets what they want and no one has any issues." I scoffed. "Little did I know, it was the exact opposite. My family struggled for years trying to get their feet on solid ground. They both worked two jobs, until my dad had an accident where he hurt his back and couldn't manage working again. So my mom had to pick up another job."

Zane's brows rose. "Damn."

"Yeah, it was difficult. I'd come home from school and would see her for an hour, sometimes less, before she had to leave to go work a night shift. But we managed, and things were finally getting comfortable again. My mom was down to one job, and my dad managed to find a job he could do from home. I had to teach him how to use a computer, but he learned pretty quick."

"You're an only child, right?"

"Mhmm." I nodded. "Just me. So, when things went to shit, I was probably the only one who could help get things back on track."

"What happened?" Zane was completely and totally engaged in my story. He was leaning forward on the stool, probably to make sure he could hear everything I was saying over the music. I could see the finer details of his face. The birthmark on the bridge of his nose. The long brushes of the eyelashes he would bat every now and then, seemingly unaware of the kind of power those things had on me.

"So the job my mother had was as a professional housekeeper. She was determined to open up her own company after she saved enough from cleaning. She landed some really rich and powerful clients, and they were paying enough to make her dream seem more and more like a reality. I was a senior in high school when the cops showed up at our house one evening, right when we were about to eat dinner, so that they could arrest my mother."

"What the fuck." Zane's jaw dropped open for a second before he picked it up.

"The family she cleaned for was accusing her of robbing a million dollars' worth of jewelry."

"Holy..."

"Yeah, so they took her away for questioning and searched our entire apartment. Of course, nothing was there, but the family kept insisting it was my mother who stole the jewelry. They said they had video evidence of her leaving with her pockets bulging. *Cazzate*. Bullshit. It was just her cell phone—they were huge back then! But they weren't giving up, and they were going to press charges."

"Jeez," Zane said, shaking his head.

"Yeah, so my mom was going to hire a lawyer, but it would have cost her entire savings account plus more. We'd go into debt for a frivolous lawsuit. So, that was when I decided I'd represent my mother myself." Zane looked impressed. "I pulled a ton of all-nighters studying up on what I needed to do and what was going to happen. Thankfully, I had already taken my finals by then, so schoolwork was basically done until college started. I had to sacrifice going to grad night or any other celebrations we were having, but that was fine because I was determined to help my mamma. It helped that I was actually really enjoying what I was doing."

"So what happened? Did you storm into the courtroom and serve up some kickass justice?"

"No. I never got the chance to. Turned out they found the jewels inside of the daughter's treasure chest of dolls."

We both laughed at that. "Seriously?" Zane asked.

"Yup. So I never got to have my kickass moment where I'd storm in wearing a cheap suit and holding an overflowing briefcase of information and evidence. Which is probably good because reality would have had me walking up to the bench and instantly blowing it by saying something dumb. There was no way I was ready for a real case back then, but the good thing was that it made me positive of what I wanted to study. I went to NYU first before transferring to Columbia, where I went to law school."

"Impressive," Zane said. He was practically eating me up with his eyes now. Maybe it was the fact that we were still in the Museum of Sex, or maybe it was just the raw chemistry between Zane and me, but I was starting to fill with lust. I moved on the stool, trying not to pay attention to my tightening briefs. "That's a really inspirational story. I don't think a lot of people who watch you on TV know about that."

"I'm thinking of maybe coming out with a book, but who knows."

"It wouldn't be a bad idea. But you're right," Zane said, "the picture book market is pretty saturated right now."

My jaw dropped a bit in surprise before I snorted a laugh. "I'll have words in it, thank you very much." I lifted my glass, finishing the last bit of champagne. "But the majority will be pictures."

We both started laughing. It was so easy letting loose with Zane. This entire spontaneous excursion was all about being relaxed and having a good time in an environment that may have freaked some people out. I figured we could take this home where we could get a little looser.

"Let's go back to my place," I offered. "It's only a ten-minute walk from here."

It was dark out, but I had Zane by my side and that gave me an ungodly amount of courage. It was like walking with a superhero. I couldn't describe it exactly, but I definitely felt safe when I was with him. Maybe it was because he'd already saved my life once that had me imprint on him like some vampire-werewolf fan-fiction story. But I doubted it. I think it just came down to Zane making me feel safe.

Not to say that I ever felt like I needed protecting. Even after the incident with the gunman, I didn't allow it to make me scared enough to alter my life. I was shaken, sure, but I wasn't going to stop walking down the street or taking the subway or doing anything else I would normally do. The one thing that did make me nervous, if I were being 100 percent honest, was the fact that the Unicorn was somewhere out there. But I couldn't let that affect me too much, either. I refused to live my life ruled by fear. Besides, a serial killer wasn't going to attack two men very capable of defending themselves out on the streets of New York, which were never empty, regardless of what time. It wasn't even that late. Only eight according to my watch.

"Let's go," Zane said. We closed out the tab and made our way out, shaking our groove things on the dance floor to one song before leaving.

The walk back to my place was filled with easy conversation and more laughs. I felt like a kid again, walking back from a high school dance with my date. Granted, back then my date was a girl who I had zero sexual chemistry with, but our friendship was great and I definitely had an incredible time. If Zane were my date back then, we wouldn't have even made it back home before we landed in some bushes, ripping at each other's dress pants. Instead, I'd walked Helen home and kissed her good night on the cheek before promising to help her decorate her graduation cap in the morning.

The thought of shoving Zane into some bushes was giving me a chub. I stuck a hand in my pocket to readjust and hold myself down. Maybe walking was a bad idea after all. Have you ever walked with a boner stuffed in your jeans?

It was hard, that was for sure.

## 25  ZANE

My fingers were itching to reach out and twine themselves between Enzo's. The entire walk to his place, all I wanted was to reach out and hold his hand, a gesture so intimate, and on the same hand so commonplace, yet it was still difficult for me to do. As a gay man, there was an added layer of complexity to hand-holding. It wasn't so much if the other person was receptive to some palm-on-palm action than it was about the people around you; were they the type to lash out at seeing two men holding hands, or would it be okay, a sign of progressing times? There was no way of knowing for sure—that was the shitty part. We could have been in the most liberal city around and there still could be someone who would fight over seeing two guys holding hands.

Imagine, how fragile did your own masculinity have to be to be offended by what me and my (incredibly hot and hung Italian) lover did?

"Hand-holding?" Enzo asked after I brought up the issue. We were two blocks away from his penthouse. It was getting late into the evening, but the Manhattan streets were still packed. People walked with headphones blaring, others with grocery bags in hand, others wearing their suits and ties as they speed walked toward the subway before they missed their train. The buildings stretched out toward the dark blue and purple sky. Cabs competed with Ubers as they honked and dodged each other on the roads.

"Yeah, what are your thoughts on it?"

"I think it's important, but also depends on who's comfortable with what. My last relationship, there wasn't much hand-holding. Even in private, he wasn't the type to display his affection. Who knows. Maybe that was a sign of what was coming." He shook his head, his gaze dropping to the ground.

A little flag went up in my head, marking a question. Enzo hadn't talked to me about his past relationships. I had no idea who he'd been with or why they'd broken up. I wanted to, especially since it seemed like there had been a heavy history there. "What happened?" I asked simply. As the words left my mouth, my hand gravitated toward Enzo's with barely even a thought, our fingers locking together.

He unfurled like a flower. "It was bad. Really bad. I had a hard time trusting people after what Ryan did to me. We were dating for a few months and things felt right, but I hadn't realized he was stealing from me until the third month."

"Fuck," I said. My hand gave a gentle squeeze.

"That wasn't the worst of it. The day before I figured out he was robbing me from right under my nose, we were having sex and he—well, I didn't realize, but he slipped off the condom midway and finished without saying anything. Inside. Cazzo. When I found that out, I almost knocked him out. I couldn't explain it, but I felt so angry and so damn betrayed. We hadn't been tested together yet, and we'd never talked about barebacking, either. I kicked him out that night, and then the next morning, I see my case of watches is open. Sure enough, one of them is missing. I looked around and realize little things that I normally wouldn't have really noticed are gone. Rings, bracelets, even some shoes. I mean, you haven't seen my shoe closet, but it's big, so he made sure to take the ones hiding in the corner, shoes I hadn't worn in years but were definitely worth good money."

I could hardly believe what Enzo was telling me. What that monster of a man did to him would be enough to shatter anyone's trust beyond repair. But Enzo still allowed me in. He still opened himself up to me. It made me even more aware of how precious Enzo's trust was. A delicate gem that needed to be cherished.

"Still not the worst." We were reaching his building now. It was tall and felt historic, with a grand entrance and a bellhop on standby regardless of the hour. "He, uhm, called me a week later. He told me he got tested and that he was positive."

The world screeched to a halt. "Oh no," I said, a knot of pure dread forming in my chest.

"It's okay, it's okay. I got tested and I'm negative. Turned out his was a false positive. But regardless, it was one of the hardest times of my entire life." Enzo swallowed, his gaze dropping. I squeezed his hand a little harder. "We were never really sure for a full three months since that's how long it could take to show up on tests. I barely got any sleep. I drove myself sick with anxiety. It was brutal, and all from a cazzo shithead who couldn't be honest with me. I stopped dating for a while after that." We walked through the golden sliding glass doors and into a large lobby decorated in an eclectic mix of old-fashioned New York glamour mixed with modernized touches throughout.

"I'm so sorry you ever had to go through that," I said, feeling like anything I said wouldn't really be enough. "He never deserved you. Not in the slightest. You deserve to be treated like a king. Admired like one. Loved like one. Enzo, I swear, I'd never betray your trust. Not like that, not in any kind of way."

We were in the elevator, the mirrored wall giving me a glimpse of Enzo's eyes, which he had kept aimed away from me. Enzo looked at me as the doors shut. "Thank you, Zane. I trust you. I never thought I'd find someone who'd piece me back together, but here you are. Chiodo scaccia chiodo."

"What's that mean?"

Enzo's eyes were glistening. It made a ball of emotion rise up in my chest. "A new nail drives out an old one. You're my new, shiny nail. Replacing the rusty piece of shit from before."

I chuckled and pulled him into me. Our faces were inches apart. I could feel his breath on my lips. Could see his pores, the flecks of yellow gold in his eyes. I could smell his cologne, intoxicating me.

"I love you, Enzo." The words came out of me before I realized what I was saying. And that was it. Once it was said, it was said. Out in the ether. I was as vulnerable as I'd ever been. Time slowed down. Enzo's lips curled into a smile, growing wider and wider.

"I love you, too," he said, his Italian accent coming in thick. Our lips collided then, just like our worlds had on the day we met. I pushed him back on the wall of the elevator, the kiss rocketing up in heat. It felt so good, having said what I'd been feeling for some time now. And it felt even better to hear it said back. To know that Enzo was on the same page as I was.

*Ding.*

The elevator doors opened. *Shit. We never pressed Enzo's floor.*

"Oh dear," said an older lady holding on to a bright pink leash connected to her yappy Pomeranian. I separated from Enzo, straightening my coat and trying to smile as charmingly as I could, even though I knew my lips were still plump and wet from getting sucked on.

"I'll, uhm, take the next one." She stepped back as the doors closed again. I turned to Enzo, and we both started laughing. He pulled his key card out of his wallet and pressed it against the sensor, pushing the button for the penthouse. The second the elevator jerked into movement, our bodies were back on top of each other. This time, it was Enzo who grabbed my hips and locked lips with me, pushing me back so that I could lean on the wall. I could feel Enzo getting hard against me, his dick pushing against mine through our pants as we ground our bodies together while our tongues danced.

I wanted him. So fucking bad. I opened my eyes and glanced at what floor we were on. We had thirty-seven more. My hand went down between us, rubbing over Enzo's bulge, and I swallowed a moan from him as our kiss burned hot. Fifteen more floors. I stopped kissing him and tilted my head so I could suck on his neck instead. I loved tasting him, and I loved feeling him buck as I sucked on his sensitive flesh. His hand moved to caress the back of my head while another went to squeeze my ass. I pushed against him harder, moving onto a new spot on his neck before I left a mark.

Five floors. I slipped a hand underneath Enzo's waistband, finding that the naughty boy wasn't wearing any underwear. I immediately felt his velvety soft length against my hand. I closed my fingers, holding him, stroking him.

*Ding.*

We tumbled directly into Enzo's penthouse, our bodies not wanting to separate for even an inch. I wanted all of Enzo, and I didn't want to wait for him. Not only was there such a relief flooding through me after hearing those three words come from Enzo's lips, but there was also a flood of endorphins—nature's aphrodisiac. I was hornier than I'd ever been, and I needed Enzo to know it. My hands dropped down to my pants as I popped open the button and pulled down the zipper. I dropped them down to my ankles, our kiss still smoldering as Enzo steered us toward his couch. Next came my coat. I threw it to the side. Enzo started doing the same, pulling off his clothes and almost tripping on his pants, but I was there to catch him.

"I didn't know you liked going commando," I teased, reaching down and cupping Enzo's balls in my hand.

"I like wearing the least amount of clothes I can get away with."

"Works for me," I responded, looking down and admiring Enzo. We laughed and kissed the rest of the way to the couch, both of us fully naked by the time we flopped back onto the soft cushions. My belly became wet with Enzo's precome as he laid me down and straddled me, rubbing himself on me as we kissed.

"Fuck," I groaned into a kiss, "you're getting me soaked."

"You make me so... *wet*." Enzo said that last part in a

dramatic tone, like an actress in a cheap soap opera, as he pulled up and batted his eyelashes at me. We both started to laugh. I pulled him back down for a kiss, wanting him to get us both even wetter.

We broke our kiss for a breath. "Sei bellissimo," Enzo purred as he sat on top of me, his breathtaking eyes pinning me down to the couch. "You're beautiful. So fucking beautiful." I didn't want to tell him I didn't need the translation for that one. He could keep calling me beautiful all damn night—I wouldn't stop him.

Another kiss. I couldn't get enough of him. "You're addictive," I said, my turn to take a breath of air. "I can't get enough of you."

"Bene," Enzo said. "There's plenty of me for you to have, bello." I noticed how much more pronounced Enzo's Italian became whenever he was turned on, which, in turn, made me harder than a fucking diamond.

"Let me have you, then," I said, reaching around and grabbing both of Enzo's cheeks in my hands, squeezing and spreading them open. "Let me have all of you. I want to be inside of you." I thrust my hips up, my cock rubbing against Enzo's crack, adding some emphasis to my sentence.

Enzo smiled down at me and pushed his ass back, rubbing himself on my stiff dick. I could feel his tight hole with my fingers. I circled around the sensitive spot, pressing down and applying pressure as Enzo rocked backward. He showed his appreciation of my touch by spilling more of his precome onto my belly. I used a free hand to run two fingers through the clear liquid before bringing it up to my lips, smiling as I sucked the fingers into my mouth and tasted Enzo on my tongue.

"Cazzo," Enzo exhaled. He stopped rubbing himself on me and pushed up on the couch. "I'll be right back," Enzo said, his tone low as he bent over and started kissing my chest. He sucked a nipple and sent a bolt of pleasure shooting through me before he stood up and disappeared into his hallway.

A few minutes passed and he was back, naked and hard, holding a navy bottle of lube and a black-and-gold wrapper. He looked so sexy standing completely naked, his cock jutting out ahead of him, throbbing gently in the air. I could see it leaking, which drove me wild. And his body, *fuck* his body was perfect. He had some meat on him (and I wasn't just talking about the Italian sausage he was packing), which I fucking loved. I never found overly muscled men attractive, which was also why I never went overboard myself at the gym. Enzo was perfect. He had strong arms, a powerful, prideful chest, and a tummy I could bite on when he got close enough.

Fucking perfect.

"Get over here," I growled.

I was sitting down on Enzo's couch, my legs out in front of me, my hard cock stiff in the air and leaking from the tip. I grabbed the base and aimed it straight up. Enzo walked toward me, eyeing my cock like it was his last fucking meal. It turned me on to no end. My gaze dropped from his eyes down to his thick cock and tight balls. Saliva collected in my mouth before I swallowed it down.

"Come sit on me." I practically growled it as a command. Enzo, his hand already lubed up, spread it on his cock before reaching behind himself and lubing his ass. I stroked myself in anticipation.

Enzo dropped down to the floor and settled on his knees between mine. He smiled as he licked from my balls to my tip slowly, sucking on skin as he jerked himself off. The air in the room grew fifteen degrees warmer. Our gazes locked as he opened his mouth and took me in, the warmth and wetness instantly sending me to another world. I let my head drop back and my eyes close as Enzo got to work with his mouth. My hands moved to twine in Enzo's hair, grabbing enough so that I could push down and shove my cock deeper down his throat. He took it and went down even farther. Saliva was dripping down, sliding down my balls.

"Fuck," I hissed, "I need to be inside of you."

Enzo looked up, grinning around my cock before he pulled off it. He got back up on his feet, his cock slick with lube and shining in the light of his living room. He moved forward so that both of his legs were on either side of mine as he reached down and grabbed my cock in his hands. He stroked, spreading the wetness up and down, making me as slick as he was. I reached over to the condom next to the bottle of lube and tore it open in record time, sliding it on as Enzo positioned himself to ride my fucking brains out. He put a knee on the couch before bringing up the other and straddling me. My cock throbbed against his ass. I pushed my hips up, lifting my ass from the couch, and rubbed myself against Enzo, aching to be inside him.

"You're so big," Enzo said as he reached behind and grabbed me in his hand. He was looking down at me, his pupils dilated like coals ready to catch fire. He bit his lip as he moved my cock so that it was pushing up against his tight hole. He took a breath before sitting back, opening himself for me, his eyes rolling back as I entered.

It was ecstasy. I wasn't even halfway inside him and I was already close to coming. He was exactly what my body had been crying out for, begging for, *needing*. I needed this. Needed him. Enzo sat down farther, wrapping heat around more and more of my cock. My hands held on to his hips as

I looked down. Enzo held his balls in one hand, giving me the perfect view of my dick disappearing inside of him.

"Fuck, that's it, sit on me." I looked back up to Enzo, our eyes locking, the fire between us ready to incinerate the entire penthouse.

With a moan, Enzo sat, taking in every last inch of me. My head dropped back, my toes curled. I pushed my hips upward, knowing that I was hitting his prostate.

"Cazzo, Zane, right there," he said, his pitch confirming what I thought. I pushed up harder and grabbed on to his hips so I could grind Enzo down. He was making small circles in my lap, hitting that spot of his harder and harder. I could feel him tighten around me.

"Bounce on it, baby." I was almost growling, my voice deep like my breath. Enzo looked down and used his knees to push himself up before he slowly sat back down, his tight hole taking me with ease. He must have been starving for this. Yearning for it as much as I was.

I started pushing up off the couch, driving myself deeper into Enzo, harder. I started fucking him, watching as his hard cock bounced and slapped on my abs, leaving behind a trail of clear, sticky precome. I grabbed him in my hand as he bounced on my cock. Fuck. I loved feeling that thick dick of his in my hand. The weight of it, the softness, the fact that I couldn't wrap my fingers around it.

And Enzo's ass. Holy fuck, that was perfect, too. Everything about the man had my body humming like an exposed live wire. I wanted that ass in my hands. I grabbed his hips again and slowed him to a stop. He came down on me, our lips crushing together, our tongues dueling, all while my cock was buried deep inside Enzo.

Bliss. Pure bliss.

"Come here," I said when we broke for breath. I lifted

him up off my dick and guided him to the arm of the couch, where I bent him over. He instantly stuck his ass out in the air, even giving me a little wiggle. I slapped it, the white skin turning pink in response.

"Ohh, do it again," Enzo said, looking back at me with a fiery smile. I gave the man what he wanted. My hand pulled up and back down, slapping the other cheek, a little harder this time.

I squirted some more lube on my hand and rubbed it over my cock before I got into position behind Enzo on the couch. "Question for you," I said, rubbing my cock against his ass. "How would a naive tourist in Italy say 'you've got the best ass I've ever seen'?"

Enzo chuckled. "Asking for a friend?"

"Exactly." I slipped the head of my cock inside.

"Oh," Enzo moaned. "Hai il miglior culo che abbia mai visto."

I chuckled. I wasn't even going to try saying what he said. "Got it," I said instead, sinking myself deeper into Enzo. With a moan from deep in my chest, I watched myself disappearing inside him. I put a hand on his lower back and another went between his legs, where I could grab on to that meaty cock of his again. I stroked him as I started fucking him, harder, pounding into him from behind. My balls slapped against his ass, and his cock throbbed in my grip. Our sounds became animalistic. Our grunts were synced with every thrust, our moans growing louder and louder. Enzo's fingers were pale as they held on to the couch. He threw his head back, giving me the perfect angle to suck on his flesh. I thrust inside him, impaling him, before I dipped down so that I could kiss on the back of his neck.

"Proprio qui," Enzo groaned. "Fuck, right there. Yeah."

I was getting close to my edge, and judging by how wet my hand was from jerking Enzo off, so was he.

"I'm so fucking close," I said into Enzo's ear. I kept driving myself into him, his ass wrapping around my entire length and filling me with an indescribable heat. I had to blow.

"Fuck, come for me, Zane." Enzo was thrusting his ass back, begging for it.

"Yeah, tell me how much you want it," I growled, pulling my cock out of Enzo's tight ass. I stroked myself, my cock still slick with lube and pulsing in my grip as I pressed the head against Enzo's needy hole.

"Give it to me, Zane. I want it so bad," Enzo said before he dropped his head and started moaning with his face in a pillow, his ass grinding in the air, telling me how badly he really wanted my come.

"Come here," I said, grabbing him so that I could have him sitting down on the couch, his hard cock jutting out between those thick thighs, red and wet.

Enzo was smiling as he grabbed my dick and rolled the condom off. He looked up at me while he started to jerk me off.

"Come for me, Zane. I want to feel it all over my face."

It was all I needed to blow. Looking down into those captivating eyes, seeing his hand wrapped around me, I couldn't hold it back even if I wanted to. I grabbed my cock from Enzo's hands, my fist tightening around my shaft as I felt the unstoppable orgasmic wave flood over me, starting at the base of my spine and exploding outward. A jet of my sticky, white come landed smack on Enzo's forehead. He jerked back, smiling and laughing as he leaned back in, my cock covering him in my seed. I was a twitching, spasming mess by the time the orgasm had finished. And Enzo looked like a fucked-up snowman.

"Holy... shit," he said, using his fingers to wipe away some of the dripping come before it landed in his eyes. "That was so fucking hot. Cazzo, Zane."

"Now it's your turn," I said, pulling him up to my level so I could lick his face clean.

## 26  ENZO

I had been hungry for Zane, and the man made sure to feed me. He gave me everything my body had been crying out for. His cock inside of me, thrusting into me, filling me; it was all I ever wanted in my life. He could have stayed inside me for the rest of time.

But no, I wanted his come; I wanted to taste it. And I got exactly what I wished for. I jerked myself off as Zane blew all over my face, covering me in his seed. I was positive I could have passed for a glazed donut when he was done. I could feel it dripping down my forehead, falling off my nose, down my chin. I looked up and smiled, continuing to jerk myself off. Pure ecstasy coursed through my veins as I wiped away some of the come and brought my sticky fingers into my mouth, sucking them clean before Zane pulled me up and devoured me with a kiss.

My cock was still rock solid. I felt ready to blow, and Zane knew exactly what to do to make me explode. He guided me back so that I was the one lying down. I could still taste him on my lips as I watched him kneeling between my open legs. He spit into his palm and brought his wet hand down onto my cock, tugging it toward him and stroking. I closed my eyes, my toes curling. My fingers tried to find some kind of hold on the couch. Zane's other hand grabbed my balls, massaging them, before he slipped his fingers between my ass. He rubbed at the sensitive flesh between my ass and my balls. He pushed at the area, making my cock throb and leak in his grip.

"That's it, Zane. Like that. Finger me, bello." I lifted my ass off the couch, giving him even more access. I was already open and ready; I needed him inside me one way or another.

Zane seemed more than happy to oblige. He brought two fingers up to his mouth and sucked, getting them soaking wet before he brought them back down to my crack, pressing in on my hole. I gasped as the pads of his fingers rubbed, the tips pushing in, my ass pushing down on him to take more of his fingers inside of me. I could feel him curl his fingers and massage on my P-spot. My eyes rolled back. I tried to express how incredibly good I was feeling, but all I could do was string together a few unintelligible Italian words. Zane had me speaking in tongues.

"You like that?" he asked, sticking his fingers in even deeper, starting to fuck me with them while his other hand formed a tight fist around my leaking cock.

"Yes, bello," I said, feeling my body tighten, every muscle getting ready for the impending release. "More—yes, there—oh fuck." I couldn't take it. "I'm going to—arghgh!"

My entire body spasmed as my cock erupted. My legs stretched out, my head fell backward, and my fingers dug into the couch. Zane, his fingers still deep inside, must have felt every orgasmic wave rock through me as my hole tightened around him.

It was phenomenal. I had never come so hard in my fucking life.

"Holy shit," I said, breathless, gasping as Zane pulled himself out. We both took a second to take stock of the situation before we broke down into laughs, our bodies drunk on the bliss.

"That was—"

"—perfetto," I said. I was still a little breathless as Zane got up off the couch. He looked so damn good, standing there naked and lightly glistening in sweat, his chest still flushed pink.

"Let's get cleaned up," I said, Zane helping me up from the couch. I was a dripping, comey mess, and I definitely needed a shower. "Then I know the perfect way we can spend the rest of the night."

"I've got a few ideas on how we can spend the rest of the night, too."

"Oh really? I'll have to hear about them in the shower."

"I'll describe them in great detail."

We laughed and joked as we went to the shower, every step feeling as if it were onto a nice buoyant, cotton-candy cloud. It was something I'd never really experienced before, this complete and total lightness. The sky could have been falling outside and it wouldn't have fazed how good I felt from being with Zane.

\*\*\*

To my surprise, there were stars that were powering past the light pollution and dotting the dark night sky. It helped that there wasn't a cloud in sight, giving us a clear view of the endless expanse. It was like looking down into an ocean, except this one was somehow hanging above us, an endless trove of mysteries hidden within its depths.

I had to close my eyes and stop thinking about it. It was starting to freak me out.

"This is such an incredible space," Zane said, his body cuddling in closer to mine. We were lying down on the wide lounge bed on my private rooftop lounge, its red memory foam cushion shaping to our naked forms. It was still cold out, but the nearby space heaters provided more than enough coverage from the chilly night air. "How do you not spend all day up here?"

"I sometimes do," I confessed, thinking back to the few days I'd spent relaxing on the rooftop. It was really more like a Zen garden. I had soil brought up and an irrigation system installed so that I could grow a colorful garden around the borders and stone pathway that led to the lounge bed and a table with four chairs surrounding it. There was a Japanese rock garden to the left of us, with tranquil swirls and perfect circles formed using the light gray stones. A koi pond gurgled nearby as water fell down from a rock formation. Overall, it was exactly the space I needed whenever I had a really difficult day in the courtroom and had to get away from it all. Normally, it was a very relaxing experience. Tonight, though, it was a magical one. My body still felt like it was floating on cloud nine with Zane by my side. I could feel him against me, his warmth, his breaths, his dick. Our feet were knotted together at the ankles, gently playing with each other.

"You know, I'm going to be honest," Zane said, rolling onto his back and staring up at the night sky. "I never pegged you for the Zen type. I always assumed you'd be into the work hard, party harder kind of life."

"Oh no," I said. "Maybe during university, but the

partying's died down. Cazzo, I haven't actually gone dancing in years, I don't think."

"Really?" Zane sounded surprised. "Are you a good dancer?"

"Pfft," I said, throwing a hand in the air. "Am I a good dancer? Of course I'm a good dancer." I puffed my chest, smiling and rolling onto my side now so that I could fit my chin against Zane's shoulder and smell his addictive scent. I threw an arm over his chest and a leg over his. "I can twerk like the best of them." I gave a few playful shakes of my ass.

"I don't believe it," Zane said.

I rolled off him, my smile competing with my offended gaze. "Wow. That hurts."

"Prove it to me, then." He was grinning. "Go, twerk for me." He propped himself up on the bed and motioned to the open space. I nodded my head and clapped my hands. I got up and grabbed my phone off the table, unlocking it and connecting it to the sound system. I pulled up my music app and went through my recently played songs. There was a mix of Italian and American, but there was one that I figured would be the best to twerk to.

I hit Play on Cardi B's latest hit and let the song start, turning to Zane while the Bronx-born rapper went in on the beat.

"Ready?" I asked, cupping my dick and balls in my hands, shaking my hips, and sticking my tongue out. Zane never failed to bring out my playful side.

I turned right when the rapper started talking about her red bottoms. The pressure was on. The time had come. Twerk time.

I dropped into a squat position, finding my balance. "This view is already five stars," I heard from behind me.

My hands went on my thighs, pushing down as I started to bounce my ass, twerking like a damn pro.

"Yes, Enzo, get it." I could hear Zane clapping over the song. I'd never thought that I'd be twerking naked in the middle of my Zen garden, but those were the kind of things that happened when Zane was around.

I made it clap for him, busting it down and twerking, turning around and moving my hips, holding myself in my hands so that I could be somewhat of a tease. Zane was grinning, clapping, and whistling as the song faded to an end.

"Wow," he said, nodding as I crawled onto the bed and back to his side. This time, both of us were sitting up on the bed's slightly curved headboard, pillows propped behind us for some support. "That was better than in some of the music videos I've seen." He was grinning from ear to ear. "Also helps that I got the most perfect seat in the house."

"Told you I could twerk." I arched a brow. "Cazzo. You didn't believe me."

"I did, trust me. I saw the twerking potential in you. That bubble butt of yours is made to clap."

"Bene. Now it's your turn." I motioned toward the impromptu dance floor.

"Oh, no." Zane shook his head. "I don't twerk. I can barely dance the Macarena."

"Well then, try. I want to see you."

"Twerking?"

"No, do the Macarena. Get up and do it. I want a show."

Zane laughed and scooched off the bed. I watched him, admired him as he stood in front of me, bathed in the warm soft light from the nearby lanterns. His muscles rippled when he moved. He had a muscular chest and wide stance. Heavy balls hung between those thick thighs. Zane was the epitome of man. He stood there, confident as all hell, on the top of a building in the middle of New York, dancing the Macarena naked for me, his laughing, mesmerized lover. He put one hand out. Then another. Behind his head. On his hips. Crossed them over.

"Jump, jump," I said, clapping. He gave his hips a shake and jumped, repeating the dance another time. It seemed like Zane was making sure he shook his junk a little more than he needed to.

When he had finished his dance routine, Zane climbed back onto the bed, laughing as he sat next to me. "That was great!" I said. "See, never say you can't do anything."

"Thank you, Enzo. You're an inspiration. Like... a guiding star." He was being overly dramatic now, putting on a Valley girl accent. "A beacon of hope inside of a thunderous storm. You help me see that I really am worth it. You're the pumpkin spice latte to my autumn." He bundled my hands to his chest and batted his eyelashes the same way I had done earlier.

I cracked up at his impression. "I'm glad to help you in any way I can," I said, playing along. We chuckled and kissed, our lips feeling so familiar now. I had a flash to the day I first met Zane, a man I wanted to devour from head to toe, but a man who seemed so far, so closed off, I didn't think this moment would have ever been a possibility.

We continued joking around with each other, lazily kissing the other, our feet casually rubbing every now and then. It was *perfetto*.

When the jokes and laughs simmered down, space for more serious conversation started developing. We began discussing our childhoods again. I told him a couple of different stories, starting with the time I helped save my mamma's big family dinner by cooking a killer lasagna

("When he was only ten years old!" Mamma would surely shout). I told him about my pa's love for bikes and how I never really acquired the fascination but still tried hard to understand it, even fixing one up with him when I was in high school. I told him about all the times my parents took me to Central Park, making it one of my absolute favorite places to be in New York.

"So that's the vibe I'm getting from the rooftop garden. It's like you tried to recreate Central Park up here."

"Yeah, I guess so," I agreed, not having thought of that before.

"And at least you tried learning how to fix bikes with your dad, that's what counts," Zane said, smiling up at the night sky.

"I guess. I almost severed a finger with one of the parts, but eh, nothing bad happened."

Zane laughed at that. "It sounds like you had a great childhood and you came out with all your fingers intact, so all in all, I think that's a win."

"I think so, too." I leaned over so I could kiss Zane's cheek. I couldn't get enough of my skin on his. The night was full of random kisses from the both of us. Each one made my heart feel that much lighter. I expected it to float out of my mouth any second now.

"Things were a little different for me growing up," Zane said. I could tell he was pulling back another layer. He was letting me in, allowing me to see a part of him that only a select few ever saw. He swallowed. "I didn't really cook much, and most of my foster families didn't show much interest in giving me hobbies like bikes or cars. Two of them tried, but that was during one of my rougher moments... I had actually stopped speaking for a couple of years. Didn't say a word to anyone."

"Whoa," I said, my hand coming to rest on his chest, feeling the heartbeat underneath.

*Thump. Thump. Thump.*

"Yeah, when the system separated Andrei and I... I sort of shut down. I still went to school and did my work, but I never spoke."

"So what happened?" I asked. "Was it being reunited with Andrei that got you talking again?"

"No." Zane shook his head. "It's crazy. I can remember that time in my life like it was yesterday. I had been so young back then, and yet I felt so old at the same time. I remembered thinking, 'Well, the world doesn't care what I have to say about my brother, why say anything else?' It was an experience that would instantly age anyone. It aged me quick."

I exhaled a deep breath, as though that would help take off some of the weight settling on my chest. I felt so bad Zane ever felt like he wasn't being heard. He must have shouted to the rooftops about how badly he wanted to stay with his brother, and still, they had split them up. It was tough to think about. Especially because my childhood had been on the complete opposite end of the spectrum. I almost felt guilty, like I shouldn't have had it all, like I should have given some of my blessing to Zane.

Clearly, that was absolutely fucking impossible, but still, I felt bad.

"It wasn't Andrei who got me talking, though. It was Steven, a boy in my class."

"A boy, huh?"

"Yup." Zane was smiling. I nuzzled closer into him. "He was a gangly thing who was obsessed with *Transformers*, which I was also secretly obsessed with, too. He always wore cool shirts and had the best haircut. I was into him, even though I barely understood it back then. He pulled me aside one day during lunch and just started talking to me. It didn't matter that I didn't say anything back, he was just talking. Two weeks later and we were having full-blown conversations about Optimus Prime, Decepticons, and whatever else we found interesting at the time." He took a deep breath next to me. I could almost feel his lungs fill with air. He let it out. "Then I was moved to another family. Never talked to Steven after that. But I was reunited with Andrei, and we were never separated again."

"So Steven was your first ever love, huh?" I asked, poking Zane in the rib. "Is that when you knew you were gay?"

"I had an idea before Steven. Since I was like seven, I think I realized something was up. But Steven was the confirmation. It took a lot more for me to actually accept it, though."

I leaned in and kissed Zane, unable to keep from showing him how much I cared for him. Loved him. This man managed to heal my trust and fill me with love, two things I never thought would happen again after Ryan had left me in such a dark place.

I kissed him again, sitting up so that I could look him straight in the eyes when we parted.

"Ti amo," I said.

"Ti amo," Zane repeated with a heart-melting smile.

Italian sounded good on him.

It looked good *on* him, too.

## 27  ZANE

The night sky opened up above us. The sounds of New York drifted up from below us. The night was cold, but Enzo had equipped his rooftop paradise with space heaters that blasted out warmth from nearby, keeping our naked bodies warm and cozy as we lounged together. I wasn't surprised by how much I was opening up to Enzo, but I was surprised at how easy it felt. Speaking about my past was hard for me, but everything with Enzo came easy. Life was that much easier with him by my side.

And so I told Enzo everything. About my foster life, about my silence, about my first crush. I hadn't opened up to anyone in this kind of way since... well, since Jose. It felt good to finally be able to connect with someone again and share my life's experience with.

I dropped my head to the side so that I could kiss Enzo's. His hair smelled good, like coconut and strawberries. "When did you come out?" I asked, wanting to hear about Enzo's experience.

"I was sixteen when I made it official. My pa wasn't having it at first, gave the whole 'must be your friends influencing you' type spew. At one point, I'm sure he even blamed it on the water I was drinking or something. Mamma had a much easier time accepting it. She said she had known from the beginning."

"Yeah, sometimes it takes a little time. Your dad is good with everything now?"

"Oh yeah. He's a hundred percent fine. Even cracks some risqué jokes now and then. One time, I had a boyfriend over for dinner and we were all eating, I asked to get a spoonful of meatballs on my plate. So he had said something like 'balls, huh, isn't that for after dinner?' Mamma almost flipped the table. She turned as bright red as the glass of wine she'd been drinking, while we all started laughing."

"He sounds like a great man," I said, laughing up at the sky. "Makes sense because he raised a great man, too."

"Yeah, they both did a pretty good job, I've gotta admit." I looked over. Enzo was smiling, his eyes bright with the ambient light.

We lay there, comfortable in the silence that followed our conversation. A good sign. It was important to appreciate the empty spaces without feeling the need to constantly be chattering about mindless things.

It was Enzo who broke the silence, something clearly entering his mind with the way he perked up. "So... nah, forget it."

"What?"

"Nothing, nothing."

"Come on, Enzo. What were you going to ask?"

He sighed. "I didn't want to bring work into this, but... do you think Ricky did it? Killed Luanne and Oscar?"

I took a breath. I didn't want to overcalculate my answer. "I'm still not sure. It's looking more likely, Enzo,

I've got to be honest. His last interview came off as desperate. Someone clutching at straws. And since he wasn't honest with us from the start, he could be hiding even more. What if he really did threaten Oscar and Luanne on that tape? If he really did say 'you'll regret this'?"

I could feel Enzo deflate a little. But I trusted in him being an adult and being able to handle my professional opinion. "I hear you," Enzo said, proving my trust was placed correctly. "It's difficult, because I really do see him as innocent. I've had to defend some bad people in my career, and he doesn't strike me as one of them. Besides, threats don't always equal crime. But again, you're right, he has held things back from us."

"Well, there's still what Tito told me, about Luanne looking like she'd just been in some kind of altercation the day he saw her. That could lead us somewhere."

"But how are we going to find out who fought her? Ricky hasn't seen many other people visit Luanne's place."

"Except her sister." I looked up at the sky, spotting a few bright stars twinkling through the light pollution. "Maybe I should give Susan another visit. She may know if Luanne had been arguing with anyone."

"She didn't even know about Tito, though. Sounds like she didn't know much about her sister."

"No, she did know about Tito, just didn't know exactly who he was. They seemed to have a fine relationship judging off social media and the way she was acting during our interview." That was when a bell rang in my head. A distant one. "Well... wait a second. She did say she hadn't been to her sister's place in a while, but Ricky said she was there all the time."

It was a question that quickly started to burn at the base of my brain.

"Huh, maybe Ricky isn't being a hundred percent correct with his statements?"

"Maybe," I said. "Regardless, I'll have an interview with her tomorrow afternoon."

"Afternoon? Wanna grab some drinks for happy hour after the interview, then? What part of town is she in?"

I closed my eyes, mentally drawing out her street in my head. "Brooklyn," I said. "But I can come back to Manhattan if you want to have drinks around here."

"Sure, that works. Then we can have another relaxed evening up here?"

"That sounds *parfetoh*." My tongue got a little twisted on my attempt at Italian, but Enzo seemed to love it regardless. He loved it so much, he started kissing me, climbing on top of me and kissing me harder, his tongue parting my lips.

"*Perfetto*," Enzo repeated, sounding much sexier than I had. I was instantly hard, and so was he.

We spent most of the night out on the rooftop, playing with each other under the blinking stars.

\*\*\*

It was hard getting out of bed. Figuratively and literally. Enzo made it difficult, when his warm body was pressed against mine under the big heavy white comforter. I knew it was much colder outside than in, and all I wanted to do was stay with Enzo, our naked bodies providing all the warmth (and entertainment) I would ever need.

But the sun was already up, although it wasn't shining. I expected a bright beam of sunlight breaking in through the floor-to-ceiling window Enzo had in his bedroom, but the day was dark. I could hear the hard taps of raindrops smacking against the window. It was going to be one of those days.

I managed to get out of bed and get ready without waking up Enzo, who didn't have to be into the office until an hour later. I liked being up early, and I felt like I needed to make sure I woke up early so I could nail down that interview with Susan. By the time I was tugging on my jeans, Enzo was blinking the sleep out of his eyes.

"Hey, sexy," Enzo said, his voice still groggy. He sat up in bed, and his chest showing above the covers was giving me another reason to stay.

"Good morning," I said, walking over to the bedside so I could steal a quick kiss.

"Drinks today, right?"

"Definitely," I said, feeling like a new man after last night. It felt as if I sold an old beat-up '94 Honda and upgraded to a brand-spanking-new Porsche. I was riding on a pure high.

"Okay, bello. I'll see you later, then."

"See you," I said, tugging on my shirt and giving Enzo one last kiss.

I left Enzo, already counting down the minutes until I saw him again. I took the subway back to my place and then picked up my car, just to have it. Enzo's building had parking, so it wasn't like I'd have trouble finding a spot for it later.

It was while I was waiting for the subway that I was able to make contact with Susan. She still sounded a little distraught and upset by the prospect of another interview with me, but I assured her it wasn't like I was some tough police officer. I sold it to her as if I were a friend, looking for just a couple more answers. She agreed to a short sit-down, asking to make sure I wasn't bringing over a big group of investigators since she was still very stressed.

The entire drive to Susan's consisted of me smiling like a goofball and listening to dumb pop songs I'd normally roll my eyes over before changing the station. I was tapping my fingers on the wheel and shaking my head and just fucking living. It had been a while since I'd sung in my car. I forgot how great it could feel. By the time I reached her apartment building (and luckily found parking right in front), I had almost made it through an entire Katy Perry album. I almost expected to step out of the car wearing some bright pink costume worn by a pop princess, as though I'd blacked out on love and changed into it.

Thankfully, I was still wearing my simple black tee and faded blue jeans.

Susan seemed to have been waiting by the door, opening it almost as soon as I knocked. Her hallway was dark and musty, so I appreciated not having to wait outside too long.

"Hi, Mr. Holden."

She stuck a hand out. I noticed she appeared a little thinner than the last time we'd spoke. I made a mental note to make sure she'd been eating properly before I left. It wasn't uncommon for someone suffering from grief to forgo meals.

"Hi, Susan. Thank you for your time."

She nodded and turned, walking toward her couch. She was wearing a stained sweater that appeared a size too big, with a pair of khakis that also needed a good wash. "Do you want anything? Water?" she asked over her shoulder.

"No, thank you, though." I stepped into her living room. It smelled like smoke and old pizza. Sure enough, I spotted a couple of boxes stacked next to an overflowing trash can. I could see there were dirty dishes in the sink, a few fruit flies dashing around them.

"Susan, how have you been doing?" I looked to her now. Her big eyes were red. Must not have been sleeping well.

"Not too great," she said, slumping down onto the couch. "I just want this all to be over."

"I know," I said, sympathizing with her. The murder happened some time ago, and by me coming over, I was tearing off whatever scab she had been forming over the wound that her sister's loss left her. "Hopefully it will be soon."

"So, what do you need from me?"

I sat down on the hard wooden chair she had next to her small dining table. "There's a couple of questions." I had to choose my words carefully. This was where being a private detective was harder than being a detective on the force. If I wanted information, I needed to coerce it out of people, sometimes by sneakily misdirecting conversations or by throwing in a few white lies here and there. Cops couldn't lie, but they could bring someone down to the station for questioning and pursue things even further if they thought someone was purposefully withholding crucial information.

"Shoot," she said.

"Okay, first I wanted to ask if you knew about anyone Luanne could have gotten into a physical fight with? I've gotten confirmation that she'd been in a pretty bad state a few nights before the murder, and I have a suspicion it could be linked to her death."

Susan looked down at her hands. She was chipping away at her nails, using her fingers before bringing them up to her teeth. "No." Her voice was tense. "We grew distant before she died. Biggest regret of my life." She threw a glance up at the door and stood up suddenly. She walked over to the door and clicked the lock shut.

"Sorry," she said, looking at me before diverting her gaze back to the floor. "It's a bad neighborhood."

She walked into the kitchen and disappeared behind a wall.

A thought invaded, like a cannonball blasting through the skull.

*Could Oscar have been with someone other than Luanne and Ricky?*

*Could he have been with Susan, too?*

"Susan," I asked, loud enough for her to hear me. "Were you and your sister fighting?"

"See"—her voice sounded strained—"I was thinking you might ask that."

Something else blasted against my skull, then. Not a thought. Something solid.

Something hard enough to knock me out cold.

## 28 ENZO

The office was busy, with interns and assistants and associates speed-walking from room to room, all suited up and looking sharp. I left my suit in the car. It just didn't feel like a suit kind of day. First, not only was it raining and gloomy, but also, regardless of the *merdoso* weather, I felt like I had a beam of sunshine directly above me at all times. I was on cloud nine. Last night had been one of the best nights of my life, and the pep in my step made that obvious to everyone around.

I didn't think I'd wake up feeling so damn happy. And I certainly wasn't expecting that euphoria to last well into my day, but sure enough, it did. Even Candice noticed something when I walked into her office.

"You... did you get fucked?"

*Merda... was I walking like a penguin?*

I huffed. "Again with the assumption. What if I was the one who did the fucking?"

"We've talked about that ass of yours."

I laughed, nodding my head. "It was a night in *paradiso*, Candice." I brought my fingers to my lips, kissing them. "Perfetto. I couldn't have dreamed of a better night."

"Damn, that good, huh?"

"Very good. And not only the sex—everything about the night was great. From the time we spent walking through a museum of dildos and sex dolls, to the time we spent talking until we fell asleep."

"Oh, stop it," Candice said, her bright red nails flashing through the air. "You had me at dildos and sex dolls." She laughed, pushing back from her desk and standing up from her chair. She was looking real sharp in an all-white pant suit. "It sounds like you found someone special. I can see it in your eyes."

"I feel it, too."

"Plus," she said, glancing at her watch, "you came in walking like a penguin."

"I did not."

She ignored my statement. "I've got a meeting with the Millers now in five minutes. Did you figure anything out on your case? The one with the murdered couple?"

I shook my head. "Nothing. If anything, the trail is starting to lead back to Ricky."

"Shit."

"Yeah." I rolled my neck, joints popping in response. Candice collected some things from her desk before turning to the full-length mirror propped against the wall. "But still," I continued, "there's no solid evidence pointing to Ricky, unless the prosecution is going to come out with some surprise."

"Is there anything they can surprise you with?"

I nodded, my lips pursed. "He had a one-night stand with the husband."

Candice's well-done eyebrows shot up. "Double shit."

"But I figured that out through Zane's investigating. I still don't think other people know about it."

"Still, you want to get ahead of it."

"Exactly." I shook my head, walking with Candice toward the door to her office. "Zane is interviewing the sister of the murdered woman now. Hopefully she remembers something."

"Hopefully." Candice opened the door and entered the chaos of the hallway. I followed behind. Phones were ringing, lawyers were arguing, and printers were singing the song of their people. The meeting rooms were on the way to my office, so I walked next to Candice. "Just work your hardest and craft a bulletproof defense, regardless of what Zane brings back to you. You can't count on the sister knowing anything. If it were my sister, she'd probably be celebrating on a cruise to the Bahamas."

"You guys are still fighting?"

"When are we *not* fighting. I wish I had a good relationship with her, but we've just never clicked, and it only got worse with time. She lived with me for a few months."

"Yeah, I remember that."

"Right. I thought maybe the relationship was salvageable. Then I find out she was stealing from me and making moves on my boyfriend at the time. I could have killed the bitch."

A spark went off in the far corners of my mind. Like when a match runs against the striker but doesn't catch fire.

"Well," I said, letting the thought take shape but not still able to put the pieces together, "we'll see what Zane gets back with. I spent a few all-nighters researching comparable cases, and I've got a mock trial set up next Friday and another one the week after. The prosecution still doesn't have any solid evidence. No DNA or witnesses. But if they paint a dark enough picture of Rick, I'm scared that a video with a veiled threat would be enough."

We stopped in front of the glass doors that opened into the meeting room. "Let me know how it goes." She grinned at me, her light red lipstick perfectly painted on. "And don't go near any zoos. They might think one of their penguins escaped."

"Ha-ha," I said, tilting my head and turning to go toward my office. I exaggerated a penguin wobble for a few steps, hearing Candice laugh behind me.

\*\*\*

I checked the clock on the wall for the tenth time in the last five minutes. It felt like the seconds were crawling by. Something felt off. I couldn't pinpoint exactly what, but it was growing worse. From the clock, my eyes darted to my phone, lying screen up on my desk. I was expecting a text or call from Zane any minute now. His interview should have been over an hour ago. He'd been there for over two and a half hours already. It wasn't like he was going over with a book of questions he wanted to ask her. And I didn't think he was Netflix and chilling with her, either.

During those hours, my mind had been swirling around the case. I kept thinking about Luanne being in a fight the day Tito saw her, and my thoughts would then swing around to Candice. *"I could have killed the bitch."* Sibling rivalries could sometimes cut deep enough to take a life. What if Susan and Luanne were fighting in the days leading up to her death? That wouldn't necessarily make her the killer, but it would definitely be suspicious.

I wanted to talk to Zane about it. I wished I had thought of the possibility last night, when we were lying under the stars together, talking about the case. I hadn't thought of it, though. Zane said that the sisters seemed to have a good relationship, besides the discrepancy with Ricardo's description of Susan always being over.

I grabbed my phone and twirled it in a circle on my palm. The rain outside seemed to have gotten angrier, pounding harder against the glass. The wind was loud, and the lightning was striking more frequently. It was the perfect kind of weather to get back under my bedsheets with a naked Zane. I thought back to how great the night had been with him. Not just the sex, but everything else, too.

*Cazzo*, was the sex mind-blowing. But so was the conversation, how he opened up to me and revealed another layer of himself. And how I did the same with him. Speaking about what Ryan had done to me was cathartic. I felt so much better about it. I was also so much more willing to trust Zane, the man who was showing me that not everyone in the world was a fucking shithead.

I had to hear his voice. What the fuck was he doing with Susan for so long? He could step out for a minute to take my call. I'd apologize as soon as he answered. I didn't want to be needy or clingy or anything like that, but I was feeling unsettled and needed to hear his voice. That was all.

I called. It rang and rang. *Click*. Sent to voicemail.

I called again. This time it didn't even ring. Just went straight to voicemail.

*Cazzo.*

## 29  ZANE

My head was throbbing, as if someone had taken a hammer and a nail right to the left side of my scalp. I went to check and see if there was any blood, but to my surprise, I couldn't lift my hand. I couldn't move my feet, either. I was tied up with thick, rough rope. My arms were bent back behind the wooden chair, the rope cutting in tight around my wrists.

It took me a few more seconds to piece everything together: the moment that led up to the blackout, the realization, and the question that followed.

"Susan," I said, my voice shaky. I looked around. Thankfully, she hadn't blindfolded me. I was still in her living room, the lights all off except for a floor lamp next to the old couch. The rain was hammering against the window, harder than it had been before. A bright white light filled the room. A loud clap of thunder followed seconds later.

"Susan," I said again, my voice stronger. Another bright, hot flash. Another booming clap. "Susan, where are you?"

I craned my head left and right. My back was to the

hallway that led to the rest of the apartment. I felt vulnerable. The door was probably fifteen feet in front of me. I could shake the chair, try to tumble over, and maybe I'd be able to get loose like that. It would leave me even more open to an attack, though, if that was what Susan was planning. I had absolutely zero idea of where her mental state was currently at. She had killed her sister and brother-in-law, she was unstable and dangerous, and I was currently tied up like a fucking pig in her living room ready to get roasted.

"Susan." I could yell for help, but I didn't think that would do me much good. Her window was closed, and the neighbors wouldn't hear anything over the rain and wind.

"Sorry," I heard behind me. "I was getting things ready." Her footsteps sounded from down the hallway, moving toward me.

"What? What are you doing, Susan?"

"There's no other way out for me, Detective Holden." She sighed, still behind me. "Not unless you die tonight. Then I can start fresh. No one will know. I can leave everything behind me and try to move past things."

"Killing me isn't going to solve any of your problems, Susan. People know I'm here. They know you would have done it. My assistant knows your exact address."

"That's what I was getting ready." I felt a cold, thin blade press against the nape of my neck. Immediately, every hair on my body stood straight up. A primal chill crawled down my neck, constricting my spine as it traveled through my body. "It's a sad story," she continued, the blade pressing harder. "A grief-stricken girl is being interviewed by a big, handsome detective, when suddenly someone breaks into the apartment. A stalker. A man the girl's already complained to the police about. The big, handsome detective, he jumps up and goes to save the day. Instead, he gets stabbed. The girl is left behind, a crying mess, traumatized as the dead detective lies on the floor. So much loss. A GoFundMe page raises enough for the girl to never have to work again. She moves out of the country to avoid the stalker, never to be heard from again."

*Fuck.*

That was when cold dread started settling into my chest. She had a plan. She knew this was coming, and she was ready for it. I was at a massive disadvantage. I took a few deep breaths, trying to center myself before panic overtook me. I had to stay sharp if I was going to make it out of this.

And how badly I wanted to get out of this. My mind immediately went to Enzo. The smiling Italian Prince Charming straight out of my dreams. The man who fixed my shattered heart. I had a profound feeling that our story wasn't over, and yet, there I was, sitting with a psychotic woman holding a sharpened blade against the back of my neck.

A literal 'the end' to our story.

"People will figure it out," I said. "People will know."

"No one will know anything." The blade disappeared from my neck. I could feel her moving around me until she was standing in front of me. She was holding a long, slightly curved hunting knife in her left hand. Her face was bloody and bruised, a fresh gash on her forehead bleeding down her brow in a bright red trail. That's what she must have meant by getting ready.

"Trust me," she said, "I've made four reports of my stalker in the past month. The cops are probably surprised I'm even still alive with the reports I've given. I'll just stage a break-in after I kill you to really get all the details right." She smiled, her teeth pink with blood. "And they'll see that the crazy man slammed my head against the wall, leaving me unconscious while the entire thing happened. I couldn't call for help while you bled to death." Blood dripped off her chin. "I could tell you were onto things. I had to get ahead of you somehow."

I took another breath. Another man entered the forefront of my thoughts just then. Jose. My first love. The man who'd taught me so much about the world. He was in this position at one point, staring down at the grim reaper as he sharpened his scythe. I felt a deep sense of helplessness take root inside me. The same feeling my poor Jose must have felt when the Unicorn took his life, extinguishing such a bright light.

Something else filled me just then. Fight. I wasn't going to die before I found out who the Unicorn was, that was for sure. For Jose. And I wasn't going to die without seeing Enzo again.

No. I refused.

I *wasn't* going to die.

"Why, Susan? Why did you do it?" I had to get her talking. The most important factor ensuring my survival was time. The more time I got, the higher the chances were that I'd walk out of this alive.

"I thought you had it all figured out, Detective." Her pupils were blown, her hair a mess. I noticed there was a tremor in her hands. She stuffed them into the front pocket of the dirty gray sweater she was wearing, the blade disappearing inside.

"You and Oscar were together and you were jealous of your sister, so you killed them both?"

"Jealousy. What an emotion, huh?" She was shaking her head, her eyes pinning me down. All the while, my hands were fumbling at the rope, my fingers trying to find some kind of purchase. "Yes. I was jealous. But I was also furious, and I was broken and sad and I was *in love*. It was always supposed to be me and Oscar. From when we were kids, he was supposed to be mine. We were the ones who went off to play together for hours. We were the ones who our parents were sure would have the perfect life together. He was supposed to be *mine*."

So it was deeper than a recent affair. Susan had feelings for Oscar dating back years. Another lightning strike filled the room with stark white light, casting ominous shadows on the dirty white walls for a few brief seconds.

Something wasn't making sense, though. I figured another question was exactly what I needed to buy some time, and she seemed to be in the answering kind of mood. My eyes didn't break contact with hers. I didn't want her to think she was intimidating me. That would only give her more power than she already had over me.

"Wait, but Luanne was cheating on Oscar. Why would she be so possessive over him?"

She narrowed her eyes and cocked her head. "Oh, you didn't figure that part out, huh?"

My fingers froze their work when Susan's eyes dropped down, then quickly came back up to mine. "What was I missing?"

"They were in an open relationship. Both of them slept around. They just got off on keeping things secret, pretending like it was something they were doing behind the other's back. Luanne told me one day after she downed a bottle of wine. She also told me that the one woman in the world she said was off-limits to Oscar was me. *Me*. The woman who he fell in love with first. I was floored. By then, I'd already been sleeping with Oscar for a year, so it seemed like he wasn't much for her rules. She didn't know, though.

No. She didn't find out until that day at her house, when we got into a fight that left me with a bloody nose."

That made much more sense. She started pacing in front of me, making a straight horizontal line on the crusty beige carpet. "How did Luanne find out?"

"I told her." She looked up. "I was sick of it. Sick of hiding, sick of wondering. Wondering when Oscar was going to leave her."

"But you both seemed so close."

"I *was* close with her. I loved her. Admired her. Even when I was secretly with Oscar, I never took out my anger on her. Not until the end."

I could see something in her eyes. A weight. She had to have been haunted by what she did, even if she convinced herself somehow that she was in the right. Maybe I could take advantage of that. It was risky. Emotions were volatile, but I had to try. "You miss them, don't you. You regret what you did. I can see it."

"He told me he would leave her," she said, the rage that seethed in her soul manifesting in her voice. "He told me—he told me I was the one. I just had to wait a little longer. 'Keep waiting, dear. Just another month.'" She was shaking. "I couldn't wait any longer! I *couldn't*. I was at home and I was drinking and I was fed up, okay? I was done!" Her sadness and anger were palpable in the air. Her arms came out of the pocket, the knife practically glowing in the dim light. "When me and Luanne fought, she told me to stop. Told me that I was a dirty whore worth nothing but a fucking shitstain. She said exactly those words. I saw red. I couldn't stop. I loved Oscar since we were kids. He loved me. Then Luanne grew breasts before me, and all of a sudden, she was the apple of his eye. She stole him from me." Her eyes were wide. Her hand was shaking. My heart beat hard against my ribs. "I went over that night. Luanne left the key in that dumb frog, so I let myself in. I wanted to scare them. That was all. I wanted to scare Oscar, show him that I wasn't toying around, that he needed to leave Luanne or bad things would happen."

The rope around my wrists felt looser. My thumb and index finger were tugging at a frayed end. The bend in my wrist was beginning to pulse with pain, but I kept tugging at the rope, trying to keep the rest of my body as still as possible.

"But then I saw them in bed together, laying there, something I could never do with Oscar—just sleep next to him. Something came over me. I don't remember seeing anything. My vision went black. I shot them. Both. The silencer on the gun kept things quiet. Bought it off some thug leaving the police station so it wouldn't be trac—"

A loud ringtone interrupted her. My phone vibrated against my thigh, still inside my pants pocket. Her eyes darted down to my pocket. My hands were almost free. If only I had a couple more minutes.

"Let's see who's calling." She walked over, the steel of the knife glinting menacingly. She reached into my pocket without walking around me. Thank God. I couldn't let her notice the knot on my wrist was loosening.

"Hm," she said, checking the phone. "Lorenzo. Oh, he's a cutie." She turned the phone toward me. Enzo's smiling face was looking back at me. It was a picture I had snapped a couple of weeks ago. Enzo was sitting in my living room, sunlight beaming on his face, shirtless, a silver chain hanging on his neck. The phone started to ring again. She rejected the call. "I better get this party started before your little lover boy shows up."

My hands were almost free. I could almost slip one out,

but I couldn't do it yet without making it obvious. Just a little longer.

"Susan, think about this."

"I already have," she said. For a second, I thought she was going to drop my phone to the floor, but instead, she started walking behind me. "I have to remember to wash this. Don't want to leave any fingerprints on it."

Shit. She was behind me. I heard her set the phone on a counter. My hands went stone-still. I held them together, tight, so that she wouldn't see a gap between them.

"Well, well, well," she said.

Shit. Shit. Shit.

"When were you going to tell me your binds needed tightening, huh? I've gotta kill you first before I set the scene."

I felt the bonds tighten again, the rope chewing into my already raw skin.

Shit.

## 30  ENZO

*Cazzo.* The frustration inside me was reaching a boiling point. I didn't have any kind of confirmation that Zane was in danger, but the feeling in my gut wasn't a pleasant one, and it made me nervous. He wasn't answering his phone, and that was odd. Even if he were in an interview that was lasting way past the scheduled time, I felt like he'd still give me a heads-up about how he was doing. I wasn't even needing a full-on call; he could have sent me a simple text message saying "talk soon" and that would have put me at ease. But there was radio silence, and it wasn't like Zane.

Fuck. Fuck. Fuck.

I paced my office and checked my watch, giving myself five more minutes. Three more minutes. One more minute.

Still nothing. I picked up my phone and sent him another text message. "Zane, I'm getting worried."

I considered dialing 911 but ruled it out. Even if I called Andrei, Zane's brother, I don't think he would have taken me very seriously. No, the cops wouldn't do anything. Zane hadn't been missing long enough for a missing person's report to be opened, and it wasn't like the cops were very fond of me to begin with. I couldn't go to the police.

But then what was I supposed to do? I felt it. Down in my gut. I *knew* something was wrong. The air around me felt weird. Thick. Like even the atmosphere was telling me Zane was in danger.

It was up to me. I was about to do something crazy, but something my mamma would be damn proud of me over. I was going to pull a page out of her book and show up to where Zane was supposed to be. She had done that a couple of times to me back in high school, showing up at a party unannounced, looking to make sure I did my homework. I never knew how she figured out the address, but she had her ways. I assumed it was witchcraft.

Unfortunately, it didn't seem like magical powers ran in the family. I needed to figure out Susan's address somehow. Zane only told me he was seeing her and mentioned that she lived in Brooklyn, but that was only a start, and a flimsy one at that. I did have one idea, though. Someone who may have known Zane even better than I knew him sometimes.

I unlocked my phone and dialed Stonewall Investigations.

"Stonewall Investigations, how can I help you?"

"Andrew, just the guy I needed." He was Zane's friendly and sharp-witted assistant; he had to know Susan's address. "It's Enzo. Have you talked to Zane in the past few hours?"

"Nope, figured his interview ended and he was hanging out with you."

"Yeah, that's what I was hoping, too. He hasn't picked up my calls or answered my texts."

I heard Andrew clicking on his computer, most likely

pulling up the schedule to try to track down his boss. "Hmm."

"What's Susan's address?"

"Huh?"

"Her address. I want to drive by and make sure things are okay."

There was a pause on the line. "Enzo, I'm not sure I'm allow—"

"Andrew, I just want to check on things, that's all."

I could hear him take a deep breath. I looked out the window of my office. There was a sea of dark gray clouds dumping a torrent of rain on the city. Lightning struck somewhere, filling the room with harsh white light.

"Okay, you got a pen and paper?"

I hurriedly grabbed a pen, almost tipping over the metallic holder, and snatched a yellow sticky note. "Go ahead."

\*\*\*

I decided to take my car to the address Andrew had given me. I couldn't risk getting stuck on a subway, especially since Zane was still completely silent. Real worry was beginning to set in. It was starting to make sense, too—Susan being the one who did it. Oscar was cheating on Luanne with more than just Ricky, and Susan ended up catching feelings. She shot them both in the chest. How poetic.

It also meant that this woman was dangerous. I had to be careful. I wasn't trained for this kind of stuff. I could easily disarm someone in the courtroom, but disarming someone in real life, that was entirely different. As I was driving, I began to get flashbacks of that night a month ago, the night Zane had rescued me.

*Cristo.* It felt like that had happened years ago.

The fear I had felt that night, so primal, so frigidly cold, was starting to creep up on me again. I had to be stronger than it, though. I focused on the road, made a mess by the downpour that had my windshield wipers working on overtime. At some points, I had to lean over the steering wheel to make sure I wasn't about to drive over a curb.

Finally I made it to the address, my fear still trying to find some kind of purchase. I looked around, noticing a police station across the street. But something else caught my attention. Through my rain-battered window, I could make out Zane's car. I knew it was his because he had that black-and-white decal of a Tardis on the rear windshield. It was a reference to a show I was surprised he watched, one that had been pretty big in my life as well.

I quickly found a parking spot and jumped out of the car, holding my jacket above my head to try and avoid getting drenched. I completely forgot to grab the umbrella from the office in my rush to get here.

I hurried up the steps to Susan's building. It felt endless, and I almost tripped on the last one. The wind was making sure I got drenched, rain slicing almost horizontally. Thunder boomed above me as I threw the heavy door to the building open. There wasn't an intercom system, so I didn't need to get buzzed in.

The building was old, its decor tired. The stairs leading up to the three floors above were cracked and wooden, the red carpet getting pulled up in various spots. It smelled musty, almost like a swamp, which I assumed the rain didn't help with. I shook my jacket and set it down on a table by the mailboxes.

Susan was in apartment 310, so I started up the creaking stairs, taking two at a time. I ran into the hall that opened up on the third floor. She was the last apartment in the hallway.

*Thump. Thump. Thump.*

My heart was in my throat. The fear had found a place to hook into. My gut felt like it was getting shredded with anxiety. This all felt so wrong.

I reached her door. I raised my hand to knock but pulled back. The door was already open. In fact, it looked as if it had been forced open. There were screws on the floor, as if someone had used tools to take out the doorknob, maybe to pry the door open.

"Zane," I called out, pushing the door open even wider.

What I saw didn't make sense to me at first. My eyes immediately went to him, but my brain couldn't process what I was seeing.

There he was. My Zane, lying in a pool of blood, sprawled on the floor. His eyes were closed, his hands to his side. He looked like he was sleeping. He had to have been sleeping. That was it. That was all.

My legs started to move while my brain was catching up. "Zane, Zane, hey, Zane, I'm here, Zane." I kept saying his name, more loudly as I bent down to hold him. I had to stop the bleeding. Apply pressure to the wound. That's what I had to do. That was it.

All I had to do.

I scanned his body, looking for the source. His shirt was soaked in crimson. I peeled it back. His chest. A stab wound, still pushing out blood.

"Zane, Zane." I tore off my shirt and bundled it up. I pushed it down onto him. He was just sleeping. That was all.

Police. Needed to call for help.

One hand stayed down on Zane, my shirt quickly turning red. I reached into my pocket and grabbed my phone. Blood stained the glass. I tapped out 9-1-1. The woman who answered sounded like Barbra Streisand, I noted. One of Zane's favorite singers. I told Barbra Streisand exactly where we were, why we needed help. She said help was on the way.

The police station was just across the street. They'd be here—

"Oh my..."

A voice sounded from behind me. It was faint. I whipped around. A woman, bleeding from her forehead, was getting up from the ground. Susan. She was looking at me with wide eyes, the kind of eyes a doe gives when a semi is barreling toward her. Fear.

"No, no," she said, a hand coming up to her mouth. "He tried saving me. Oh God. Please, no."

"Save you?" It sounded like someone else was speaking, not me. Was that Barbra still on the phone?

"My stalker. He broke in while Zane was interviewing me. Oh no, no. I can't lose someone else."

She looked shaken to the core. I turned back to Zane. His eyes were closed, his skin pale. He was still breathing. "Come, help me hold this. We can save him."

Susan stood there.

"Now!"

She burst into action, running to Zane's other side and kneeling down, adding to the pressure.

"Come on, Zane. You'll be okay. Just wake up." I couldn't feel the tears that slid down my face, only saw them as they fell down onto Zane's.

"Come on, come on."

Sirens. Police were so close.

"Go grab extra towels," Susan said, nodding toward her bathroom. She was looking at the open door. "We need more towels."

I didn't want to leave his side. I didn't give a fuck about towels.

"Go get them," she said, sounding more insistent.

I looked down. *Wake up. Wake up. Wake u—*

"Zane!" His eyes were fluttering open. Susan stood up. I looked at her, angry. She had a job to do.

"Enzo," Zane rasped. He coughed. "She did this."

Instantly, I knew. Everything clicked.

"Shit," Susan hissed, looking down at the both of us, her face twisting into something resembling contempt. "I really thought he was dead."

She was turning to bolt. She was about to run right out of the room, possibly escape. I wasn't going to let that happen. I exploded into action, jumping up like a fucking great white going after a seal. My arms were wide as I flew through the air, and I clamped them around her and threw us both to the hard ground, landing with a thud on Susan's side. She struggled underneath me, kicking and spitting like a rat inflicted with rabies.

"Fuck, it was going to all work out. Fuck," she spat as she kicked out, hitting a side table and almost splitting the cheap wooden leg in half.

Footsteps sounded down the hallway. The police. Help was here.

I continued holding her down. Someone came up to us and lifted us both.

"What's going on here?" the man said, his voice commanding the scene.

"She stabbed him," I said before Susan could spew any of her lies.

*Zane.* I ran to him. The EMTs ran in right after the police and immediately started work on stabilizing him. I held on to his hand. His eyes were still open. The EMTs were saying something, but all I heard was Zane. His voice was soft. "I love you."

"Mio amore. I love you. You're going to be okay, Zane. I promise." I looked to the blonde EMT, her concentration laser focused on stabilizing Zane. "Right? He's going to be okay, right?"

"The stab wound appears to have missed any vital organs," she said.

That wasn't really an answer, but I took it anyway. I kept holding his hand, memorizing the feeling, committing it to heart, never wanting to let go again. It felt like I held on to Zane's hand from the second the police got there, to the moment he was being laid down onto the stretcher.

It was when Zane was taken into surgery that the immensity of the situation hit me, threatening to crush me under its weight. I had to step outside of the hospital while I was waiting, even though the day was still shitty and raining, I couldn't be inside. I couldn't sit there not knowing how Zane was doing.

Needless to say, I was overjoyed when the doctor found me to tell me that Zane had made it out of surgery and was in stable condition. He said that Zane was tired but awake, and that a five-minute visit wouldn't cause any harm.

I hurried to the recovery room. The elevator felt like it took decades to get to me. When it opened on his floor, I hurried out and searched for his room. When I found it, the door was ajar, and so I pushed it open, then walked into a small room with a single hospital bed and a window that was streaked with rain. A television was hung on the wall, playing *NCIS* on mute. I looked to the bed and saw Zane, color back in his cheeks. He looked like a mess, but a mess that was alive.

I broke down. This time, I was well aware of the tears that streamed down my face. "Zane. My bello Zane. I thought I lost you." I went to his side, my feet moving on autopilot. He smiled at me. Actually smiled. It wavered a little, but he managed to keep it on his face. A machine monitoring his vitals beeped next to the bed.

"I'm not going anywhere," he said, looking up at me. I bent down and kissed him softly on the lips.

"Bene," I said, feeling my heart swell with a gratitude I'd never felt before. It was deep and profound and lifted by the powerful love I felt for Zane. "Neither am I."

# EPILOGUE

**Zane**
*Four Months Later*

I was woken up from a hazy dream by the morning sunlight breaking in through Enzo's bedroom window. He had thick, dark red shades, but there was a slit down the center that allowed the light to sneak in and land right on my face. I stretched underneath the covers, rolling over and throwing an arm over a still-sleeping Enzo. He could sleep on the sun itself, it didn't matter how much light there was. I joked that his eyelids must have been abnormally thick. He'd then joke that his eyelids weren't the only thick thing about him.

I smiled as I pulled myself closer to Enzo. There were butterflies in my stomach, as if they had been asleep with me, waiting until the second I woke up to activate. Today was a big day, one I'd been looking forward to for months now. Since the second I walked out of the hospital, really. I knew that I wouldn't be able to wait for much longer after that.

We were both naked under the soft white covers. I could feel his body heat mixing with mine. It had my morning wood throbbing against Enzo's ass. I kissed the back of Enzo's head and glided my hand up and down his side. He was starting to stir. My hand stopped on his hip before dropping, my fingers feeling Enzo's hardness before closing around it. I gave a few slow, lazy strokes. He gave a small, sleepy moan and started to gyrate his ass, softly at first, onto my hard dick. I pushed myself into his crack while I continued jerking him off and kissing the back of his neck, using my teeth to graze over the sensitive skin before sucking it into my mouth. He was moving harder onto me, moaning more frequently. Sleep was giving way to lust. He was tilting his head, giving me access to more of his neck.

I sucked a little harder, moving my hips more, my cock leaking onto Enzo's ass.

"Good morning," he said with a moan as he rolled over onto his other side so that he was facing me. His eyes were still cloudy with sleep, and his hair was messy from the pillows. He looked so fucking cute. I was so grateful that I got to see Enzo's face every morning. I went in for a kiss, unable to resist. Underneath the covers, our legs entwined and our cocks pressed together, intense heat emanating from the both of them. I brought a hand up to Enzo's head.

"Good morning," I said into the kiss. Meaning it down to the core. Every day I woke up next to Enzo was guaranteed to be a good morning. Our tongues were soft and slow at first, warming up from a night of great sleep. I pushed my hips forward, rubbing more of myself on him. I could feel my stomach getting sticky and wet from our mixed excitement.

"You're so sexy in the mornings," I said when we broke from the kiss, a hungry smile on my lips.

"Just in the mornings?" Enzo asked, reaching down and grabbing me in both his hands.

"You make me hard twenty-four seven, Enzo."

"Bene," he said, slowly stroking me. "That's what I like to hear." He grabbed both our cocks in his hands. I closed my eyes, enjoying every single second of this.

"Keep going," I moaned, loving how it felt when he jerked us both off. He listened and continued his strokes, holding a little tighter. My balls ached. I pulled away before I blew too early. I hadn't even put him in my mouth yet.

"Come here," I said, propping myself up on the bed and throwing the comforter aside so that we were both exposed. I moved lower on the bed, admiring Enzo's body on the way: the light covering of hair, the soft rise of his stomach, the biteable thighs that were wide open, giving me more than enough space to kneel between. Oh, how I loved this man's body. I fucking cherished it. Every day, I felt blessed to have him, to be able to kiss him. Especially after I stepped onto Death's doorstep, only to turn around at the last second. That gave me a brand-new appreciation on basically everything in my life. And if I ever forgot about that appreciation for some reason, I had a five inch scar on my chest that served as a permanent reminder.

I bent down, sucking him into my mouth. He gave a deep moan and stretched out his legs. My tongue swirled around his head, rubbing over the sensitive slit, tasting his sweetness and wanting so much more. He throbbed between my lips, my own cock responding in kind. I started jerking myself off with one hand while my other went to work on Enzo, stroking whatever real estate my tongue couldn't cover. Enzo was one gifted man. I didn't have to wonder where the term "Italian stallion" came from, that was for sure. He was hung, and I couldn't get enough of it.

I tried fitting as much as I could into my mouth, looking up to see a blissed-out Enzo, his head pushing back on the pillow. His hands came up to my head as his legs rose up as well. I knew what was coming. And I wanted it. I craved it.

With purchase on the bed and his hands on the back of my head, Enzo started thrusting upward while simultaneously pushing my head down onto his cock, fucking my face and driving me absolutely wild. He went faster, his cock pushing deeper down my throat. I was getting teary-eyed, but I wanted more. He kept going, groaning and saying something in Italian I couldn't make out.

When he stopped and I came up for air, his cock was left soaked, a rope of saliva dripping down onto his groin. He reached down and used it as lube, but instead of using it to stroke himself, his fingers slipped down between his ass. He looked up at me and licked his lips, a sight that almost made me blow right then and there.

"I need you inside me, Zane."

That was all I needed. I reached over and opened up the drawer in the bedside table. Inside was a sleek black bottle of lube. I grabbed it, the already slippery bottle almost slipping out of my grip.

"Cazzo, you're so sexy, Zane." Enzo was practically purring as he watched me squirt some of the lube on my cock. I stroked, spreading it on myself before pouring some more on my hand and rubbing it between Enzo's legs, all over. I grabbed his cock, stroked, and then went down to his balls. He moaned and lifted his ass up from the bed, giving me the space I needed to slip a hand down beneath him, my finger curling and finding his tight hole.

"Ohhh," Enzo said as he ground his ass down on my

lubed finger, his hole already taking me in deep, my finger disappearing inside him. My cock was throbbing in the air, ready to be buried inside my man. I slipped my finger out. He looked so hot, lying there for me, his dick hard and leaking. I grabbed his legs and lifted them onto my shoulders. I kissed his leg as I moved forward on the bed, pressing my cock up to his hole. We had gotten tested together and left the condoms behind the second we got our results.

Sinking into Enzo was pure, unadulterated bliss. The kind of stuff a drug addict feels after their first hit. Except this was how I felt every time we made love. It was always such an intense high. Especially when I was looking down on him, our eyes locked, his mouth agape as my cock sunk in deeper, past the head. I could feel the warmth spread. He was so tight, and the heat was insane.

"Oh fuck," I hissed, pushing myself in until I was balls-deep. I held myself there for a moment, leaning down so that I could kiss Enzo, relishing in his warmth.

"I love you," I whispered to him. I began to slowly move my hips.

"I love you, too, Zane." He was looking me straight in the eyes. Our lips met again. My hips moved faster as we became one. I righted myself back up and held on to Enzo's legs as I began to go even faster.

"Yeah, Zane, yes. Faster, bello. Faster."

I gave him exactly what he asked for. I started pounding into him, driving myself deep with every thrust, picking up my pace so that the room was echoing with the sound of our bodies slapping together. His cock bounced against his stomach. Enzo grabbed himself and started jerking off while I continued to fuck him. I looked down, watching my cock get lost inside of Enzo. I could feel myself getting closer and closer.

"Cazzo, Zane, right there. Oh, fuck, I'm going to come, baby."

"Do it. I want to see you come all over your chest."

"Yeah?"

Seeing him so close to coming was all I needed to launch myself over the edge. "Fuck, Enzo, you're going to make me come."

"Fill me, Zane." His eyes were burning with a passion I found hotter than anything else. My head fell back and let out an animalistic grunt. My thrusts became erratic as my cock began to explode inside of Enzo's ass. I plunged myself in deep, plugging Enzo, opening my eyes to see him coming all over his chest, just like how I wanted. I could feel him tightening around me with every blast. It was almost enough to make me come twice, back-to-fucking-back.

When it was all over and I was sure I wasn't going to spontaneously pass out, I collapsed onto Enzo, kissing him and relishing the feeling of having him underneath me, our bodies still shaking with aftershocks. We were both catching our breaths. The morning sun felt like a spotlight, and we had just given one of the best performances of our lives. Well, until the encore. Then I was sure that performance would only top the last. And so on and so on.

"Good morning," I repeated again, sounding much more awake than I had earlier.

"Excellent morning," Enzo said, *also* sounding way more awake.

"Well, get ready, because the day's only going to get better."

"Oh really?" Enzo asked. "I'm having a hard time seeing how."

"You'll see," I said, smiling.

*He really has no idea what I have planned, does he?*

\*\*\*

## ENZO

I had absolutely zero fucking idea of what Zane had planned for us. The concrete jungle rose up around us as Zane drove through the busy streets, which he'd been doing for the past hour or so.

"Are you trying to throw me off?" I asked, when he had made the same left turn twice in the span of ten minutes.

"What? No, relax."

It was a Saturday, so everyone was out and about. It was a bright, breezy spring day with plenty of big, puffy clouds crossing the blue sky above. I was trying to figure out where Zane was driving to, but he kept taking weird side streets, and his driving pattern didn't really make any sense. At one point, I thought we were heading toward the Bronx; another moment I thought we were about to get on the bridge to Jersey.

I didn't really know what Zane had planned, but I was going along for the ride, regardless. I had found that closing my eyes and doing what Zane told me to do usually ended up with the both of us being very happy, so what was one more time?

I looked over to Zane. He was looking incredibly handsome in a light blue short-sleeved button-up shirt, his strong biceps pressing against the fabric of the shirt. He had gotten a haircut a few days ago, short on the sides and a little longer on the top. I reached across the center panel and put a hand on his thigh, giving it a good squeeze before Zane's hand came to find mine.

"Still don't know what we're doing?" he asked.

"No idea."

"Okay, good." He pulled the car into a dingy parking

lot. I looked around but couldn't really figure out where we had gone. We pulled into a spot when Zane's phone started ringing. He glanced at the screen, and his brows drew together.

"Huh?" I asked, sensing something was up.

"It's Collin. Weird he'd call me on his day off."

"Pick up," I said. Collin was the detective assigned to work on the Unicorn case. Everyone at Stonewall had their eyes and ears open to any clues of who the monster could be, but Collin was the one Zane had chosen to take the lead.

"Hey, Collin, what's going on?" I watched Zane's facial expression change from curiosity to disappointment to anger. Collin's voice was loud, but not loud enough to make out any clear words.

"Fuck, okay. Keep me updated." Zane hung up and slipped the phone back into the pocket of his dark jeans.

"What was that?" I asked, curiosity piqued.

"Nothing, nothing."

I arched a brow. "Didn't sound like nothing."

Zane sighed. "I didn't want to dampen the mood, but the police found another Unicorn victim."

"Merda." My head dropped back on the headrest. The last time the Unicorn struck was six months ago. It was long enough for the community to start letting down their guard, which was probably exactly what the Unicorn wanted.

"Let's not get hung up on evil right now." Zane started getting out of the car. I followed, still unsure of what the hell was going on.

"Did he have any details?" I asked as we walked toward the street.

"We'll get the full rundown later," Zane replied, clearly wanting to change the subject. I looked around, trying to pinpoint exactly where Zane had taken me.

"Okay," he said. "Before we keep walking, you have to put this on." He reached into his pocket and pulled out a thick black cloth. I looked from the cloth dangling in his hand to him and cocked my head, my heart rate starting to pick up a bit. What the hell was Zane planning?

I stood there while he tied the velvet cloth to my face, covering my eyes and blocking out all the light.

"Okay, I can't see anymore," I confirmed. Zane's hand went on my lower back and started to guide me.

"Perfect," I heard him say from my left. "Just how I wanted."

"That doesn't sound sadistic whatsoever."

Zane chuckled as he continued to lead me. He grabbed my hand, and we walked, and walked, and walked. It felt weird, walking through the streets with the sounds and scents suddenly emphasized. "Are we even still in New York?"

"Yup," Zane said. Finally, we started to slow down. I had only tripped about fifteen times trying to get to wherever spot Zane was leading us to.

"Okay," he said. "Finally, we're here." I could hear the smile in his voice. I could also hear a bunch of other people around me. There was the loud sound of conversation, and was that... an opera singer?

"Enzo," he started. I felt him walk behind me, his hand leaving mine and trailing across my lower back. He reached up and I felt my blindfold come loose. The next thing I knew, the blindfold was off and the sun was beating into my eyes. I shut them before I could get used to it.

When I opened my eyes again, I immediately recognized where we were. The Bethesda Fountain, a statue of an angel with her wings spread, was spouting water in front of me. It was one of the iconic symbols of Central Park built back in the eighties.

That's why Zane had to blindfold me. There'd be no other way to get me toward the center of Central Park without me knowing otherwise.

But the fountain was different. There were rose petals, a bed of them, floating in the water. And that wasn't where the roses stopped. There were petals on the ground as well. And they were laid out in a peculiar shape. They spelled out words. They...

"Enzo," Zane said again. Realization of what was happening hit me in the face. "The second I met you, I knew you were the one who'd teach me to love again. I may not have admitted it in that moment, but there was no denying it. Deep down, I knew. Then life threw us a few curveballs, and we handled them like experts. Expert ball handlers." We both laughed at that. Zane dropped down to one knee. My heart was in my throat. Behind him, the rose petals spelled out the one question I knew was on its way.

"You showed me that love doesn't die, Enzo. A lesson I would have never learned if you hadn't come into my life when you did." His eyes were getting wet. Were mine? Were those tears I felt going down my cheeks?

"Enzo, the love of my life," he said, looking up at me with those eyes that told a thousand love stories, written only for me. In his hands was a velvet navy blue box holding a matte silver wedding band. "Will you marry me?"

I didn't hesitate. "Yes," I said. "Sì!" I was laughing and teary-eyed and an overall mess, but I was also *happy*. More than happy. I was over the moon, to the stars, *past* the stars. Zane slipped the silver ring on and got up from the floor, pulling me into an embrace, our lips meeting to seal the deal. I thought I heard clapping and cheering, but all I could focus on was the man who completed me in every single way.

THE END

IF YOU ENJOYED Zane and Enzo's story, consider listening to it on audio, narrated by the incredibly talented Greg Boudreaux!

Receive access to a bundle of my **free stories** by signing up for my newsletter!

Tap here to sign up for my newsletter.

Be sure to connect with me on Instagram and TikTok **@maxwalkerwrites.**

WANT EVEN MORE MAX? Then join Max After Dark for exclusive stories, audio excerpts, chat room, and much more.

Happy Reading!
Max Walker
Max@MaxWalkerWrites.com

A LETHAL LOVE

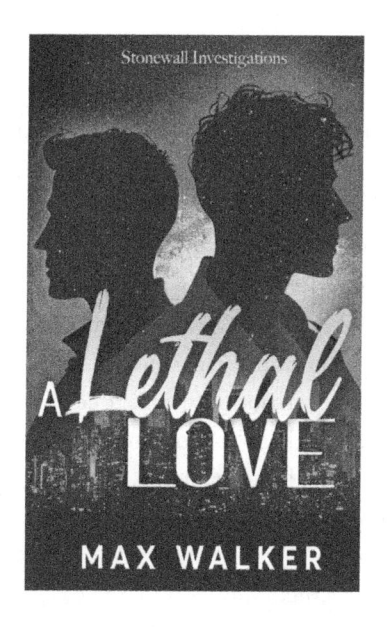

## CHAPTER 1- GRIFFIN

There shouldn't have been so much blood. *Fuck*. There shouldn't have been *any* blood. Why was there so much blood? It was a deep red, almost maroon. A pool on the floor next to her, reflecting the light from above. It was a color I'd immediately come to hate. There was a smell, too. A scent that stung my nose and rolled my stomach. Like a metal tang, something rusting in the air. My head hurt. Pounded. I looked around the room trying to establish where I was. The familiar eggshell-white walls of my brownstone were surrounding me. There was a handprint on the far wall, as red as the blood on the floor.

Underneath the handprint was Veronica, my roommate.

My dead roommate.

*Holy shit.*

*Fuck. Fuckity fuck fuck.*

She was dead. There was no question about it. She had been wearing a white shirt that was soaked through in the dark red. The shirt was sliced at the chest, where it appeared she had been stabbed. There were a handful of other stab wounds across her body. Her skin was a bluish white and her eyes were wide open and—my lunch shot up my esophagus. I swallowed it back down.

I was laying down on the couch, looking at my dead roommate, my head throbbing as if it had been hit a hundred times with a hammer.

Full panic flooded through me. I stood up. Slipped. Fell hard on my ass. That was when I realized I slipped on blood. My brain was firing off nerves that had been fried, their ends burned to a crisp. Like live wires that whipped around in a storm, frayed and broken, sparking, searching for a connection that made sense but finding nothing. That's always how my brain felt after the medication.

Especially when I followed the meds with wine. Lots of wine. Red wine. Almost as red as the blo—

Police. I needed to call the police.

But, wait! Tires screeched inside the folds of my brain. *They're going to think I did this. What am I going to say?*

It didn't matter. She was dead. In my apartment. What the fuck else would I do? I looked around for my phone, spotting it on the far end of the couch.

Shit... what happened before I blacked out?

The phone was in my hand, my fingers moving over the numbers automatically. Nine-one-one. A sweet-sounding guy answered. I'm sure I sounded much less sweet.

"My roommate!" I yelled louder than I thought I would. "She's dead. I don't know what happened. I was, uh, shit. I was—"

*Passed the fuck out.*

"Sir? Is the location you're in safe? Just you and the deceased?"

*Deceased. Shit. Fuckity fuck.*

"Yes." *As if that doesn't seem at all suspicious.* "I—it wasn't me. I don't know what happened. I blacked out."

"That's okay. Just stay calm, police will be there shortly."

I stumbled back, away from the blood. I hit a wall with my back. I hadn't even noticed I was moving. Slowly, the floor rose to greet me. Or did I sink down to it? Couldn't really tell anymore. Everything was still fuzzy; nothing made sense. The sharpness that came from the adrenaline wasn't sharp enough to cut through the fog completely.

What had happened? Why was Veronica dead?

I didn't... no, I couldn't have. Never.

Not unless...

Sirens sounded through my living room. The window was open, letting in all the noise from outside. I lived in a brownstone in Chelsea, Manhattan. It was just me and Veronica, who had moved in only two weeks earlier. No one else was inside from the last thing I remember, which was... what were we doing?

Shit. I couldn't remember.

The sirens were louder now, directly outside the window. I got up, surprised I was able to stand with how shaky my legs were.

Legs. That's right! Veronica was practicing a dance routine she was going to do for an audition. I was watching her, drinking on the couch, pointing out when she'd miss a step. That was at... one in the afternoon. She had the audition at four. And it was now... fuck, eleven o'clock at night.

---

THE POLICE STATION STANK. There were homeless people, drunk people, regular people here for who only knew what. Overall, it was a shit time. All compounded by the fact that I had woken up to my roommate dead in the living room.

It still wasn't fully hitting me. Maybe I was still in shock. Maybe it was the mix of alcohol and medication still numbing my system. I'd realize what happened in slow bursts. The ride to the station had me bursting out into random cries. I pulled myself together, though, insisting we would find whoever did this. I had been scared that the cops would accuse me of doing it, but thankfully, the two officers that showed up seemed compassionate and willing to help. They sounded like they believed my story, as crazy as it sounded while I was saying it.

*Seriously. I need to stop doing this. Drinking. Blacking out.*

At the station, the two officers walked me to a room I assumed was reserved for interrogations. Lucky for my sanity, there was a window in this room. I hated tight spaces, so being able to look out at the police parking lot helped calm me down a bit. It was dark out, the streetlamps on and glowing their orange light down onto the hoods of the police cars.

It felt like another two hours before anyone came into the room. It was a police officer, but I didn't know this guy. He was dressed in a regular navy polo shirt and dark jeans. I knew he was a cop by the badge hitched onto the waist of his jeans. He had big bushy brows that framed intense brown eyes. He had a couple of scars on his forearms and face. He'd obviously seen some shit.

Well, guess I'd seen some shit now, too.

*Fuck... I need a beer. Just one beer.*

It still didn't fully click into place. Drinking was what

had me sitting in this dingy police station. If I hadn't opened that bottle, I wouldn't have blacked out...

*I'm going to need one to go to sleep tonight.*

"Griffin Banks."

"Yes," I replied, even though the cop's tone didn't sound like he was asking anything.

"I'm Detective Dawson. Want to tell me what happened tonight?"

I was sitting in an uncomfortable chair on one side of a sturdy white table. The cop took the seat across from me, his chair scratching against the big gray tiles underneath. My head pounded. Exhaustion was overcoming the adrenaline. Someone outside the room was yelling something about the Illuminati. I wanted to cry and sleep and drink, although I wasn't sure exactly in what order.

"I mixed up my medication with my liquor. I blacked out for something like eight hours. When I woke up, Veronica was dead."

"How often do you mix the meds with alcohol?"

"Not often." We both knew that was a lie. The detective sat back in the chair. He had big brown eyes, the kind that made you feel at ease. But the way the rest of his face was set told me this guy wasn't someone who went easy on people. He looked like a bulldog chasing down a bacon strip. Something in my brain was trying to push forward in that moment, shouting at me, fighting for my attention but I just couldn't pinpoint it.

"Griffin," he said, his voice sounding as soft as his eyes. "You've gotta be upfront here. Honest. We want to help find who did this to your friend."

"Right, right." It was hitting me. Slowly. "Fuck." I coughed. Or was that a cry? "I, um... shit. I don't know what happened."

"When you woke up, do you remember seeing a murder weapon anywhere?"

My eyes widened. I hadn't even thought of that. Of how she died, and with what. It was bloody, and I was panicked. "No." I shook my head. "I didn't see anything."

"Hmm."

"Jesus... I don't even know. How did it happen?"

Dawson cocked his head, his eyes sparking. Something was replacing the warmth. Something else was shouting in the farthest parts of my brain. Louder. Getting louder.

"How?" I asked again.

"What was your relationship like with Veronica?"

"It was good. She needed a place to stay, so I offered mine. What happened to her, Detective?"

"That's what I'm trying to figure out." The spark in those warm brown eyes was transforming. His eyes narrowed as he scanned my face. I looked out the window, getting uncomfortable. The seat I was sitting on was getting hotter and hotter.

*Shit. Is the sun coming up? How long have I been here?*

I took a deep breath, feeling myself spiraling. I was a total mess; I'd been a mess for years, and now it was all catching up to me. If only I'd been awake. Not fucking blacked out like a newly initiated frat douche. Maybe I could have stopped whatever happened to Veronica. At the very least, I'd have been able to be more help.

*But wait... why was I left alive?*

The question hit me with the speed of a bullet train. Whoever killed Veronica decided to leave me behind. Why? Because they felt bad? Doubtful.

"Griffin." There was my name again. This time, it sounded like the detective was using his voice as a blunt object, banging it against my already aching head. "This isn't looking good. You have an excuse, but not necessarily an alibi. The murder weapon wasn't found, and there are no other witnesses. We've talked to neighbors, two of which weren't home and another who said they heard tires screeching away but didn't think much of it. So, whatever you can remember, whatever tiny detail you can pull up from your drug-addled brain, bring it up."

*Shit.* Realization washed over me as if someone had pulled down a lever and opened up the floodgates. I was suspect number one. Everything I said was being viewed through a suspicious lens. The detective wasn't on my side. He was on the side of getting answers, and I was sure that he'd force some of those answers if he wasn't finding them. I swallowed back what felt like a stone, dropping right down to my gut.

"I need to go."

"You need to answer my questions."

The bulldog was transforming into a pit bull. His face turned tight, the muscles in his jaw twitching as he pressed his teeth together. I was sweating. I adjusted in the uncomfortable seat, the legs sounding in protest underneath.

"Am I under arrest, Detective?" The question felt like bile in my mouth.

He waited a moment before answering. "No." He shifted his weight, looking directly at me. "We don't have enough. Yet."

The last bit sounded very much like a threat.

"I really hope you find whoever did this to Veronica," I said, meaning it with every single fiber of my damn being. The chair protested louder as I pushed back and got up. The world outside, through the window, seemed so inviting. The sun was breaking through the morning haze and painting the street a light blue, as though night still wanted to cling on.

I had to get out there. To fresh air. And then I had to get home, drink a beer or two, and knock the fuck out.

*Shit... I can't even go home. It's a goddamn active crime scene.*

Maybe this was all a really bad dream. Maybe I could go to a hotel, sleep after downing a bottle of wine, and then when I woke up, everything would be back to normal.

Hopeful, huh? Nah.

Even I knew that was mostly just dumb.

"Griffin, be available for more questions."

"Yeah, right," I replied. Dawson was standing now, his eyes drilling a hole through me. I knew the only reason I wasn't behind bars was because of who my father was. A regular Joe Schmo would probably have to be bailed out with the flimsy excuse I had. But I knew money talked in most situations, and sometimes money shouted loud enough to bring down entire police departments, and that meant the police would need an airtight case before chucking handcuffs on me. But that still didn't mean I was immune to being wrongly accused, and that part terrified the living shit out of me.

The detective walked me out of the station, telling me to call him the moment I remembered something. The pit bull in him seemed more restrained toward the end. His shoulders were less tense and his eyes less narrowed. But that didn't mean I could let my guard down. He was after something, and I could tell he wasn't going to give up until he got it.

Before ordering a car to take me to a hotel, I pulled up another number. I had to make a call. One of the only real friends I had, and that wasn't saying much seeing as I had to pay him a sky-high fee most times I talked to him.

"Ciao, Griffin, how are you?" my lawyer answered.

"Hi, Enzo." I sighed, wishing the ground would just split open and swallow me whole. "It's been a day."

## CHAPTER 2- ALEJANDRO

"*Coño!*" I cursed, jumping backward before the jar of marinara smashed on my toes. The glass shattered, flying in large shards across the tiled kitchen floor. Thick red marinara sauce exploded out from the center. The smell of basil and garlic and tomato sauce wafted up from the floor. I almost rolled my eyes but resisted the urge. It would be about the hundredth time I did it since I woke up thirty minutes ago, and I was sure that they'd get stuck by the hundred and first time.

Instead of grabbing myself a bowl of cereal, I cleaned up the mess and opened a vanilla protein drink after giving it a few good shakes. I took a few gulps and walked back to my bedroom, my muscles slowly waking up. By the time I had buttoned up a simple light-blue shirt, I could confidently say I was functioning at eighty percent.

Ninety once my pants came on.

My phone rang, clattering against my nightstand. I leaned over my bed and reached for the phone, grabbing it with the tips of my fingers and almost dropping it.

"Hello?" I said, seeing my mom on the caller ID.

"Hola, hijo. You're working today, right?"

"Yup. Why? Everything okay?"

"Great! Everything's great. Just wondering if you'd be home, that's all."

"Why?" I was becoming suspicious. The sounds of traffic in the background didn't ease those suspicions. Usually, my mother's residence wasn't filled with the sound of traffic horns. No, that sound was a city's signature, one I was very familiar with.

I glanced at the clock on my bedroom wall. It was 7:00. I liked getting to my desk by 7:30 at the latest. Aside from putting on my shoes, I was ready to go.

"Well..." my mom's voice sang on the other end of the phone.

"Just tell hi—"

"Shh! Coño, chico!" I could practically hear the slap on the chest my mom had just given my dad.

My doorbell rang. I cocked my head, my brows drawing together. "Mom..."

All I heard from the other line was a stifled laugh. That gave me all the confirmation I needed. I hung up the call and massaged the tension out of my forehead before getting up from the bed. I looked in the floor-length mirror set against the off-white wall, an exhausted face looking back at me. I definitely needed a haircut, which I'm sure my mother would remind me of the second I opened that door.

I wasn't even exhausted because of anything in particular. Life had just been so... *meh*. It was the same thing day in, day out, and that shit made me tired. Some people loved it. The monotony drove them. They enjoyed routine and thrived off it. Don't get me wrong, I didn't want to live life like a loose cannon, running around the city creating chaos. But I still wanted some excitement in my life, and I just wasn't getting it. Things were going fine, but nothing was going *great*.

I'd been working at Stonewall Investigations for two years now, and although I loved what I did, for the past few months I'd found myself on a streak of basic cases. Everyone who came to me wanted to know whether or not their partner was cheating on them, or if their neighbor was stealing their packages, or if their sexy personal trainer preferred boxers over briefs.

Okay, so obviously no one hired me to figure out underwear preferences for them, but damn, it was starting to feel that way. And the fact that my love life wasn't exactly full of fireworks and adventure meant that my main source of entertainment was mostly the gym and puzzle apps on my iPad.

I know, I know.

Such a thrilling life.

I left my bedroom and started toward the front door, knowing that the surprise my mom was talking about was sooner rather than later.

My apartment wasn't big. It wasn't a closet space either, though, thankfully. New York was definitely hard, especially when you weren't rolling in the dough. I didn't necessarily mind it. I didn't need a huge space to be happy. I liked living in a one-bedroom, seven-hundred-square-foot apartment. I found the place at a steal in Hell's Kitchen, a trendy area that was close enough to Stonewall Investigations I could bike there most days.

The small space did have its downsides, though, and I was about to experience one of the biggest ones. Guests.

Accommodating them was difficult, especially when they were my parents. We had a close relationship, but by age thirty-one, most men would have told their parents to go find a place to stay. But I didn't mind it as much so long as they didn't overstay their welcome. Maybe it was from going what we had to go through as a family that bound us stronger than most.

"Hola, mi hijo!" my mother said as soon as I opened the door, throwing her hands in the air before jumping forward to hug me. My dad was right behind her, smiling, his balding head reflecting some of the morning sunlight. "Ay, sorry if we're bothering you. I just wanted to surprise you. And then this one almost ruined it over the phone."

"Surprise!" my dad said, laughing and hugging me after my mom was done almost cracking all my ribs. When greetings were over, I helped them move their two rolling suitcases into the apartment.

"Okay, guys." I clapped my hands together. "Not a bother at all. Make yourselves at home. Mi casa es tu casa. I have to get to work, though, so you guys will have to find something to do in the meantime."

"That's okay, that's okay." My mom waved a hand in the air. I noticed her hair looked freshly colored, a really nice auburn brown, with waves of light brown running through. Her colorful bangles rattled on her wrist as she sat down on the couch. "Go, go. We'll see you tonight for dinner. We're only here for the day, then we fly down to Miami for a *sex* cruise."

"A what?" My eyebrows almost shot through the ceiling.

My mom started cracking up. "That's what your dad read on the brochure, and I haven't stopped laughing since he said it out loud."

My dad was turning bright pink. "My vision isn't like it used to be."

"Okay, well, I'll chip in to get you new glasses, then," I said, laughing at the two of them. They were always like this. Since I was a kid, they would always be teasing and joking with each other. It was fun to watch.

Well, maybe saying they were "always" like this was misleading.

"Bueno," I said, grabbing phone from the dining room table. "There's a great new Cuban place that opened up across the block, Mondo's Pizza, if you guys want a good lunch." I was slipping on my shoes. I chose the tan wingtips from the shoe rack by the door.

"Wait..." I said, stopping midway through the door. "Did you think it was a sex cruise before or after you booked it?"

My parents started cracking up then, and both turned a slight pink shade. I got the answer I never even needed and closed the door.

---

STONEWALL INVESTIGATIONS WAS LOCATED in a classic brownstone with emerald-green ivy clinging to the exterior. It was a narrow street, a bodega with some great sandwiches was on the corner, a great place for lunch when I wasn't in the mood for a walk. The sign above the heavy white door read Stonewall Investigations with a subtle rainbow streaking through the middle. It was an incredible place to work in, made even better by the people who worked inside. I was one of the newer detectives to have joined, and even then, I felt like I'd been welcomed into the family from the start.

And that's no exaggeration. We felt like a genuine family. Hell, I saw some of them more than I saw my own family. I'd become especially close to Collin over the last few years. And of course, there was Zane Holden, founder of Stonewall Investigations, who had taken me in all those years ago when no one else had seen my potential, not even me.

I walked into the cozy lobby area, where Andrew's table sat in the right corner. It was a big enough room to serve as a reception and small waiting area, with two comfortable couches on the side opposite of Andrew. There were stairs that led up to Zane's office and a hallway straight ahead that went to the others.

Andrew looked up from the computer, smiling and sitting back in the leather chair. "Morning!"

I smiled back. "Hey there," I said, knocking on his desk as I drew close. "How's your morning gone?"

"Can't complain," Andrew replied. He had an impeccable sense of style and wasn't scared of experimenting either. Thankfully, Zane didn't enforce any kind of uniform policy because I didn't want to see Andrew's flair for fabric snuffed out. He was currently wearing a light-blue Hawaiian shirt with a black undershirt underneath, a thick silver chain sitting around his neck, and a pair of tailored dark jeans that rounded out his look.

"How's the coffee this morning?" I could already smell the sweet notes drifting up from Andrew's steaming Harry Potter mug, black ceramic with the classic thunderbolt printed on one side and a Hufflepuff crest on the other.

I always teased Andrew for his house, even though I secretly loved those loyal little badgers. Still, not as cool as a Ravenclaw, of that I was pretty certain.

"It's good!" Andrew said, picking up the mug as if he'd

just been reminded of its existence. "Wanda brought some with her from Hawaii, and you know they don't play when it comes to coffee. I feel like I'm ready to run a marathon and wrestle a shark, all while auditioning for *RuPaul's Drag Race.*"

I almost snorted at that image. "Well, I'm sure your audition tape would get you in."

"If my heart doesn't collapse before." He opened his eyes wide to add dramatic effect. We were both laughing when the door opened again. I expected to see one of the detectives coming in since a couple of them were more night owls than early birds, but instead, a young man came walking into Stonewall. His eyes weren't finding a place to settle, and his gait told me he felt uncertain. Scared. But there was something else.

I narrowed my eyes as the man looked up from the floor and fixed his gaze on me, the same uncertainty still there, though more apparent now. But that something else was there, too. I swallowed.

"Can we help you?" Andrew asked. I hadn't even realized neither of us had said anything.

"Right, yeah, I need a private investigator. I need someone to help me figure out who killed my roommate." He was squeezing his hands together, his big brown eyes no longer shifting around but instead locked in on mine. A strong scent of breath mint was coming from his slightly parted lips. "Before the cops end up thinking I did it."

I took a breath, processing the information while also taking in the entire situation. Detective work was about details, and it started even before the client paid a deposit. The recent run of boring cases that had fallen in my lap didn't necessarily require intense analysis, but I immediately felt like this one was different. This man's case was nothing like the more mundane cases I'd been dealing with lately.

And so I looked him over, breaking eye contact. He appeared very well put together, in a pair of clean white sneakers and light jeans that hugged his thighs, looking particularly full in all the right areas, leading me to think he spent money on getting them tailored. His shirt was a simple red tee, but the logo of a small fox on the chest told me it cost at least two hundred dollars. His hair was freshly cut with a fade on the side and the top styled in a way that made him seem like a model on one of those salon magazines.

Nothing about his immediate appearance told me he was any kind of troublemaker, much less a killer. It was the total opposite. I was being drawn into this stranger like a bass hooked on a pro fisher's line.

"I'm Alejandro Santos, a detective here at Stonewall. I'd love to help you." I put my hand out, holding it between us, as our eyes locked again. I found that I didn't mind how his hand felt over mine.

"Thank you, Mr. Santos. I'm Griffin Banks."

*Griffin Banks...*

The name sounded vaguely familiar. He must have registered the look on my face. "You probably know my father, Thomas Banks." We broke our handshake, his warmth lingering on my fingers. "He's the creator of Silo."

Silo. Only one of the biggest video-streaming platforms found worldwide.

This was *definitely* not going to be a basic case.

"Good to meet you, Mr. Banks. I'm looking forward to helping you out. Let me get my office set up while Andrew checks you in and gets some basics down."

I turned to disappear down the hallway, toward my

office. I stopped at the third door on the left and unlocked it, stepping in and realizing that, for once in a very long time, I actually felt *alive*. Electricity was sparking through my bones, excitement buzzing in my veins.

I was ready for this, even though I really had no idea what *this* entailed.

## CHAPTER 3- GRIFFIN

Wow. *Shiiittt.* I was not expecting Ricky fucking Martin to be my detective. When my attorney suggested I look into Stonewall Investigations, I was picturing the detective as being some older guy, wispy hair and maybe a few moles here and there, cheap glasses and a dusty suit. But nope. Instead, I got a full-on hunk of man meat sitting in front of me.

The light was filtering into the room through two open windows, lighting him in a way that made me wish I had a camera in my hands. If he was as smart as he was attractive, then hell, I may as well consider the case solved.

*Good, because I need to put this all behind me.*

We sat in his office. It felt a little like a therapist's office, which I happened to be very familiar with. There was a vibrant green fern potted in a rounded white pot sitting in the corner, soaking in a strip of bright sunlight beaming in through the partially covered window, the thin brown blinds hanging lazily against the glass. There was a long table neatly organized, with a couple of frames depicting Alejandro with whom I assumed were his parents. They were tilted more toward Alejandro's side of the table, so I couldn't really get a great look at them. There was a Rubik's cube sitting next to his keyboard, and a few tiny succulents made their home on the opposite side of the desk.

The room made me feel comfortable, but that wasn't the only source of comfort. Aside from the medication, of course, there was an intense calming effect I felt by being in Alejandro's presence. It was difficult to describe, especially since this was probably the first time I'd ever really felt something like this, but *damn*, it was strong. And it wasn't just because he was a hot man sporting a mouthwatering five-o'clock shadow—that was a given. But there was something else. I felt like I could let some of my guard down around him. Not just for the case, but in terms of other things. I could be more relaxed with him.

And did I mention he was hot? Wow, wow, *wooow*. I couldn't figure out what I thought was the most attractive thing about him. My eyes went straight for his lips, but the rest of his face was just as delectable. He had a strong chin, dark brows, a nose that had never met a fist. His teeth were flawless, and his eyes shone a bright blue, which mixed with his dark hair to create an effect that had me mesmerized.

So much so, I hadn't even realized Alejandro was speaking to me.

Or... maybe it wasn't that I was drunk off Alejandro's smoldering looks; maybe it was the shot of vodka I'd had before coming here.

"You okay?" he asked, those baby blues scanning me. I shifted in the seat, breaking my gaze from his face and looking out the window over his shoulder instead.

"Yeah, sorry, just thinking."

"No need to apologize. You've been through the ringer."

I nodded, still looking out the window. The colors were

bright, overly so, as if whatever the sunlight touched was somehow enhanced. The greens of the leaves on the tree just outside were like twinkling emeralds, with the bright pink flowers popping off the branches like tiny stars.

*Shit. Did I take two shots or just one?*

"Let's start with what you think happened?" Alejandro was trying to command my attention again. I allowed him to. My eyes went back to his. The blues resembled the calmest, bluest ocean water I'd ever seen. I wanted to jump in. Dive headfirst. Explore the depths so that I never came back up for air.

"I... I don't know. I woke up and my friend was murdered... I was passed out. I'm bipolar and have been taking medication for it, but I've also been drinking, too." I could feel my cheeks flush pink with warmth. "And, uhm, yeah, I mixed too much of it and passed out cold. I've got no idea what happened."

I wasn't holding anything back from the detective. Mainly it was because of those eyes. The deep-blue pools had a hypnotizing effect on me, making me want to divulge every little thing about me.

But also the vodka I had before coming here. That also had me speaking with less of a care.

"Okay, and this friend, Veronica." Alejandro turned to his computer and started typing up notes as he spoke. "How did you know her?" I noticed he remembered her name even though he probably had a total of ten minutes to read my case before that cute Andrew guy let me in. Something about that made me like Alejandro even more than I already did.

"We weren't best friends or anything. We'd known each other from high school, but she moved to California and we lost touch for years. It was last month when I got a text from her out of the blue. She was in a rough spot and needed a place to stay while she found her feet again, so I offered her mine."

"And why do you think you she reached out to you instead of maybe a family member?"

"She explained when she got here. Her life was rocky after high school. She got into some bad stuff and stopped talking to her parents a little after her twenty-first birthday."

"And she was twenty-seven when she died."

"Yeah, so for six years she never talked to them."

"Did she ever say what caused the rift? What bad stuff she got into?"

"Nope." I shrugged. "I tried getting it out of her, but she only ever told me it wasn't anything that would land her in jail, so I stopped asking. I figured she'd open up to me when she felt comfortable enough."

"Boyfriends? Girlfriends? Hookups?"

"There were, I think, three one-nighters that I never saw again. All three definitely looked… sketchy. Like the kind of guys who'd steal my expensive alcohol. Only one guy came around for more than a night. Apparently they met at one of her auditions or something like that. Oh, and I saw her ex-boyfriend when he came to visit her. I don't remember his name, but I could point out his face from anywhere. He had a couple of shitty tattoos on his face and a scar on his chin."

"Did you catch the other guy's name? The one she seemed to be seeing from her acting class?"

I stretched my brain, reaching for anything.

"Nothing." I shook my head, feeling more and more numb by the minute. "I don't think they were a thing, though. I think he was just a friend." That was totally useless. Another useless fact? I couldn't feel any of my extremities. I'd definitely had two shots, not one.

*Well. That's one mystery solved.*

"That's okay," Alejandro said. He had a deep voice, with a small accent under the words. It lured me in. Made me feel comfortable. I wanted him to keep reassuring me, to tell me it was okay, to promise me it would be. There was something in the tone of his voice, like a warm blanket, the electric kind, the ones that stay warm. He felt like that.

"When you woke up, did you see anything that stuck out to you? Like something valuable being stolen? Or furniture that was moved?"

I took a deep breath. Closed my eyes. To be honest, I tried not to think much about the moments after waking up. All I could picture was a sea of red. It had only been two days since I'd woken up to find a friend dead, and I didn't think I'd dealt with it properly yet.

But for Alejandro, I would try. For that damn voice. I kept my eyes closed, drawing the scene in my mind, leaving out the blood and body. Tried to, at least. But of course, thoughts were an uncontrollable force of nature.

I opened my eyes, unable to keep digging. All I saw was red. I locked on to Alejandro's gaze. He looked concerned, sitting across from me, his back straight and brow furrowed. Even with the concern on display, there was a deep sense of calm in his blue eyes, and I clung on to that. They were practically shimmering.

"Nothing," I repeated. "Shit, I'm sorry. I'm useless."

"Not at all, Griffin." He leaned in, over his desk. For a split second, I thought he was going to reach over and grab my head in his hands. My heart rammed up into my throat, immediately dropping back down to my chest upon realization that no heads were being grabbed. "Listen, I can't make any promises in regards to results, but I swear, I'm going to work my damned hardest to find out who did this to your friend. I know you've been through a lot, but you can't break yourself down. Don't apologize and don't consider yourself useless." He was looking straight down the barrel, his eyes locked on mine. "Ever."

I didn't respond. I wanted to, but words weren't forming. It was a word soup in my head, and none felt appropriate to say out loud, so I kept quiet.

"Okay," Alejandro said, leaning back in his chair, his eyes still probing mine. "What can you tell me about Veronica? Her personality? What she loved? Favorite hangouts?"

A round of softball questions. I appreciated it. Words formed clearer sentences, rising up from the murky soup. "Veronica. Yeah, she was a good friend. We watched a lot of dumb reality shows while we ate dinners together, more so when she first moved in and less as time went on. She definitely had a fiery side to her, though. We'd sometimes get into arguments over dishes and shit, but never anything crazy, although I witnessed a few of her arguments get out of hand before. One of our conflicts was over rent. I didn't ask her to pay rent, but she insisted that she did, and she didn't even bat a lash doing it. Always paid in cash, too."

Alejandro's brow arched. His fingers were dancing across the keyboard, the satisfactory clicking sounds filling the room, punctuated by hard taps on the Space bar. "How much?"

"At first she wanted to give me two thousand, and I told her absolutely not. She settled on a thousand."

"A month?"

"Right."

"So she wasn't exactly a struggling artist?"

I shook my head. "No, she got work out in California. Told me about a couple national commercials she was in. Those pay really well from what I can tell."

"Ever seen the commercials?"

"Nope."

More typing. I watched his fingers dance across the keyboard. For a second, I could see the letters float up from the keys as his fingers tapped them, like tiny ghosts rising up to form words in the air.

I shut my eyes and shook my head. When I opened my eyes, the letters were no longer floating. Alejandro's face captured my attention now. He was looking over the notes while the sunlight played off the crests of his cheekbones. His complexion was smooth and his skin clearly kissed by the sun. Picture-perfect. I shifted in my seat, feeling a heat inside me rising.

It definitely wasn't the vodka, I was sure of that one. This heat was different—from a different source. Then, when Alejandro looked away from his computer and toward me, I had to dart my eyes away, out the window. I couldn't look into those light-blue gems again. Nope. Even though it felt like the walls were beginning to cave in, and even though I already knew I could find comfort in those eyes of his, I couldn't meet his gaze. So I continued looking out the window while he asked his next questions.

We went through a list of them, me answering as best I could, coming up with nothing for most of them. It was definitely frustrating. Toward the end, my fists were already balling up in my lap. My throat was dry. My neck felt like a solid column of tensed-up muscle.

I needed another drink.

"All right, Mr. Banks." Alejandro's voice commanded my attention. I instantly snuffed out my vodka-fueled daydream. I dared to look at him again. "You've been a great help." I could tell he was lying. That was fine. I'd take it. "I have a few people I want to question, starting with Veronica's parents. I'm also very interested in her time in California, along with her source of income. My first thought is that she was running from something. What that was, I have no idea." His blue eyes lit up. "Yet. But I'm going to make sure I figure this out."

I believed that one. I could tell he was fully invested in my case, and that, to absolutely no one's surprise, filled me with comfort. This guy might as well have been the human embodiment of a Tempur-Pedic fucking mattress, and all I wanted to do was lie on top of him.

Take that as you will.

"Thank you, Alej—" I couldn't finish. A loud crash filled the room and cut me off. It sounded like it came from right out front of the building. I shot up from my chair and darted out of the room, running for the street without a second's hesitation.

-----

Read the rest here!

ALSO BY MAX WALKER

**The Book Club Boys**

Love and Monsters

**The Gold Brothers**

Hummingbird Heartbreak

Velvet Midnight

Heart of Summer

**The Stonewall Investigation Series**

A Hard Call

A Lethal Love

A Tangled Truth

A Lover's Game

**The Stonewall Investigation- Miami Series**

Bad Idea

Lie With Me

His First Surrender

**The Stonewall Investigation- Blue Creek Series**

Love Me Again

Ride the Wreck

Whatever It Takes

**Audiobooks:**

Find them all on Audible.

**Christmas Stories:**

Daddy Kissing Santa Claus

Daddy, It's Cold Outside

Deck the Halls

Made in the USA
Monee, IL
28 January 2025